KU-277-658

LONDON BOROUGH OF BARKING AND DAGENHAM
LIBRARY SERVICE

This book is due back on the last stamped date

– 1 OCT 2015		
– 5 APR 2016		

24 hour renewal line 0115 9 293 388

BARKING & DAGENHAM

906 000 001 24302

Also by Rebecca Muddiman

Stolen

REBECCA MUDDIMAN

Gone

MULHOLLAND
BOOKS
HODDER

First published in Great Britain in 2015 by Mulholland Books
An imprint of Hodder & Stoughton
An Hachette UK company

First published in paperback in 2015

1

Copyright © Rebecca Muddiman 2015

The right of Rebecca Muddiman to be identified as the Author of the Work has been
asserted by her in accordance with the Copyright, Designs and Patents Act 1988.

All rights reserved. No part of this publication may be reproduced, stored
in a retrieval system, or transmitted, in any form or by any means without
the prior written permission of the publisher, nor be otherwise circulated
in any form of binding or cover other than that in which it is published and
without a similar condition being imposed on the subsequent purchaser.

All characters in this publication are fictitious and any resemblance
to real persons, living or dead is purely coincidental.

A CIP catalogue record for this title is available from the British Library

Paperback ISBN 978 1 444 79158 7
eBook ISBN 978 1 444 79160 0

Printed and bound by Clays Ltd, St Ives plc

Hodder & Stoughton policy is to use papers that are natural, renewable
and recyclable products and made from wood grown in sustainable forests.
The logging and manufacturing processes are expected to conform
to the environmental regulations of the country of origin.

Hodder & Stoughton Ltd
Carmelite House
50 Victoria Embankment
London EC4Y 0DZ

www.hodder.co.uk

To Mam and Dad

LB OF BARKING & DAGENHAM LIBRARIES	
90600000124302	
Bertrams	25/08/2015
AF	£7.99
CRI	

PROLOGUE

11 December 2010

Middlesbrough

"The body was found in woods near Blyth earlier today . . ."

DI Michael Gardner watched the images of the place he'd once known so well with a sinking feeling. It shouldn't have made any difference. It wasn't his problem. Not any more.

"Though police say it's too early to confirm the identity of the woman, it's believed that identification found with the remains was that of Emma Thorley, who has been missing for eleven years. A police search was conducted for Miss Thorley, who was sixteen when her father reported her missing in July 1999."

He turned the TV off as the news segued into the weather. He didn't need to be told what the weather was like – he knew it was bloody freezing. Gardner sat back, watching the snow slide off his shoes and drip onto the carpet. He remembered Emma Thorley well. Not the girl herself – he'd never met her – but the case. He remembered her dad and the photos of his little girl he'd shoved into Gardner's hands. All the photos in the world wouldn't bring her home.

But maybe if things had been different he would've looked harder, dug deeper, and then . . . Would they still have found a body today?

* * *

I

Louise's hand gripped the remote, her thumb hovering over the power button. The news caught her off guard. Even though Emma Thorley had been gone eleven years, it felt so sudden, hearing it like that. The smile on her face as she'd found the perfect gift for Adam dissolved when she'd heard it. Replaced instead with the dread filling her from her gut – ice and fire at the same time.

She needed to do something. Needed to move. But she was frozen. Staring at the images of the place she used to call home.

The sound of the front door snapped her back to the present. She turned the TV off as Adam appeared in the doorway and she somehow managed to find a smile. As Louise watched him walk away, into the kitchen, she knew that it was over.

Sooner or later they'd find out what she'd done.

Blyth

Lucas Yates lit a cigarette and felt his heart race. Emma Thorley. He hadn't heard that name in years – at least not from anyone else. Heard it plenty in his head. He dreamed of her; even now, after all this time.

He thought about the days they'd spent together when she should've been in school. A good girl going off the rails. There was something different about her. Different to all the other little slags who came knocking at his door, wanting something from him. The blonde tart off the news had said there was something on the body, something that made them think it was Emma. Weren't saying what, though. They were keeping that to themselves.

He'd been lying there all morning thinking about the last time he'd seen her. Thought about the anger that'd coursed through him. He'd been looking for her for weeks. And when he'd finally found her he could barely control himself. It was more than anger. It was fury. Hate. It stayed inside him, bubbling up.

She was in his head again. Lucas punched the wall and the knobhead in the room next to his banged back.

He stubbed out his cigarette and stood up. As he walked to the small window he could see his own breath in the air. He looked down at the street and watched people passing by and wondered when that knock would come. If the police would come asking when he'd last seen Emma Thorley and bring up all that shit from the past. He knew it was going to happen. He just didn't know when. The police weren't the sharpest tools in the box but between them they might be able to put two and two together.

Him and Emma had history.

I

13 December 2010

DS Nicola Freeman sat at her desk and looked at the clock above the door. She hated this. They were pretty sure that the dead girl was Emma Thorley – from what they could piece together the body appeared to be the right height and age. But there needed to be no doubt before she made an official statement. Before she confirmed things for Emma's dad. It would've been so much easier to get a DNA comparison but Emma Thorley had no living blood relatives. Or at least no known ones. The only family that remained was her dad, Ray, but he'd adopted Emma. Nothing was ever simple.

The phone barely got out its first ring before she snatched it up. 'Freeman,' she said.

'Hi, Nicky, it's Tom.' Tom Beckett, pathologist and the most laid-back man Freeman had ever met. She usually hated being called Nicky. Only her little brother, Darren, had ever called her that, purely because she hated it, but with Tom she let it slide. To be honest, he could call her whatever he liked. The man was wasted spending his days with dead people. He should've been made to come and work with the living, who'd appreciate him.

'Tell me you've got something,' she said.

'I have, but you won't like it. Our disorganised dentist definitely does *not* have Miss Thorley's records any more.'

'Brilliant,' Freeman said.

'Not that it would've mattered a great deal. There's not a lot left to work with. *But* what I can say is that it looks like your mystery girl was attacked twice, possibly once post-mortem.'

'What do you mean?'

'Well,' Tom said, 'it appears she was beaten. The injuries to the face suggest that someone really had a go, probably with their fists. And it's likely whoever did it was left-handed. The injuries were predominantly on the right side of her face. But then there are marks on some of the teeth that appear to have been made with a weapon. Possibly a hammer.'

'So someone was trying to prevent identification?'

'Looks like,' Tom said. 'Only they didn't quite manage to finish the job. We didn't retrieve all of the teeth but a few were in the grave and there were a couple still intact. Looks like your killer was sloppy.'

Freeman sighed. 'So there's nothing that I can take to Ray Thorley?'

'There's not much else to work with in terms of identifiers. There's the broken arm. I checked medical records and there was no match but that doesn't mean to say she didn't break it later on. If she did it during one of her disappearing acts then it's possible she didn't get it treated.'

'And possible her dad didn't know,' Freeman said. 'Okay. Thanks, Tom.' She hung up. She wished she hadn't been forced to involve Ray Thorley so soon. Wished she hadn't had to go into his home and re-open old wounds without definitive proof that it was his daughter's body out there. But the leak to the press about the ID in the pocket of the tracksuit top had forced her hand. At least they hadn't mentioned the gold necklace. At least she still had some-thing the rest of the world didn't know. The papers were already suggesting the police had failed Emma Thorley and her father back in the day. She didn't want to be accused of the same thing now.

Freeman looked at the clock again. Her stomach rumbled and she wished she'd grabbed something to eat before she left this morning, but at 6 a.m. she just hadn't been able to face anything. She took out her mobile and found the number for her doctor, her finger hovering over the call button before she threw the phone down on the desk and went back to the information she'd pulled on Emma Thorley. Her own shit could wait.

Emma's dad had filed three missing person reports in total. The first in February 1999, which was resolved when Emma returned of her own free will a month later. The second in April of the same year, which was quickly retracted by her father. And finally in July that year when she disappeared for good. Ray Thorley had told her that Emma's problems had started after her mother died. Emma was fifteen and it hit her hard. She'd never been in trouble before then. She worked hard at school. Wasn't an 'A' student but she tried. She was quiet. She had a group of friends but didn't socialise with them outside of school very often. She dreamed of going to university. Ray had been saving for a long time. In the end he'd spent the money searching for his daughter and on posters saying 'Have you seen this girl?'

Freeman sat back in her chair. It was funny how things, how people, could change, just like that. One minute they're good, heading for a life of security and friends, marriage and kids. And the next they're gone. The person they were, destroyed beyond all recognition. Suddenly they're monsters.

She took a breath. She wasn't going to go there. She couldn't think about him any more. It was too hard. He'd chosen his path. And now there was nothing she could do. Nothing anyone could do. He was long gone. She hoped he was finally at peace.

DC Bob McIlroy stomped into the office, shouting across the room at the top of his voice. The man didn't have any volume control. Ignoring his greeting of 'Morning, Nana' – his nickname for her on account of her glasses (which bore little to no resemblance to singer Nana Mouskouri's) – she watched him as he passed her desk, shirt buttons straining against his gut. She felt nauseous and turned her attention back to Emma Thorley.

She skimmed through the reports until she found what she was after – the officer in charge of the investigation last time, a DC Michael Gardner.

'Hey, Bob,' she said and he turned around, clearly surprised she was talking to him.

'What?' he said and pulled a pack of gum from his pocket. Since someone had told him his breath stank like rotting eggs he'd been chewing gum constantly. It hadn't helped.

'You know a cop named Michael Gardner?' She saw McIlroy's face darken. 'I'll take that as a yes,' she said. 'Friend of yours, is he?'

McIlroy snorted. 'Hardly,' he said. 'Why? What's it to you?'

'I need to speak to him,' she said. 'Where can I find him?'

'He left,' McIlroy said.

'Where did he go?'

'Don't know. Don't care.'

'What did he do to you? Make fun of your bald patch?'

She could see McIlroy's chest rise and fall. He was pretty pissed off. This Gardner must've done something bad to warrant that; McIlroy usually couldn't be bothered to get angry, it wasted energy he could've used eating.

'He screwed over another copper,' he said and then waved his hand in front of him. 'No, scratch that. He killed another copper.' He turned and walked away, shaking his head.

Freeman watched him go. He killed another cop? She saw

McIlroy stop and say something to Fry, his drinking buddy. Fry turned to look at Freeman and then muttered something undoubtedly strewn with four-letter words.

What the hell had happened with Michael Gardner?

2

14 January 1999

Lucas slid the money into his back pocket and watched the scruffy little shite scamper off with his gear. He hated this place and all the little retards in it. He'd have preferred to do business outside but his punters apparently liked the ambience of the place, damp seats and all. He needed a change of scenery. He downed the rest of his pint and slid the glass along the bar towards Tony. Unlimited refills were one perk of working in a pub run by a spineless twat.

He looked around at the place. He hated the fact that it was well into January and there were still remnants of Christmas decorations hanging in the corners of the pub. He hated that the same people came in every night and expected something different. He hated that he was one of them.

'All right, Lucas.'

He turned and saw Jenny Taylor staggering towards him. She was the dirtiest slag in Blyth and proper stalking him.

'Piss off,' he said as she draped herself over him, picking up his pint and taking a swig before handing it back to him. 'Fuck's sake,' he muttered and pushed the glass away. Tony took the hint and got him another.

'D'ya wanna come to the toilets with me?' Jenny said, her words slurred.

Lucas pushed her off him and she toppled onto the sticky

floor. He stepped over her and walked towards the pool table where Dicko was currently making a killing. Lucas watched the smug look on his face melt away as he realised that whatever he won would be going in Lucas's pocket, not his.

Someone had left a pack of fags on the edge of the pool table. Lucas took one out and found his lighter. He slid both the lighter and the remaining fags into his pocket and watched a girl cross the road outside, head down, sleeves pulled down over her hands.

Whoever was losing to Dicko asked Lucas to move out of the way so he could take his shot. Lucas ignored him. He realised who the girl was. He'd seen her with Tomo a few days earlier. She hadn't said a word. Just stood there, looking at the floor. Didn't look very old but Tomo said they were in the same year so that made her fair game. She kept pushing her blonde hair behind her ear but it fell back every time. She was proper blonde, not like some of the other skanks he knew. He'd hoped she'd stick around but she reckoned she had to get home. He hadn't stopped thinking about her all night. Even asked Tomo where she lived. And now here she was again.

Lucas pushed the door open and went outside. He stopped in the middle of the pavement and watched her. She almost collided with him before she realised anyone was there.

'Sorry,' she muttered and went to walk around him.

'It's Emma, isn't it?'

She stopped and looked up and down the street, as if she shouldn't be there. Or at least not with him.

'I met you the other day, didn't I?' Lucas said. 'With Tomo.' Emma nodded but kept her eyes on her feet.

'Do you want a drink?'

She shook her head. He stepped a little closer and she finally looked at him properly. 'Come on. You can't stay out here by yourself. All sorts of scumbags out here. Come on,' he said again. 'Just one drink and then I'll walk you home. Promise.' He smiled and he could see her soften. 'Good girl,' he said.

They sat in the back. Every time someone headed their way he warned them off with a glare. The shop was closed. By her third drink she still hadn't said much, but she'd smiled.

'Give us a triple this time,' Lucas said to Tony, before looking back at her. 'Fucking cunt,' he muttered and walked back to their table. Jenny was standing over Emma, up in her face.

'You fucking get me?' Jenny screamed and Emma nodded. Lucas grabbed hold of Jenny from behind and dragged her away, pushing her against the fruit machine. Her hair fell over her face, blonde but not like Emma's. Jenny's was bleached. Dirty.

'Talk to her again and I'll smash your fucking ugly face in,' Lucas said, his face an inch from hers. He shoved her away and walked back to Emma. 'You all right?'

Emma nodded but he could see it was time to go. 'Sorry about her. She's a proper psycho.' Lucas held out his hand to her. 'Come on,' he said. Emma stood up and took hold of it. He led her out, past Jenny, who glared at them but didn't say a word.

Outside, the cold air made her face flush. She stumbled as the effects of the alcohol hit her and he held on to her hand tighter. 'Come on, we'll go back to mine. It's closer,' he said.

3

13 December 2010

Lucas stood on the corner of the street, looking at the house. He'd wondered if there'd be reporters hanging around, but if there had been any they'd all gone home. And who could blame them? It was freezing. The street was empty except for a little old woman walking a dog that looked almost as old as her. Not much had changed in the last eleven years. Nothing ever did around here. People had no money then, they probably had even less now. The place was a dump. Rusting cars resting on bricks and piles of junk cluttering the front gardens. The houses were a mismatch of styles and sizes. Too many were pebble-dashed in some fit of insanity by the builders. At least it was quiet now. When he'd been here back in the day, back when he'd been watching Emma, all the scruffy kids were out causing trouble, making the place unbearable. Asking him for tabs or to go to the offy for them. They did his head in. These days they all stayed inside.

He remembered standing in the exact same place all those years ago, waiting for her to come out. Seeing her looking at him from the window upstairs, knowing he was watching her. He'd enjoyed the way it made him feel.

He'd questioned coming back today. But he needed to know if her dad would recognise him. If he'd be able to start pointing fingers when the cops came round. They'd never actually met. But he'd stood outside so many times that it was possible her dad had seen his face.

Lucas stared at the house. He wondered if it would be the same inside. If Emma's room would be the same. Perfectly preserved. He'd only been in a couple of times. Once when her dad was out. Once when they were both out. He'd gone into her room. Lay down on her bed. Done what any man would do in the bed of a teenage girl. He'd always wondered how she'd felt when she found it.

The old woman with the dog finally shuffled her way past him and he crossed the street. More than needing to know if the old man recognised him, he needed to go inside, needed to see her things.

He straightened his tie and thought about taking it off. Emma's dad wouldn't expect one of his daughter's friends to be that respectable, would he? She was a junkie, a loser. But it was too late now. He'd already knocked. He tapped his feet as he waited, and watched as a figure emerged from somewhere in the gloom of the house and approached the door, disfigured by the glass. Lucas took a breath and put on his game face as the door opened.

An old man stood hunched in the doorway, dressed in brown polyester trousers and a beige cardigan. Lucas didn't know what he'd been expecting but it wasn't this. Not a red-faced pensioner with last week's tea crusted onto his shirt.

Ray Thorley looked at Lucas expectantly. Maybe he thought he was police.

'Mr Thorley?'

'Yes. Is it about my Emma? Is there news?' he said.

Lucas smiled at the old man and stepped forward. 'May I come in?'

Ray stepped back and ushered Lucas in. 'Have you heard something?' he said as he closed the door.

Lucas walked through into the living room and took in all the pictures of the girl he used to fuck. 'May I sit down?' Lucas asked as he took a seat. Ray continued to stand, waiting for him to speak. 'Mr Thorley, I just wanted to offer my condolences—'

Ray slumped down into his chair and made a noise as if the life were slipping out of him. 'So it *is* her,' he said.

A heat rushed through Lucas's body. The police weren't sure it was Emma. Was that a good thing? The news hadn't confirmed things but he'd assumed the police were just holding back. Keeping their cards close to their chest. But maybe they really didn't know. Maybe they wouldn't be knocking on his door after all.

Lucas looked at Ray Thorley. He was staring, waiting for a response. 'I think you misunderstand. I just came to offer my condolences. I was a friend of Emma's. A long time ago. When I heard I was so upset.'

Ray pointed at Lucas with a shaky hand. 'You're not a policeman?'

'No,' Lucas said. 'You don't remember me?'

'I'm sorry, son, I don't,' Ray said, searching Lucas's face.

Lucas held back his grin. 'I was friends with Emma. Knew her from school.'

'Oh,' Ray said. 'Of course.'

Lucas sat forward. 'I'm very sorry, Mr Thorley.' He stood. 'Would you mind if I used your toilet?'

Ray nodded and pointed in the vague direction of the stairs. Lucas closed the living room door behind him and climbed the stairs. The sign on the door of the bedroom caught his eye.

EMMA'S ROOM. KEEP OUT!

It was one of those tacky signs bought from a souvenir shop in a crappy holiday town – Whitley Bay or Scarborough. He remembered seeing it all those years ago. She was embarrassed by it. It was loose on one corner where she'd tried to pull it off. Lucas pushed open the bedroom door and went inside. Nothing had changed except for a hint of mustiness, the way the box of Christmas decorations smells when you get them out of the loft. The smell of her cheap body spray was long gone.

Lucas sat down on the bed. He remembered touching her. How she'd pulled away from him, scared her dad would come home, scared he'd hear. She thought she was a bad girl but she couldn't quite follow through.

He looked at the headboard. Still covered in stickers of the Spice Girls and Take That. Some half peeled away when her tastes had changed. He could still see her huddled against it, wondering if she'd made a mistake saying she wanted to leave it all behind.

Lucas walked to the window and looked down the street. It was raining again, a cold sleet, coming down almost horizontal. He opened a box on the windowsill, full of jewellery and loose change. He rummaged around and pulled out a familiar silver locket. The one she'd rejected. He wrapped it around his fingers before slipping it into his pocket.

He could hear movement downstairs. Closing the jewellery box, he slipped out of the room and headed back down to Emma's father, who was standing by the fireplace, holding a photo of the family on holiday. He seemed oblivious to Lucas's return.

Lucas cleared his throat and Ray turned. 'I'm sorry to have bothered you,' he said.

Ray shook his head. 'All this time and I never thought she was dead. I thought I'd know. I'd feel it here,' he said, moving a shaky hand to his chest. He drifted off and looked at the clock above the fireplace. Lucas glanced at the clock and realised it bore no resemblance to the actual time. He wondered how long to let the old man talk before leaving. 'Even when he didn't come, I thought maybe—'

'He?' Lucas said. Had Emma found someone else?

Ray frowned, his train of thought gone.

'You said when *he* didn't come.' Lucas waited for the old man to recall his words, convinced the old guy was batty.

Ray nodded and pointed at Lucas again with his unsteady hand. 'Yes. The man who came before. He'd come and tell me my Emma was okay. He helped her out.'

'Who?' Lucas asked.

'He'd come and tell me she was doing okay and would be back soon. He was nice, a friendly sort. He'd tell me not to worry. I thought she'd gone like the first time, but he brought a letter from her. I don't know.' Ray looked around as if trying to place where he'd put it. 'And then the last time . . . I waited and waited and I started to think something bad could've happened but I didn't feel it. I thought I would but I didn't. I always thought—'

'Who was he? The man who came?'

'Oh, I . . .' Ray shook his head and tapped his fingers on his lips. 'Oh, what was his name? Damn and blast. I should remember.' He shook his head again. 'He came from the clinic. He was helping her with her problem.'

Lucas felt something stir inside him. *He'd* been there, at her house. Where else had he been? What else did he know?

Ray shook his head again, trying to shake free the memory. Lucas offered Ray his hand. 'Again, I'm very sorry about your daughter,' Lucas said, and Ray thanked him. With obvious effort he walked Lucas to the door. Lucas said goodbye and walked down the path.

'Ben!' Ray shouted behind him. Lucas turned. 'The man from the clinic. His name was Ben.'

But Lucas already knew who he meant. Knew the prick who'd been hanging around Emma like a bad smell, trying to get between them. But how much did he actually know?

Maybe it was time to get reacquainted with Ben.

4

13 December 2010

Gardner closed one eye and aimed the small paper ball at DC Don Murphy. To be fair, you didn't need to be a sharpshooter to hit the target. He was big enough. But the rules were clear: one point for the gut (easy target), two for the forehead, and three for the mouth. Gardner was going for the money shot. He let go of the paper and watched it sail across the office, landing right in Murphy's open mouth. Murphy coughed and sat up straight. Gardner raised his arms in victory and DC Carl Harrington tried to claim cheating. PC Dawn Lawton looked up from the corner, smiling at Murphy's angry bear impression before getting her head back down to whatever she was doing. At least someone was working. Usually Gardner would be the one telling Murphy to get off his lazy backside and do some work but to tell the truth, there was nothing doing. Sure there was paperwork, chasing up a few loose ends, but nothing to really *do*. He couldn't decide if he wanted to jinx it by mentioning it or not.

'I could go to HR about this,' Murphy said and shuffled off towards the kettle.

'I do believe I'm winning by ten points,' Gardner said to Harrington.

'Nine,' he said.

'Whatever. I'm still kicking your arse.'

The phone rang and Harrington picked it up. There was nothing like a sore loser. Gardner wondered what Lawton was up to. The last big case they'd had was a missing teenage girl who'd told her separated parents she was staying at the other's house for the weekend and had then run off with a teacher. There'd been nothing to suggest the girl had been forced into anything but she was only fourteen. Everything since then had been straightforward, solved in a couple of days. Nothing to get his teeth into. He supposed he should be grateful. After a case like Abby Henshaw's, which had taken over five years of his life, he should've been pleased when things were sorted out so quickly.

Gardner leaned back in his chair, the high from his win wearing off. He needed to stop thinking about Abby Henshaw. They hadn't spoken for weeks. Months, maybe. He'd done his job; it was time to move on. And he was trying.

In a moment of madness he'd signed up for online dating. He'd spent hours tinkering with his profile and drank more than should be necessary in order to send it into the world. He wondered whether admitting to being a copper was a good idea. Or if lying about hobbies would be considered breach of contract. He did *have* a mountain bike. He just never used it. But he definitely regretted putting the photo on, despite, or maybe because of, the man in the picture being almost a decade younger than he was. To be fair, that was less about vanity than the fact no one had taken his picture in almost a decade. He'd panicked afterwards that someone he knew might see it, might find out what a loser he was, but he guessed if they were on there too they must be as sad as him.

And though he'd had no luck so far (it'd only been three weeks), in that the sole response he'd had was from someone who listed knitting hats for her cat as her only hobby, it was almost addictive checking his inbox. He was itching to check again but the last thing he needed was anyone in the office finding out what he was up to. Least of all Carl Harrington. He would never live it down. He'd have to transfer somewhere else.

'Oi,' Harrington said, holding up the phone. 'For you. A DS Freeman from Blyth.'

For a moment everything stopped. Gardner felt like the whole office was staring at him. Waiting for a response. How could one little word – the B word – feel like a punch in the guts?

His own phone started to ring and Harrington indicated he should pick it up. But without wanting to sound like a five-year-old, he didn't want to and no one could make him. He didn't want to talk to anyone from Blyth. He didn't want to get involved.

The phone kept ringing and now people *were* staring. Gardner snatched up the phone.

'Gardner,' he said. DS Freeman introduced herself and Gardner recalled the name from the news. He knew what she wanted, he just didn't know what he could do to help. If he'd had any ideas about Emma Thorley he would've found her eleven years ago.

When she'd exhausted every avenue, DS Freeman finally hung up and Gardner released the breath he'd been holding. He could see Harrington lurking, waiting for round two, but suddenly he didn't feel in the mood.

He clicked onto the BBC website and found the story about the body in Blyth. They still hadn't confirmed it was Emma Thorley but Freeman had suggested it was looking that way. She must have been there all along. Lying in those woods while he'd told her father that Emma would come back when she was ready. Like she had before.

He wondered what would be better: that it *was* Emma

Thorley so her father could finally have some closure after all these years. Or that it wasn't her, that there was still hope.

If only he hadn't been so caught up with his own shit, then he wouldn't have failed her all those years ago.

5

12 July 1999

DC Gardner tried not to let his impatience show as Ray Thorley dug around in an old biscuit tin, searching for photographs of his daughter.

'There must be a more recent one than this,' Ray said, sifting through memories of holidays in caravans and birthdays defined by cakes.

Gardner looked at the half-dozen pictures of Emma her father had already handed over. Most were a couple of years old. Emma aged thirteen or fourteen – smiling more than most teenagers do in photos with their parents. The girl in the picture was pretty but looked young for her age.

'This one was last year,' Ray said, handing over another picture. Gardner took it from the man and noticed the happiness levels were down a little. Emma sat beside her mum on a hospital bed, clutching her hand.

'Thank you,' Gardner said and put the collection down on the coffee table in front of him. 'Mr Thorley, I wanted to ask you about Emma's boyfriend again. Lucas Yates.'

'He wasn't her boyfriend,' Ray snapped. 'I'm sorry. But that boy was not her boyfriend.'

'Okay. But she *did* stay with him, didn't she? The first time you reported her missing in . . . February. That's where she went. Is that correct?'

Ray gave a quick nod. 'But she's not with him now, if that's what you're thinking.'

'What makes you so sure?' Gardner asked.

'Because she wasn't seeing him any more. She can't stand him. He hurt her.'

'How did he hurt her?'

'I don't know,' Ray said, his voice catching, his eyes welling up. 'She wouldn't talk to me about things like that. It was always her mum she talked to. But I know my Emma and she wouldn't have gone off with him again. She wasn't a stupid girl.'

Gardner felt for the man, he truly did. He'd not long lost his wife and then his daughter had gone off the rails. But grief had made Ray Thorley blind.

'Mr Thorley, Emma had problems with drugs, didn't she?'

'Not any more. She stopped all that.'

'Okay. But it's not always easy to just stop. Perhaps she was using again and Lucas Yates is a known dealer—'

'No!' Ray Thorley closed his eyes, shutting Gardner out. Gardner waited a few minutes before standing. No matter what her father thought, he knew the best way to find Emma was to find Lucas Yates. So far he'd had no luck with that, but he'd turn up eventually. Come out from beneath whichever rock he was hiding under.

Emma Thorley needed help. That was a certainty. It just wasn't the kind of help her father imagined.

He watched Ray Thorley sit there, head in hands, refusing to listen to reason. It was pointless. They could sit there all night, going round in circles. He'd keep looking for Yates but it'd have to wait until tomorrow. He was tired. All he wanted to do was go home and chill out.

Gardner stood. 'I'll be in touch,' he said and left Ray sitting amongst his tins of old photographs.

* * *

Gardner scraped the leftovers into the bin. He was starting to wonder why he bothered at all when nothing was good enough any more – too salty, too garlicky, too whatever. She was like Goldilocks. They should've got a takeaway every night, at least then it'd be someone else's fault. Usually she still managed to eat it, or enough to make him wonder if she just wanted to complain for the sake of it. But tonight she'd barely touched it. She'd lost weight. She was going to the gym more and more.

He walked into the living room with a bottle of red. There was never anything wrong with the red. He expected her to be sitting staring at the blaring TV, feet tucked up beneath her, but the room was quiet. She was standing by the window, arms around herself. He saw her jaw clench. So much for chilling out. She had something to say. He tried running through his day. What could possibly be the problem now?

They never had real arguments – no fireworks – just a few carefully chosen words and ominous silences.

She stood staring at him as if he was supposed to know what was wrong.

'What's up, Annie?' he said and put the bottle down on the table without finding a coaster. She didn't even blink. Now *that* was strange. He sat down, sinking into the worn leather settee. He couldn't be arsed with whatever it was. It had been a long day.

She stayed standing. He could see tears starting to well. Oh fuck, he thought. Someone's dead.

Gardner leaned forward, reaching for her hand, but she pulled away. Turned to the window.

'Annie?'

'I'm seeing someone,' she said, almost whispering.

Seeing someone? Gardner tried to work out what she was talking about, whether he was supposed to know. Had she mentioned this before? 'A therapist? Why?' he said.

A sound came from her, part laugh, part sob, and she covered her mouth, real tears coming now. She turned back to him and looked at him pleadingly, head tilted as if she were talking to a three-year-old.

'Michael,' she said.

'What are you talking about?' he said, shaking his head. 'You're seeing someone?'

She nodded, barely perceptibly. Suddenly things were falling into place – a kid's toy with slots for shapes – all glaringly obvious to everyone but the stupid kid trying to force a cube into a circular hole. He didn't want to acknowledge it, didn't want to make it real. But he could feel it. He could feel it running through his veins, zigzagging its way through his body until every last cell was aware of what was happening.

'Who is it?' he asked.

Gardner stepped closer, stood looming over her. She stepped back and he wondered for a second if she thought he might hit her. If she thought that's who he was.

'Who?' he said.

'Just sit down. I'm not talking to you like this.'

'I'm not going to fucking sit down,' he said and felt a lump in his throat. He squeezed his eyes shut. Please don't throw up, not now. 'Just tell me who.' Annie started to walk out of the room. Gardner caught her by the elbow. 'Tell me.'

'Stuart Wallace,' she said and pulled away from him. She started running up the stairs.

'Stuart fucking Wallace?' He couldn't move. Wanted to follow her but couldn't. 'Stuart Wallace is a fat, fucking prick,' he shouted after her.

He heard the bathroom door slam and the sound of his own breathing filled the spinning room.

Stuart Wallace. He'd introduced Annie to him. He'd been

forced to go to a Christmas party at his shitty nouveau-riche house. They'd laughed at his decor.

He knew where he lived.

Gardner grabbed his keys from the table. He started to walk out, first stopping to pick up the bottle of red from the table. He smashed it against the wall that held the shabby chic photo frames she'd insisted on and threw what remained of the shattered bottle against the opposite wall.

'There's a red wine stain on your fucking carpet,' he shouted up the stairs and then slammed the front door.

6

13 December 2010

Freeman sat and looked at the door to the house. The small garden was overgrown and strewn with litter. She wondered if the toll of eleven years of not knowing where his daughter was had done that to Ray Thorley – robbed him of all desire to live his life, to take care of himself, to do his garden – but as she got out of the car and walked towards the house she noticed that most of the other gardens on the street were in a similar state. The place was hardly a candidate for Britain in Bloom. Freeman brushed away the crumbs from a hastily eaten ham and cheese sandwich and knocked on the door.

Ray Thorley answered and a look of confusion morphed slowly into recognition. Freeman had thought last time she'd spoken to him that perhaps he was a little senile. He seemed to take a while to recall certain words and when he had offered her a drink he'd disappeared into the kitchen for fifteen minutes and then returned empty-handed. Freeman wasn't immune to the occasional blank when writing reports or remembering her shopping list but there was something about Ray's behaviour that reminded her of her granddad. Perhaps that was why she had liked him so much.

Ray stepped back and showed her into the warm house, muttering something about it being all go. Bloody reporters. They hadn't even positively ID'd Emma yet and already they were hassling Ray. If she got her hands on the little shit who'd leaked it to the press, she'd cut his balls off.

As she walked through into the living room she unwrapped her scarf and shoved it into her pocket. Ray was right behind her.

'Have you heard anything, Miss Freeman?' he said.

Usually she bristled at being called Miss and would correct whoever had spoken, usually some macho guy who didn't take kindly to a woman in a position of power, telling them, 'It's Detective Sergeant.' But with Ray somehow she didn't mind. It seemed kind of sweet.

'Not yet, I'm afraid,' she said. 'The post-mortem did show a broken arm – the left arm. I was wondering if Emma—'

'Never had a broken bone,' Ray said and smiled. 'I remember her crying one day, telling me all her friends at school had had a cast except her. Thought it was very unfair.'

That didn't necessarily mean anything but she let it go. Freeman wondered why he wasn't making more fuss. Why he wasn't shouting at her to do more. She wondered if he'd always been this kind, this understanding, or if all the years had just beaten the fight out of him.

'Mr Thorley, I'm trying to retrace Emma's steps before she disappeared. Did you know any of Emma's friends? Anyone she used to hang around with before she disappeared?'

Ray shook his head. 'She was always a shy girl. She never played with other kids very much. Not really. There were a few girls from school but by the time she was, well, when she was having the trouble she stopped seeing them. She kept to herself.'

Freeman nodded. She'd bet Emma hadn't kept completely to herself. If she was doing drugs she wasn't doing them alone. And of course there was Lucas Yates keeping her company. 'What about boyfriends? She ever tell you about anyone in particular?'

She noticed Ray's face darken a little but he shook his head. 'She wouldn't talk to me about those things.'

Freeman nodded again. 'But there was someone when she started . . . when the trouble started?' Freeman had noticed that Ray never used the words 'taking drugs'.

Ray looked anxious again. 'There was some boy. She went off with him the first time, the silly girl. I knew he'd hurt her,' he said and twisted his hands on his lap. 'She came back and was so upset but she wouldn't tell me what happened. I was just glad she was back so I didn't push it.'

'Did she get back together with him?'

Ray shook his head. 'No. She wouldn't have done that. He was no good. I knew that much. He used to come here sometimes. I remember she stopped going out for a while. She'd look out the window. Up and down she'd be. Checking outside. I asked her if she was waiting for someone.' Ray turned towards the window. The net curtain had yellowed from the sun. 'I saw him hanging about one day. Across the road. I said I was going to call the police but she told me they wouldn't do anything. I went to go outside myself, to tell him to bugger off, but she wouldn't let me. Said it didn't matter. When I looked out later he'd gone.' Ray stood and picked up a photo of Emma from the mantelpiece. 'She left again shortly after that.'

'And that was in April. Was this when the man from the clinic came to see you?' She searched through her notes, recalling what she'd read from the original investigation. 'Ben Swales, right?' Ray nodded. 'But he never came when she disappeared the last time?'

Freeman saw his hands shaking as he put the photo back. 'No. He never came again.'

'Was there anyone else who might've seen Emma before she disappeared? Any other friends you can think of?'

Ray sat down again. 'There was a girl she was at school with.' He shook his head. 'It'll come back to me. They'd been friends since primary school. I know they stopped seeing each other so much but she might know something. Emma could've told her something about the boy.' He shook his head again as if trying to dislodge his memories. 'Diane. That's it. Diane Royle. I'm sure your lot spoke to her last time.'

'Great,' Freeman said. 'I'll check.' She pulled her scarf out of her pocket and made a move to go. 'If you think of anything else, could you give me a call?' She got to the front door when Ray appeared in the doorway of the living room.

'I'm sorry I couldn't help.'

'You've been very helpful,' she said. 'Thanks.' She opened the door and winced at the cold wind. At least it had stopped raining.

'Maybe that boy could help,' Ray said and Freeman turned around.

'What boy?' she asked.

'He came this morning. He was a friend of Emma's, he came to offer condolences. He was very nice.'

Freeman felt a jolt of excitement. Finally someone who might be able to offer some insight.

'What was his name?' she asked.

'His name?' Ray frowned again and Freeman felt a stab of guilt as she wished he'd answer faster. 'Oh, I . . .' Ray closed his eyes and shook his head. 'I don't know. I don't know if he said. I'm sure he must've but I don't remember.'

'What did he look like?'

Ray closed his eyes for a little too long. 'He was a nice boy, well dressed. Dark hair, I think.' He opened his eyes. 'I'm sorry, Miss Freeman. I can't remember.'

Freeman let out a sigh and smiled at Ray. 'That's okay,' she said. 'But if you remember or if he comes again, will you call me?'

Ray nodded and looked like the whole world was on his shoulders, like he'd let his daughter down. Freeman smiled again, hating herself for making him feel that way.

7

13 December 2010

DCI Routledge leaned back in his chair and yawned. Freeman assumed she wasn't boring him, but instead chose to believe he'd had a late night. And judging from the state of him, that wouldn't be an unreasonable assumption. Apparently Christmas had started early for some.

'Anyway,' she continued, 'I spoke to DI Gardner in Middlesbrough—'

'DI?' Routledge said and pulled a face. Freeman wanted to ask what it was about this Gardner that got people's backs up, but doubted Routledge would spill. He still had *some* professional discretion.

'*Anyway,*' she started again, 'it was pretty much a waste of time. He couldn't tell me anything that wasn't in the reports. There'd only been two real people of interest at the time. One was a drug counsellor, Ben Swales, who apparently helped Emma and had acted as a go-between for Emma and her father the second time she went missing. Gardner interviewed him and ruled him out.'

'Well, I suggest you speak to him yourself,' Routledge said and Freeman thought, *no shit.*

'The other was Lucas Yates – Emma's ex-boyfriend and from what I read, a real charmer. Gardner spoke to Yates but nothing came of it and as far as I can tell, he was

32

convinced the pair had run off together, despite what Ray Thorley thought.'

'Which was?'

'That she wouldn't go anywhere near Yates. And I have to say I agree with her dad.'

'Why? She disappeared with him the first time, didn't she? She was a smackhead, wasn't she?'

Freeman counted to five. She didn't have time for ten. And she didn't have time to stand there explaining things to Routledge. She hated the way half of her colleagues seemed to see addicts as second-class citizens. It seemed that no one gave a shit about Emma Thorley – then or now.

'Despite Emma's problems with drugs, she was never actually in trouble with the police. The only records we have are her missing person reports. Whereas Yates is a scumbag. He's a known dealer. Been arrested dozens of times. Drugs, assault, burglary, sexual assault, stealing cars, driving without a licence, without insurance—'

'I get it. He's quite the Renaissance man.'

'He finally went to prison in 2000, seven years. But there's been nothing on him since he was released.'

'Maybe he found Jesus,' Routledge said.

'Maybe,' replied Freeman. 'But either way I really want to speak to him.'

'Fine. But as we don't even know if it is this Thorley girl yet, just tread lightly.'

'I always do,' Freeman said and closed the door before he could respond.

8

9 February 1999

Emma listened as Jenny and the others shouted at a couple of pensioners across the street. The woman kept her head down but the man shook his walking stick in their direction, telling them they should be ashamed of themselves. Emma turned her face away but it only egged the others on. All except Lucas. Lucas was quiet. Watching. Watching her. She could feel his eyes on her, heavy and possessive. It made her feel safe.

She hated the rest of them, hated that the only reason they seemed to have for getting up in the morning – or more likely, lunchtime – was to make other people's lives hell. That was all they did. That and the drugs. She hadn't tried anything yet, despite their taunts. Despite Lucas's offers to make her feel good, to help her forget all the other shit. She'd been tempted but that was all. She had more willpower than to just give in to it.

She sometimes wondered what she was doing there, with them. The kind of people she would've crossed the street to avoid before. People she would've looked down on. But that was before. And was it really better to be sitting at home, watching her dad weep? Sitting in school, trying to ignore the pitying stares? Sitting alone in her room, wondering why her mam had left her alone.

'Catch.' Someone threw a can at Lucas. He opened it and

took a swig before offering it to her. The sour smell of cheap, warm lager made her stomach turn. She shook her head and Lucas shrugged, downing the rest of the can before crushing it and throwing it over the wall they were leaning against.

Emma looked across the road and saw someone staring. Her face reddened as she realised it was Diane. She'd been ignoring her calls. Couldn't bear to talk to her any more. She still had a mother, she didn't understand.

'What's up?' Lucas said, turning her to look at him.

'Nothing,' she said and looked into his eyes. Sometimes she couldn't believe he'd chosen her. He could've had anyone but he wanted her. He made her feel special. If only the rest of them didn't come as part of the package, she could be happy. If it were just the two of them she knew that she could be happy again.

'Tell me,' he said.

She shrugged and looked at the ground. 'I'm just sick of it.'

'Of what?'

'All of it. My life. Dad's so . . . One minute he's treating me like a five-year-old, checking I'm okay every five minutes. And then he goes all distant as if I don't exist any more. And I hate school. Everyone thinks they know how I feel but they don't. None of them do. And I hate being in that house. It smells of her and I hate it . . .' She realised she was crying and felt ashamed. He'd think she was a baby. She rubbed her face with her sleeve and noticed Diane was still standing there. Why didn't she just go away? Leave her alone.

'You could come and live with me,' Lucas said. 'Fuck the rest of them.'

Emma looked up, tried to work out if he was taking the piss. But his eyes flashed with something more serious. The same look he'd had when he'd said he wanted to touch her. When she'd let him.

'Lucas,' Jenny shouted, breaking the spell Emma was under. They both turned and saw Jenny mooning another group of unsuspecting pensioners. Jenny cackled as the little old ladies blushed and Emma couldn't help but notice that Jenny's arse was now aimed in Lucas's direction. She was pathetic.

Lucas looked at Jenny with revulsion and turned his attention back to Emma. He moved himself closer to her, pushing her against the wall. 'What do you think?' Lucas said, his hand on her hip, fingers dipping beneath the waist of her jeans. 'It'd be just you and me.' His hand pushed further down and Emma's heart raced. Someone was going to see.

'Lucas,' she whispered. 'Not here.' She pulled away from him, her face burning despite the bitterness of the wind.

Lucas's hand wrapped around her arm and pulled her towards him, before slamming her into the wall. She felt the pain reverberate down her arm. He stared at her for a few moments, his eyes flashing again, and then he dropped his gaze and her arm and walked towards his mates for another can.

Emma told herself not to cry. Not now, anyway. She took the can Lucas offered her and then looked across the street and saw Diane walking away.

9

13 December 2010

Yates' probation officer had given Freeman the address of the bedsit where he was currently residing. She'd been there before. It was quite the place. Full of delightful young men and run, if she remembered correctly, by a little old woman who was more frightening than the residents.

She pulled over across the street. Three storeys of faded period-glamour. Much of the street had managed to retain respectability but Yates' home was verging on an eyesore – the gate was hanging off its hinges, the front door dented, no doubt from when one of the residents had forgotten their key, lager cans littered the windowsills and the one, solitary, dead-or-dying bush at the front. The run-down pub and takeaway less than a minute away only added to the value of the place. If she had to live there she'd probably be out robbing the nearest bank so she could escape it. Sometimes she wondered how anybody could move on and become a good person when they were forced to live like this. But then she'd talk to them and start to think they deserved it.

She spent a lot of time thinking about that. About punishment, about rehabilitation, about why she'd become a copper in the first place. That all these scumbags were someone's son, someone's brother. But in the end there were no answers so she just got on with it. The criminals did their jobs and she did hers. The world keeps turning.

She'd wondered whether she was doing the right thing by hauling Lucas Yates in so soon. It was hard to pin a murder on someone without a positive ID on the body. But she needed to speak to him, needed to see his face when she asked him about Emma. True, she couldn't hold him. Not unless he confessed, which was unlikely. But she needed to do it. She wanted him to know he wasn't going to get away with it. Everything she'd read about Yates convinced her that if the girl *was* Emma then he would be the one who had killed her. One of the first things you learn as a detective is never to assume anything, but this, this was more than an assumption. Besides, who else would want to hurt Emma?

Freeman watched as a couple down the street argued. The woman shoved the man against a low wall and stomped off as best she could in the platform heels she was balancing on. The man gave her the finger and walked off in the other direction. She was forming uncomplimentary judgements when she recalled the night she'd told Brian to piss off for the last time. It had probably looked a lot like this. Without the heels.

She turned back to Yates' bedsit and saw someone walking towards it. Between the grim grey of the architecture and the battered cars, the man looked out of place. A decently fitted black suit and blue tie stuck out like a sore thumb. She started to turn away, thinking he must be a solicitor. But at the last minute she glanced back at him and realised who she was staring at. Apparently Lucas Yates was not your usual tracksuited scumbag. She got out of the car and started to cross the street.

'Mr Yates,' she said and he turned around. 'DS Freeman.' She showed him her ID and for a split second she thought she saw fear. But he quickly composed himself and reached into his pocket for a pack of cigarettes.

Freeman stopped in front of him and felt, not for the first time in her life, like a small child. The picture of Yates she'd seen didn't quite match, nor do justice, to the man in front of her. Seemed like he'd taken up weights while he was in prison. Though maybe only five-ten at most, he was imposing. But to her, *everyone* was tall. She'd had to ask ten-year-olds to reach for things in supermarkets before today.

'Can I help you with something, officer?' Lucas said, and lit his cigarette.

'I was just wondering if you'd mind coming down to the station with me, to answer a few questions.'

'About what?' he said.

'Emma Thorley.'

Freeman detected the faintest hint of a smile. He took another drag and then flicked the cigarette towards the door of his bedsit.

'If you like.'

Freeman led the way towards her car. She could feel him walking too close to her. She moved to the side and fell back to walk beside him.

'Nice suit,' she said and opened the car door for him. 'Court date?'

'Job interview,' he said and slid into the passenger seat.

'Can I get you anything?' Freeman asked as Lucas sat down on the hard plastic chair in the interview room. Her boss had warned her again to tread carefully. She promised she was only going to ask him the same things she'd ask any of Emma's old acquaintances. When did you last see her, what was she wearing, who was she with? Nothing wrong with that.

Lucas looked around as if he'd never seen a police interview room before. 'A cup of tea would be nice,' he said, smiling at her.

Freeman ducked out of the room and waited a few seconds before going back inside. 'Someone will bring one in for you,' she said and pulled up a chair across from him. 'So. I'm assuming you've heard about the body being found,' she said and Lucas nodded. 'You read the papers?'

'Only the broadsheets,' he said.

Freeman smiled. 'Well, some of those papers have suggested it was Emma Thorley.' He nodded again. 'I bet that must've come as a shock.'

'I don't always believe what I read in the papers.'

Freeman waited. She wanted to knock the smug look off his face.

'So it *is* her, then?' Lucas said.

Freeman took a moment, looking him in the eye. There was something he was trying to hide. Guilt, maybe. Panic. She chose to continue. Do what she'd promised the boss. 'When was the last time you saw Emma Thorley?'

Lucas stared at her for too long. His blue-green eyes made Freeman feel uncomfortable but she refused to look away first. He knew something and she wanted to know what it was.

Lucas shrugged. 'Can't remember. It was donkey's years ago.'

'You must have a vague idea. You were together, weren't you?'

'In a manner of speaking,' he said.

'What does that mean? You either were or you weren't.'

'We went out for a bit. Then we broke up. We weren't exactly compatible.'

'How so?' Freeman asked.

Lucas shrugged again. 'We were just kids. Kids always break up.'

'You weren't a kid. You were . . . what, six, seven years older than Emma?'

'Are you accusing me of being a kiddy-fiddler, Detective Freeman?' he said, leaning forward, the smile fading. 'Because I might be many things, but that isn't one of them.'

Freeman raised an eyebrow. 'So if I can just go over a couple of things with you to try and establish a time frame. Emma ran away from home and stayed with you for a month when she was . . .' Freeman paused and looked up, pretending to think. 'Fifteen, right?'

Lucas never took his eyes off her but the smile had gone.

'And then she went home again. Is that because you broke up?' Lucas just nodded. His foot tapped beneath the desk. 'And then she went missing again in April that same year. Do you know where she went then?'

Lucas made a face, the muscles in his jaw flexed. Finally he shook his head. 'No idea,' he said and looked away.

'She came back again after that in May, according to her dad. Did you see her between then and the last time she disappeared? In July 1999?'

'Maybe. Can't really remember.'

'Did you get back together?'

'No,' he said. 'I was done with her by then.'

'But you saw her?'

'I can't remember. It was years ago.'

'Can you remember seeing her *after* July 1999?'

'No.'

'You're sure about that? Even though you can't remember other stuff from back then? You're *absolutely* sure you never saw her after her dad reported her missing again in July?'

'If she was missing, I wouldn't have seen her, would I?' Lucas said. Freeman waited. He was getting agitated. 'And anyway, I moved around then so I couldn't have seen her.'

This time Freeman sat forward. 'Where to?'

Lucas sniffed. 'London. For a bit.'

'What for?'

'I got some work there.'

'Where? Doing what?'

Lucas looked up at the clock on the wall behind Freeman's head. 'I can't remember,' he said.

Freeman smiled. 'Well, it *was* donkey's years ago.' Lucas looked down at her and folded his arms across his chest. 'So you left shortly after Emma disappeared for the last time. Was it because life was too hard to bear without her? Must've been a hard break-up.'

'Is that when she died? July?'

Freeman stared into his eyes, ignoring his question. He knew better than her when it'd happened. She could imagine a young girl like Emma falling for his charm, for his eyes. She could also imagine how he could change in a split second and how afraid she must've been. Lucas Yates put Emma into the ground. She knew it. He was just playing games.

They both waited out the silence. He broke it first with, 'Where's that cup of tea you promised?'

Freeman ignored him again. 'You recognise this?' she asked and slid a photo of the necklace towards him. Lucas stared at it, his fingers resting on the image.

'It's Emma's,' he said. 'She wore it all the time. Was obsessed with it.'

Freeman took the picture back. Ray had already identified it as being Emma's, given to her by her mum. She'd also shown him a photo of the tracksuit top. He'd paled at the sight of it. Not surprising as it was covered in blood. He'd been unsure if it belonged to his daughter, but then how many dads could identify their teenage daughter's clothes?

'What about this?' she said and passed the picture of the tracksuit.

Lucas stared at her as she slid the photo towards him, a grin barely below the surface. But then he looked at the picture and something changed. Freeman sat forward as Lucas's jaw clenched and he swallowed, moving his hand away. She hadn't expected him to be squeamish.

'You recognise it,' she said. Not a question this time. Lucas ignored her, just looked into the photo. 'Is it Emma's?'

Lucas shoved the picture away. 'Don't know.' His eyes flicked back down. 'Could be.'

He was panicking. Maybe he thought the top wouldn't have lasted this long, thought the worms would've eaten it. But here it was, covered in Emma's blood. She was still waiting on the lab to confirm that was all there was on it.

Freeman took the picture back and slid a notepad towards him. 'I think that'll do for now,' she said. 'If you could just give me a contact number in case I think of anything else.'

She watched as he scribbled something down. Left-handed. Who'd have thought? She took the notebook back and checked there were enough digits. It was a landline. 'No mobile?' she asked.

'Nope,' he said and stood up. 'You can get me at the bedsit. Speak to Mrs Heaney. Lovely woman.'

Freeman nodded and pocketed the piece of paper.

'Well, thanks for your hospitality, Detective Freeman. Let's do it again sometime.' He pushed past her to the door.

As he walked away Freeman muttered, 'Wanker,' under her breath. She was now more certain than ever that Yates had killed Emma. She just prayed there was something solid to prove it after all this time. She went back up to her office and picked up the phone. She listened to the ringing and waited for the answerphone to kick in. Again. She'd already left two messages.

'Mr Swales, it's DS Nicola Freeman again. Please could you call me back as soon as you get this message.' She hung up. She'd already left all the information he needed.

It was probably a waste of time, but even if Ben Swales knew nothing about Emma's death, maybe he could shed some more light on Lucas Yates.

10

13 December 2010

Gardner was on his way out to find something slightly more edible than the canteen sandwiches when Lawton found him. He'd been avoiding her all day. He'd already heard several members of the team discussing a drink on Friday night to celebrate her birthday. It didn't seem like Lawton's sort of thing. But apparently her invite for a quiet drink had turned into a full-blown *thing*, thanks to Harrington.

To be honest he wouldn't mind a quiet drink with Lawton. He liked her. He'd have no problem buying her a drink or two and then getting home in time to watch one of the many DVDs he had piled up. He kept telling himself he was going to finally watch the Three Colours trilogy but in reality he knew he'd end up watching *The Dark Knight*. But now that the quiet drink was a *thing*, he couldn't be arsed. He'd only ever been to four work things in the whole time he'd been in Middlesbrough. Two retirement parties he'd felt obliged to attend. One Christmas party, which had been the worst night of his life that didn't involve a dead body. And the surprise fortieth birthday party his team had thrown him for which he'd never forgiven them.

Lawton stopped in front of him, her hands shoved into her pockets, fringe falling over her eyes. Gardner thought about feigning some kind of emergency but he couldn't do it.

45

'I don't know if you've heard,' she said, her eyes on the dirty carpet, 'but a few of us are going to go for a drink on Friday for my birthday if you want to come.' She glanced at him and then looked past him. 'No big deal. Just let me know if you fancy it.'

'Let me get back to you,' Gardner said. Lawton walked away and Gardner felt like he'd just kicked a puppy. If he wasn't going to go, he was going to have to come up with a pretty good excuse.

As he made his way downstairs he wondered if perhaps he should go. Ease himself back into a social life. A few drinks with his colleagues. Talking shop 'til the drink took effect. How hard could it be?

He kept wondering about DS Freeman. If she knew about him; his past. She'd seemed fairly polite on the phone.

He knew it was completely irrational. He was never going to speak to her again. What did it matter what she thought of him? And anyway, what'd happened was in the past. It was history. Everyone had moved on. It was possible most of the officers he'd known weren't even there any more. Freeman was new. Maybe no one had told her.

It'd been eleven years since it happened. Eleven years since he'd left the place and tried to move on. And most of the time he managed it. He knew deep down what he'd done was right. He knew that he hadn't forced Wallace to behave the way he did, to do what he did. None of that was Gardner's fault. He knew that. He *believed* that. But he knew what other people thought, he knew that whatever their opinions on Wallace, they all felt the same about Gardner. *You did it for revenge. You got what you wanted.*

Gardner knew that wasn't true. He was just doing his job. His personal feelings for Wallace had had nothing to do with it. He'd been saying that to himself for a decade. But sometimes, usually at night when he couldn't sleep, he wondered. A little nagging voice asking if he actually believed it. If there hadn't been an element of revenge in his actions. Usually he ignored it because, if he was being honest, he didn't want to think about the answer.

True, it had started with Annie's affair with Stuart Wallace, but would he have done what he did if the affair hadn't happened? Would his colleagues have reacted in the same way if the affair hadn't happened? It was impossible to say.

In the end the affair *had* happened and then Wallace was dead.

I I

14 July 1999

Gardner walked in and almost tripped over a suitcase in the hallway, the cerise one he'd been embarrassed carrying around on their honeymoon.

He could hear her moving around upstairs. Drawers slamming, the wardrobe door banging against the wall, no doubt making even more of a dent in the paintwork. She didn't even know he was there and she was still slamming things. She was all about the drama.

He knew he should go up and face the music but instead he walked through into the kitchen and poured himself a glass of water. There was a bottle of vodka on the worktop, holding a lot less than it had two days ago, but he ignored it.

There were dishes in the sink. Looked like she'd got her appetite back. And nice of her to leave him the washing-up.

'Michael.'

He hadn't heard her come down the stairs. Hadn't had time to put his game face on. Hadn't had time to work out what his game face was.

'I was worried about you,' she said, leaning against the door frame, her red hair falling in front of her eyes. 'Where've you been?'

Gardner ignored her. He didn't want her to know he'd been staying in a crappy B&B. The thought of knocking on someone's door and asking for refuge on their sofa-bed was too depressing. A single bed in a damp room was far more appealing.

'You're going, then?' he said. Annie crossed her arms and sighed. 'You're not even going to bother talking about it? You don't even care what I've got to say?'

'I assumed you didn't have anything to say, Michael. You ran away from it. I haven't seen or heard from you for two days. What was I supposed to think?'

'Oh, I don't know, maybe that you told me you were cheating on me and I needed to let it sink in?'

'You could've at least called me and told me that,' Annie said and turned to walk away.

'Wait a minute. I'm not the one in the wrong here. You're the one fucking someone else.'

Annie shoved the cerise suitcase out of the way and stomped back upstairs. Gardner followed, dodging the luggage.

'And if we're talking about people running away from things, how about you announcing you're seeing that prick and that's it. End of conversation. No explanation or anything.'

Annie spun around, halfway up the stairs. 'What do you need me to explain? I'd say it was pretty self-explanatory.'

'Oh, sure. Fucking someone else needs no explanation at all. It was bound to happen about now. I must've forgotten to check the calendar.'

'Fuck off, Michael,' she said and ran up the rest of the stairs and into the bedroom.

'All I want to know is why,' Gardner said, following her in, taking in the mess. The room looked like a bomb had hit it. 'Why is that too much to ask for?'

Annie picked up her make-up bag, clinging to it like it was a life raft. 'Why do you *think*?'

Gardner shrugged. He honestly didn't know. Things weren't

perfect. They were hardly romantic novel material, but they were all right. They were *married*. They shared a bed. They had sex when it hadn't been a long week. They ate in front of the telly most nights when he was home. They talked about crap they'd seen on the news. Occasionally they went out. They were married. They were like his parents, her parents. Like *everyone* who's married.

'Okay,' she said. 'How about the fact you're never here. Or that everything is about your job or this stupid fucking exam. Or that you come home and barely speak to me because you're too busy thinking about some poor bastard's family who've just buried their son.'

Gardner laughed. 'Is that why you're fucking another copper, then?'

'He's different.'

'Is he? I'll give you six months and you'll change your tune.'

Annie looked away from him, lips pursed.

'It's been going on for more than six months?' Gardner asked. He could feel the familiar burning in the back of his throat, behind his eyes. 'How long?' Annie's eyes filled up. 'How long?' he said again, slowly.

'Almost a year,' she said.

Gardner looked at his wife. His chest was tight. She'd been lying to him for a year. Stuart Wallace had been laughing at him for a year. Who else knew? He sat down on the bed amongst the detritus of their marriage.

'I'm sorry,' Annie said and sat beside him. She put her hand on his. He wanted her to move it but it was probably the last time he'd touch her.

They sat there for a long time. The light changed outside. Next door's cat was on their fence. He hated that cat. He'd always wanted a dog but Annie didn't like them and she'd only end up looking after it while he worked day and night.

The cat jumped down and slunk away until he couldn't see it any more in the rapidly dimming light. Annie stood up and carefully folded her work clothes into a holdall.

'Stay,' he said.

Annie stopped. She bit her bottom lip and shook her head. 'No.'

'Please,' Gardner said and took the holdall from her. 'Please. We can talk it through. We can get through this. Please.'

Annie shook her head again. 'I've already made my decision. I decided weeks ago.'

'That's why you told me?'

Annie nodded.

'Where are you going to go?'

'Where do you think?' Annie said.

'What, Wallace's wife and daughter are going to put you up in their fancy fucking house?'

Annie's fist clenched. 'We've got a flat. He's already there,' she said.

Gardner tried to keep the quiver from his voice but failed. 'I don't understand why you're choosing him over me.'

Annie picked up her holdall and took one last look around the debris of the wardrobe.

'Because I love *him*,' she said. 'I'll come back for the rest later.'

Gardner watched as she hauled her bags out of the room. He wanted to call out to her, to stop her. But what was the point? She didn't love him. She didn't love *him*.

The front door slammed shut and Gardner slid off the bed onto the floor. He let the tears come for the first time, let them come until he was sitting in the dark, exhausted.

He thought about Ray Thorley. He wondered how the man had felt when his wife had gone, taken by cancer rather than by some fat, fucking bastard copper. He knew deep down that death was worse but the way he felt now it was pretty stiff competition.

Gardner shifted and realised his foot had gone to sleep. He hauled himself back on to the bed, not bothering to move the remains of Annie's stuff. He felt overwhelmingly tired. As he started to drift off he thought that even though he'd let Annie go, Wallace wouldn't get it so easy. Stuart Wallace would pay for what he'd done.

12

13 December 2010

Adam Quinn walked in with the post and flicked through it. 'Boring, boring,' he said and then held one letter up. 'You have your first Christmas card.' Louise came in, towelling her hair. There were dark brown splodges around her hairline where she'd been dyeing it. She turned down Lady Gaga, who was blaring out at him. He hated Lady Gaga. Couldn't see what Louise liked about her or how she tallied with the folky-Americana music she usually listened to. But that was Louise. A surprise around every corner. He handed her the envelope, expecting her to tear into it like she normally did. Instead she turned it over in her hand before leaving it on the mantelpiece, unopened.

'What's up?' Adam asked, pulling her towards him, arms around her waist.

'Nothing,' she said. 'I just don't feel too good.'

'Need me to give you a check-up?' he asked and kissed her neck. Louise pulled away from him. 'What?' he said.

'Nothing. I told you – I don't feel well.'

Adam looked at her with more concern. He reached his hand to her face, brushing his fingers across her cheek. 'Why don't you go and lie down for a bit? I'll make us something to eat.'

'I'm not really hungry,' Louise said and Adam dropped his hand from her face, wondering if he'd done something to

53

upset her. She'd been quiet the night before, went to bed before him, something she rarely did. Unless he'd managed to piss her off somehow.

'All right. Let me know if you change your mind.' He slumped onto the settee and turned on the TV. The news was on – something about a body being found. He'd heard about it the day before so went to switch over to something less depressing. Before he could pick up the remote, Louise turned the TV off, and stood in front of him, about to say something. Here it is, he thought. The reason I'm in the doghouse.

'I might put the Christmas tree up tomorrow,' Louise said, glancing at the space beside the window.

Adam tried to get his brain around the shift in mood. But if it meant she wasn't pissed off at him, he didn't really care. Instead he played into their yearly ritual. 'Tomorrow?' Adam said. 'It's too early.'

'No it's not. It's December.'

'Yes. December the thirteenth. It's wrong.'

'You're such a Grinch,' Louise said. 'Loads of people have got them up by now.'

'So?'

'So? You get your money's worth if you put it up early.'

Adam laughed at her logic. The same argument every year. The same one he lost every year.

'Please?' she said, making puppy-dog eyes; Adam rolled his and gave in.

'Fine. I'll get it out of the loft in the morning.'

'Thank you,' Louise said.

'But you're doing the lights. I hate doing the lights.'

'Deal,' she said and bent down to kiss him. He took her face in his hands and held her there. Her eyes glistened and he knew there was something else. She gave him an almost smile and he let her go.

13

14 December 2010

'Emma.'

He couldn't help it. Every time he slammed into her the name came out. Like a mantra. Emma. Emma. Emma.

His hands were tangled in her hair. Caught like a trap. He could feel the sweat dripping from his body onto hers. But he couldn't look at her. Couldn't bear to see her face.

He needed this. Needed to let all the anger out. The hatred. Bitch. Slut. Junkie. Whore.

Emma.

He pulled his hands free and moved them to her neck. He could feel her pulse against his hand.

'Emma. Emma. Emma.'

Her eyelids fluttered.

And it stopped.

Lucas woke up. His breath caught in his throat. He'd come back to the shithole after visiting the police station the day before, and had fallen asleep. He must've been asleep for a good twelve hours, longer maybe. He sat up, head in hands. His elbows dug into his thighs as he tried to erase her from his thoughts.

His head was pounding. He got up and turned the cold tap on. The water sputtered out and he gulped it down. His heart rate slowed and he looked around for his cigarettes. He pushed one from the pack and stood at the window.

You'd have thought that in a dump like this they wouldn't care about the smell of smoke but Mrs Heaney, the shrivelled-up landlady, was always giving him grief about it. If you have to smoke, do it outside. Lucas had nodded like a good little boy. There was something about the old battleaxe that reminded him of his nana. She was tough as old boot leather with a face to match and had been the one to look after him most of the time when he was a kid. It wasn't long after she'd died that he'd started getting into trouble. Maybe he could write one of those misery memoirs about it and make a killing. Anyway, he'd agreed not to smoke in his room but it was too cold to go downstairs and outside so he just stuck his head out the window instead. It's not like they'd notice the cold air coming in. The old crone was too stingy to put the heating on in any case. Lucas relied on a little portable heater he'd nicked from the alcoholic upstairs.

He flicked his cigarette out of the window and laughed as it floated down onto a girl walking past, no doubt doing the walk of shame. Why else would she be up at this time of the morning? He closed the window and put his hands over the heater.

He'd been thinking about Ben ever since Emma's dad mentioned him. Wondering what he knew, how hard it'd be to keep him quiet. But after talking to the dykey copper, he wondered if Ben was the least of his worries. He had to admit, seeing the photo had rattled him. Brought it all back. But he couldn't get his head around it. Couldn't work it out at all. He was in trouble and he knew it, but as long as he stayed one step ahead of the coppers maybe things would work out fine. Maybe finding Ben was the only way to go after all. Find out what he knew. He was always lurking around Emma, poking his nose in. He'd even tried to get his claws into Jenny – that's how desperate he was. Always hanging around. So it was likely he knew something about how the body ended up in the ground. And Lucas needed to know what it was.

14

10 February 1999

Lucas glanced around at all the crap – the teddy bears, the knick-knacks, the half-used make-up from Boots. The cans of Impulse scattered about the place, uniting to create a smell that stuck in his throat. She wasn't bringing all that shit.

He tossed the red velvet box towards her and leaned back on her bed. He could see she was tense, expecting her old man to burst in at any moment. It was the first time he'd been in her room. The first time he'd been in her house. It'd probably be the last time. They weren't coming back after this. Get what she needed and they were gone.

She was scared about what her dad would say if he caught her packing her bags. Lucas wasn't stupid. No matter how much Emma tried to act like the bad girl he could see her for what she really was. Daddy's girl. Her mum had died not long back. That's what all this was about.

Emma picked up the box. She looked over at him but didn't seem that grateful. The girl barely cracked a smile, rarely spoke either. Suited him. The less they said the better, as far as he was concerned. But sometimes he did wonder what was going on in her head. There was something different about this one. The other slappers he usually hung around with were all the same. Desperate for attention, couldn't keep their gobs shut or their knickers on. Emma was different.

She opened the box and took out the necklace.

'Real silver, that,' he said, nodding at the chain in her hand. She turned it over. 'Silver plated, anyway.'

'Thanks,' Emma said and put it back in the box.

'Put it on.'

Emma rubbed the heart-shaped pendant between her fingers and Lucas moved behind her. He started to take off the gold piece of tat from around her neck but she pulled away.

'What?' he said.

'Nothing,' Emma said, her fingers clutching her neck. 'It's just this was my mam's.'

'So? This one's off me. Put it on.'

She stared at the worn pink carpet and said nothing. He could see her hands were balled up. She was in one of her moods. She didn't want it. Ungrateful cow.

'Put it on,' he said again, walking up to her, holding the necklace in his open palm. Emma reached out to take it. 'Take that one off first.'

'I can wear both,' she said.

'I don't want you to. Take that one off.'

She was silent again, staring at the floor. Lucas took hold of her chin, forced her to look at him. He waited for her to do as she was told. Kept waiting.

'Well fuck off then,' he said, throwing the chain against the window. Emma flinched and Lucas pushed her away.

'I'm sorry.' She tried to take his hand. 'Don't be in a mood with me. I love the necklace but this is my mam's.'

Lucas ignored her and opened the bedroom door. 'Just get a shift on.'

Emma started to collect things together from drawers and shelves. Lucas watched her and wondered if he'd been wrong. If she was just like the rest of them. She was doing his head in. How long did it take?

'Just leave it,' he said eventually and took the bag from her hand. 'You don't need any of this shit.'

'But—'

'Let's just go, for fuck's sake.' He pulled her out of the room by her elbow. She could say goodbye to all the teddy bears and knick-knacks. That life was over.

15

14 December 2010

Lucas finished his cigarette and stomped it out, glancing behind him, expecting to see Detective Freeman hanging around. When she'd approached him outside the bedsit his first thought hadn't been 'cop'. She looked more like one of the Goth kids he used to torture at school. Long black hair with a streak of blonde at the front, and head-to-toe black clothes with a pair of dykey boots too. But as soon as she opened her gob he could hear it. Had that way of talking down to him like all coppers do.

Lucas watched people dribble in and out of the clinic. He didn't recognise any of the faces. He supposed the junkies he'd known were either dead or had no intention of quitting after all this time. He'd known a few people in the past who'd come here, who reckoned they were going to quit and make something of their lives. He knew better. None of them ever did it. Most were back on the smack or whatever was their pleasure within weeks, if not days, and the ones who did give up had either topped themselves or were living an existence as crappy as when they had been addicts – but minus the bubble of comfort the drugs gave them. It was pointless. People like that never changed.

He wondered if any of the scumbags would recognise him. The staff wouldn't know him, he'd never set foot in the place.

He started walking towards the door. A young girl was leaving and he held the door open for her. She didn't even look at him.

'You're welcome,' he muttered and walked through the reception area. The middle-aged woman behind the desk didn't look up as he approached. They might teach sobriety but they didn't teach manners.

'Hang on,' she said and scribbled something on a notepad. Lucas said nothing but continued standing over her, watching as her thin hand shook.

The woman finished her note and sighed, 'Yes?' She looked up and did a double take. Lucas knew what it was. The shirt and tie. No one wore a shirt and tie in these places. The woman looked over her shoulder as if dealing with a shirt and tie was something she was incapable of, not in her job description. 'Can I help?' she asked, possibly more to herself than him.

'I'm looking for Ben,' Lucas said with a smile.

The woman frowned and shook her head. 'I'm sorry, who?'

'Ben. Sorry, I can't remember his surname. He works here.'

The woman looked at him blankly. '*I* don't know him,' she said.

'Well, it was a while ago. He helped me get my life back on track.'

The woman looked behind her again, starting to get flustered.

'I just wondered if he was here, or if you knew where I could find him?'

The woman shook her head. 'I couldn't tell you that, even if I knew. I could ask and see if anyone knows him. What was it regarding again?'

Lucas smiled. The woman had probably been on a week-long training course in customer care. 'I just wanted to thank him. He saved my life. I wanted him to see what he did for me.'

The woman nodded slightly. Maybe that was too much. He doubted many of the customers here actually were a success, never mind came back to thank anyone. That wouldn't have been in the training.

'I'll go and have a word with my supervisor,' she said and opened a door that connected the reception to an office behind. Lucas saw two more members of staff sitting drinking coffee: a young man who looked like he was on something stronger than coffee and was wearing sandals in December, and a blonde woman with tight jeans on. From behind she looked quite fit but as she turned around he could see she must've been at least late forties. Either that or the drugs had hit her hard.

The woman from the desk had left the door open. The pair were discussing something that'd been on TV the night before. Something about fat people. The receptionist stood, hovering until they noticed her.

'What's up, Catherine?' the blonde woman asked.

'Where's Jessie?'

'She's gone out. She won't be long,' the blonde replied.

'Something *personal*,' Jesus-sandals said. 'Andrea reckons she's gone to the clap clinic.'

The blonde shoved him. 'I never said that.'

Catherine stepped forward, interrupting their flirting. 'Well, there's a man here who wants to speak to someone called Ben?' She shrugged. 'I don't know who that is.' Lucas smiled and gave a little wave as they all turned and looked at him. 'I said I couldn't give any information anyway,' Catherine continued. 'He said Ben got him clean and he wanted to thank him.'

'Well, Ben doesn't work here any more,' Jesus-sandals said. 'He left ages ago.'

'Oh, Ben! Ben Swales. I remember him. Aw, he was so lovely. Went back to take care of his mum, didn't he?' the blonde one said and received a silencing look from Jesus-sandals, who stood up and walked out to the reception area.

'Ben doesn't work here any more,' he said to Lucas. 'I'm sure he'd appreciate your coming, though.'

'Do you know where he went?' Lucas asked, glancing back at the blonde with the big mouth.

'I can't tell you that,' Jesus-sandals said.

'I only wanted to thank him,' Lucas said. 'Your colleague mentioned his mum.'

'Yeah, well, Andrea shouldn't have said anything,' said Jesus-sandals, and crossed his arms.

Lucas nodded. He knew he wasn't going to get anything else. 'Well, thanks anyway,' he said and turned to leave. As he got to the door he stopped and looked at the blonde, who'd come out of the office. 'And thank you too, Andrea,' he said and walked out.

He booted an empty can across the road, thinking about the twat in the sandals. Smug bastard. He shoved his hands into his pockets. He supposed it hadn't been totally pointless. At least he knew his full name now. There had to be another way of finding Ben Swales. He wondered what time the library closed. And where it was.

16

14 December 2010

Freeman rolled her eyes and played the third message. 'Nicola, it's me. Again. I know you told me not to call you and I know you'll be threatening to send one of your colleagues round to knock me about a bit. But I miss you. Just please call me back and we can talk about it. We can go out for dinner. My treat. I just want you back. Call me.'

She deleted the message. 'Prick,' she said under her breath. How come she hadn't noticed how irritating Brian's voice was when they were together? They say love is blind but apparently it's also deaf. Ugh. As if she'd ever thought she'd been in love with Brian. She barely even liked him. There's a lot to be said for standards during a dry patch. In the future if she was stuck for a little male company she'd hire someone from an escort service and have done with it in a few hours. It had to be better than six months with some loser you didn't even like who then had the gall to cheat on you. If he kept up the constant phone calls, then he *would* be getting knocked about a bit. Except it wouldn't be a colleague doing it.

She walked through into the office to find a pile of notes on her desk and DC Colin Lloyd loitering behind it.

'What's all this?' she asked.

'That,' Lloyd said, 'is everything you ever wanted to know about Emma Thorley but were afraid to ask.'

Freeman raised an eyebrow. 'I already know quite a lot about Emma Thorley, but go on.'

'Okay,' he said, 'that is everything *else* you wanted to know about Emma Thorley but were afraid to ask.'

'Such as?'

'Such as a list of known associates of Emma's and, probably more relevant to a murder investigation, associates of Lucas Yates.'

'Okay,' Freeman said and pushed Lloyd aside so she could sit down. 'Tell me what I don't know.'

'Right.' Lloyd perched on the edge of her desk. 'James Thompson. Known as Tomo to his mates. He was expelled from school for taking heroin into his maths class. Clever little bugger. Nothing on him for a long time but no doubt he just hasn't been caught. Dirty little skaghead.'

'Just because he's a heroin addict doesn't mean he's a criminal,' Freeman said.

'Whatever, Mother Teresa. Anyway, I'll give you one guess as to which school he went to and when.'

'Emma's?'

'Yep. Same year. Knew each other since they were little kids. I'll bet you anything he was the little shit got her hooked on heroin.'

'I think you'll find Lucas Yates did that,' Freeman said.

'Well, I bet *Tomo* was the one that introduced them.'

Freeman sighed. 'I'll look into it. Next.'

'One Christian Morton. Arrested alongside our boy Yates in '98 for brawling outside a pub in town. Nasty piece of work – he'd already done time before then for ABH and . . . something else,' he said, flicking through his notes. 'Committed suicide in 2006.'

Freeman threw up her hands. 'How about you just tell me things that are actually useful?'

'All right,' Lloyd said, 'calm yourself. I'm building up to the good stuff. Morton was from Morpeth. As was Jenny Taylor. Another little charmer by all accounts. Says here she was picked up for soliciting – dirty cow. And then, and this is the moment you've been waiting for . . .' Lloyd did a drum roll on her desk and Freeman fought the urge to do one on his face.

'Jenny Taylor knew Emma. They were all part of a little gang, liked to hang around the same pub. One night it all kicked off, pub was a war zone from the sound of it. Police hauled the lot of them in – Emma included.'

'What?' Freeman said, sitting up straight. 'I didn't come across that before.'

'What can I say?' Lloyd replied. 'I'm just better than you.' The look on Freeman's face clearly showed him that she wasn't in the mood. 'Emma wasn't arrested. Wasn't even questioned. Neither was Jenny, for that matter.'

'Lucas?' Freeman asked.

'Nope. Just Christian Morton. Trashed the pub and then kicked some poor uniform in the balls when he tried to break it up. But in his statement he claimed it kicked off because of Jenny. Apparently Jenny had quite the crush on lovely Lucas, and the green-eyed monster got the better of her. Had a go at Emma, threatened to glass her. Lucas stepped in in his own inimitable manner and threatened Jenny, someone took offence on the lady's behalf and it all kicked off.'

'So what happened?'

'Christian was charged. Everyone else slept it off in the cells. No mention of Emma.'

Freeman sat back and thought about it. 'And when was this?'

'February '99.'

'You don't happen to know if Emma's arm was broken, do you, wise one?'

'Dunno,' Lloyd said. 'But I reckon you should have a word with this Jenny Taylor. Maybe *she* offed Emma.'

Freeman rolled her eyes at Lloyd but wondered if it was beyond the realms of possibility that a teenage girl could've killed Emma Thorley. If she'd already threatened her with a broken glass, probably not.

'See if you can find her,' she said.

17

15 February 1999

The flat was cold but she wasn't going to ask again if she could put the heating on. She'd learned by now that it'd go on when he thought it was cold enough and not before. Maybe she was just too coddled. Her mam always had the heating on. But it wasn't just the heating. It was other things. He expected her to clean up after him. Pay her way, he said. That was fair enough, but he was so critical of everything. She didn't wash the dishes properly. There was an order, apparently. And her cooking wasn't up to scratch. They were relying on takeaways most of the time. And they cost money. His money.

But there were other ways to pay her way, he said.

He wanted it all the time. And she didn't mind so much, she just wished he'd use a condom. But he hated it. Said it didn't matter. Said, 'You're clean, aren't you?'

The first time had hurt so much she thought she was going to cry. The second time a little less so. And now they'd done it so many times she'd lost count, but it was starting to hurt again. There'd been blood the last time, just like the first time. And of course he got pissed off and said she'd ruined his sheets and that she should've said she was on the rag because it was disgusting. But she wasn't. It wasn't that time. It was something else.

She shivered and tucked her feet in between the cushions

on the settee to try and warm them up. That was another reason not to ask for the heating on. He'd just say, 'I know how to warm you up,' and then he'd get her to take off her clothes and make her stand there while he watched, while she got even colder, and then he'd start. And when he was done he'd leave her alone and go and watch TV or play on his PlayStation or even go out and just leave her in the flat by herself answering the door to all the scumbags looking for a score.

Feeling the pinprick of tears, Emma closed her eyes, trying to stop them from coming. She'd been here less than a week and already she was wishing she'd never left home. She felt bad for her dad. She could've at least told him where she was going. But she hadn't told anyone, so now no one would come looking for her. No one would rescue her and take her home. She'd thought Lucas was the one who was saving her, taking her away from her shitty life, but she wanted out of this, too. She wanted her dad and school and everything else back. She didn't want to be this girl.

'Emma,' Lucas said, and nudged her arm. She opened her eyes and he nodded towards the door. She realised someone was knocking. She got up and answered and two of Lucas's mates barrelled in. Except they weren't really mates, they were customers. Lucas acted as though he liked them while they were there, while they were putting money in his pocket, while they made jokes about all having a go with her. And then when they left he called them wankers. Told her maybe she should stop acting like a slut next time people came round and then maybe they wouldn't say shit to her.

She watched the familiar routine of Lucas acting the genial host – but only when the money had been handed over. He listened to their bragging about who they'd kicked the shit out of or what they'd nicked from the offy. He let them shoot up in his living room sometimes but only if they were really good customers. He didn't want the hassle of someone overdosing in his flat unless they were worth something.

She'd watch them shoot up and slip into happiness. She wondered if that's what she needed. A security blanket of drugs.

One of the men took out his kit, laying it out on the low table. She wondered if she'd be able to memorise the ritual. If she could do it while Lucas was gone. Make the day pass more bearably.

'You want some?'

Emma stared at the man. He was grinning. Taking the piss. But the fact was she *did* want some. She looked at Lucas. He was half-smiling. He said nothing but his face was a dare. He'd offered her stuff before but she'd refused.

But now? What did she have to lose?

18

14 December 2010

Freeman waited while the receptionist finished her phone conversation, her finger held up in the air indicating, she assumed, that she'd be right with her. For a woman who worked in such a depressing place she seemed awfully chipper as she cackled into the receiver. Freeman tapped her fingers on the counter and made no attempt to hide the fact she was listening in. Behind the reception desk a door opened and an older woman walked out, causing the receptionist to glance over her shoulder and abruptly end her call.

'Catherine, what did you do with those letters I asked you for?' the woman asked the receptionist, her eyes cast down, reading through some notes, apparently oblivious to her employee's phone call.

Catherine stood up and glanced from Freeman to her boss before rummaging around on the desk and coming up empty-handed. 'I'm sure I left them here. Maybe Andrea took them,' she said and walked away into an office behind the desk.

If Freeman was a betting woman she'd put all her money on Catherine never having done the letters. She cleared her throat and the older woman in front of her looked up.

'Can I help?' she asked.

'I'm DS Freeman,' she said and showed her ID as the

woman's eyebrows rose. 'I was hoping I could ask you a couple of questions about Ben Swales.'

'Ben?' the woman said. 'He doesn't work here any more.'

'I know,' replied Freeman. 'I've been trying to get hold of him for a couple of days. I wondered if anyone here was still in touch or had his mobile number.'

The receptionist returned, hands remarkably free of any letters. 'Jessie?' she said to the older woman.

'Yes, Catherine,' Jessie said.

'Andrea doesn't have the letters.'

Jessie stared at Catherine. 'So where are they, then?'

Catherine glanced around her desk and shrugged. Jessie rolled her eyes and took a deep breath, looking from Catherine to Freeman, probably trying to weigh up which annoyance to deal with first. 'Give me one minute,' she said to Catherine, then turned to Freeman. 'I haven't spoken to Ben in years. I doubt anyone else here has either.'

'Why's that?' Freeman asked.

'Someone else—' Catherine started but Jessie cut her off with a raised hand.

'One minute,' she said and Catherine stood with an open mouth before scuttling off into the office.

Jessie showed Freeman to another room where the walls were covered in posters with inspirational quotes and flyers for helplines.

'Ben was never really a part of this place,' Jessie said.

'What do you mean?'

'Well, he never really . . .' Jessie looked at the ceiling, searching for the right word, 'gelled.'

'Gelled?'

'He didn't socialise with anyone here. He kept very much to himself.' Jessie stopped and looked at Freeman as if she'd just realised for the first time that she was talking to a police officer. 'Don't get me wrong,' she said. 'He was quite good at his job. Very committed.'

'But?'

'I don't know. Something about him always struck me as being a little odd.'

'In what way?'

'Can I ask what this is about?' Jessie said.

'I'm investigating a possible murder. I'm just looking to speak to anyone who might've known the deceased. I have reason to believe Ben knew her.'

Jessie almost raised an eyebrow. Freeman could tell she wanted to ask more questions but knew as well as she did about confidentiality.

'Ben was good at his job,' Jessie repeated, leaning forward a little, lowering her voice. 'But sometimes I worried he was a little too involved with some of his clients.'

'Which clients?'

Jessie looked away for a second. 'Some of the girls,' she said.

'What made you think that?'

'Well, he spent a lot of time with some of them. And not always at work.'

'He saw them outside work? In what capacity?' Freeman asked.

Jessie just shrugged. 'I have no idea. I just saw him in the town with a few of them. One of them used to hang around outside, waiting for him to finish work.'

'Do you know who it was?'

'I did recognise her. The name escapes me now. It was a long time ago.'

'Was it Emma Thorley?' Freeman asked, and saw Jessie's eyes light up.

'The girl from the woods?' she said. Freeman didn't respond. 'You know, I think it might well have been.'

Freeman nodded. *Might well have been* wasn't the sort of thing the CPS liked to hear.

'But you're not sure – not absolutely certain?' She had to push; had to know for sure.

'N–no, not certain, but . . .' She trailed off.

'Why did Ben leave?' Freeman asked, hoping for something a little more concrete.

'He left to go and take care of his mother. It must've been ten, eleven years ago now, I suppose.'

'Eleven years?' Freeman said, perking up. It had been eleven years since Emma Thorley disappeared. Eleven years since Ben Swales left town too.

19

14 December 2010

Freeman knocked on the door and waited a few minutes before Ray Thorley opened up. He looked bleary eyed, like he'd been sleeping despite being fully clothed. He took a minute to focus his eyes and recall her name from the depths of his mind and then smiled a kind of weary smile.

'Miss Freeman,' he said. 'You're back again.' He edged back just enough to let her through, clearly trying to minimise the amount of cold air that got in.

'I hope I'm not disturbing you,' Freeman said. 'I just wanted to ask you a few more questions.' As she'd driven over she'd told herself it was probably a pointless exercise – Ray Thorley was unlikely to remember any more about his daughter's friends and associates, even if he had once known. But anything was worth a try.

Ray led her through to the living room and the sudden heat from the ancient gas fire made Freeman's cheeks flush. The TV played in the background, some American show from the seventies or early eighties, one that only the elderly or unemployed knew of. Ray muted the volume and took a seat in his chair.

'Mr Thorley, do you know if Emma had a friend called Jenny Taylor? Did she ever mention her?'

Ray shook his head. 'I don't know. I don't recall her

friends too well.' He looked down at his hands and rubbed them. Freeman wondered if he had arthritis or something. He couldn't possibly be cold with the heating turned up that high.

'There was one girl. Diane,' he said. 'She still saw her now and then, I think.'

'Right. Diane Royle. You mentioned her. And you were right, someone interviewed her when Emma disappeared.' Freeman made another mental note to read Diane's statement. She doubted there was anything useful in it if the girls had no longer been close. 'Was Diane in trouble too? Did she—'

'No, no,' Ray said, shaking his head. 'Diane was good as gold. But I know she came around a bit even after my Emma started with it all. She might know something about this other girl.'

'Do you know where I could find her?' Freeman asked.

Ray closed his eyes and shook his head as if he were angry with himself. 'Not Diane, but I used to see her dad down the club,' he said. 'Frank. Frank Royle. That was it. I think he still lives down by the hospital.'

'Thank you, Ray,' Freeman said. 'You've been very helpful. I'll be in touch.'

Freeman got back in her car, hands frozen from just the short walk from the house. She dialled Lloyd.

'All right, boss,' he said.

'I need you to find a number for me. Diane Royle. I've got no idea if she's still local but you could try her dad, Frank Royle. Apparently he's still living by the hospital.'

'Okay,' Lloyd replied. 'Who's this, then? Another smackhead?'

Ignoring his comment, she asked, 'How're you getting on with Jenny Taylor? Emma's dad's never heard of her.'

'Still working on it, boss.'

'Let me know when you've got it,' she said. 'And if Routledge's asking for me, I'm going to see Ben Swales. Just like he asked.'

20

15 July 1999

'Take a seat,' Gardner said and Lucas Yates slunk into the chair. The last thing he wanted to be doing this morning was talking to some smug little shit about a girl who'd probably show up in a couple of days anyway. But here they were. His head was pounding and Yates was pissing him off already. He really wished he hadn't finished off that bottle of vodka the night before.

'Where's Emma?' Gardner said.

Yates looked up at Gardner; his eyes creased as if he were staring into the sun. 'Emma who?'

Gardner dragged out the chair opposite Yates and sank into it. 'Emma Thorley.'

Yates shrugged. 'Don't know,' he said and pulled his pack of cigarettes from his pocket. Gardner just stared at him and Yates grinned, turning the box round and round in his hand.

'When was the last time you saw her?'

Yates shrugged slowly. 'Who knows?' He smiled again, showing his crooked teeth, and Gardner wanted to reach over and punch them down his throat. Yates wasn't the most obnoxious person he'd sat across from in this room – he'd have to go some to win that title – but he'd chosen the wrong day to piss Gardner about.

'Emma was living with you for about a month in February. That right?'

'Yeah. And?'

'Is she living with you now?' Gardner asked.

'No.'

'You mind if we check your flat?'

Yates' jaw clenched. 'You got a warrant?'

'No,' Gardner said, slowly. 'I'm asking your permission.'

'And I'm telling you she's not there,' Yates said, each word slower than the last.

'Prick.' Gardner stood up and went to the door.

'Can I go?'

'No,' Gardner said and slammed the door behind him. He'd already spoken to Ben Swales that morning and he'd pretty much agreed with him that the most likely place to find Emma was with Lucas Yates. Yes, she'd tried to get off the drugs, but according to Swales it hadn't gone as well as Ray Thorley had suggested.

He squeezed his eyes shut and prayed for the hammering in his head to stop. When he opened his eyes he saw PC Griffin walking towards him. 'Any luck?' he asked.

Griffin shook his head. 'Nothing.'

Gardner sighed. He knew full well that Yates wasn't going to let them into his flat without a fight. Hence bringing him in for a while so that Griffin could go and take a look unhindered. It was worth a try. And just because she wasn't there right now didn't mean she hadn't been with him at all.

'Thanks anyway,' Gardner said and headed back to the interview room to let the little shit go.

Lucas watched the door to the interview room open but instead of DC Gardner, with his face like thunder, it was DS Stuart Wallace and his fat little sidekick McIlroy.

'All right, Lucas,' Wallace said, and checked the corridor before closing the door behind him. Wallace was a prick.

Thought he was a clever bastard, playing both sides, but he'd made himself useful once or twice before. 'I heard you were darkening our doors again,' Wallace said, resting one foot on Gardner's vacated chair while he pulled a pack of gum from his pocket. 'Hope you've not been a naughty boy, Lucas.'

Lucas glared at Wallace. He'd tell him to piss off but he wanted to see how it played out. See what Wallace could do for him.

'Has our DC Gardner been giving you a hard time? You want me to sort him out?' Wallace looked at McIlroy and they giggled like kids.

Lucas sighed. 'What do you want, Wallace?'

'Nothing,' Wallace said, standing up straight again. 'I just thought I'd come in and say hello, see if I could be of assistance, but if you're going to be like that . . .' Wallace shrugged and walked back to the door. McIlroy was still standing there, folded arms resting on his gut.

'What do you know about Emma Thorley?' Lucas asked.

Wallace frowned, as if he were trying to get his brain into gear. 'Not a lot to know. Missing junkie. Gone for a week or something. Why? You know her? One of your slappers, is she?'

Lucas shrugged. 'So that's it? Just a missing person. Nothing else going on?'

'No. Why, you got something you want to tell me, Lucas? A dirty little secret?'

Lucas just glared at him and Wallace laughed. 'Chill out, mate. Just kidding. Don't worry about it. There's nothing to this. Heard Gardner talking to the boss. Reckons she'll turn up in a few days, always does.'

The door opened and Gardner looked even more pissed off than when he'd left.

'What the fuck are you doing in here?' he asked Wallace and McIlroy.

'Just talking about our love lives,' McIlroy said and winked at Lucas before walking out. Lucas watched as Gardner's face reddened, his fingers curling into fists. He could hear Wallace whistling down the corridor. Tuneless git.

'You. Out,' Gardner said and Lucas wondered what he'd missed. But he didn't need telling twice. He walked past Gardner, waiting to be escorted out of the building. Instead Gardner slammed the door behind him, leaving Lucas wondering what the fuck had just happened.

21

14 December 2010

Freeman headed for Alnwick and turned on the stereo. Bikini Kill came on, blasting out 'White Boy'. She turned it off and switched to the radio. She didn't need to fuel her anger, she needed to think. She found Radio 2 and listened to someone being interviewed about something or other and let her mind wander. Wondering what Ben Swales would say when she showed up at his door.

She pulled up outside the address she had for Ben. There was an old car on the drive, even crappier than hers. Freeman looked at the house. It was nothing special, just an ordinary semi, but she'd bet it'd cost a lot more than the same kind of houses at home. She could barely afford to rent the piece of crap she was living in, so how did Ben Swales afford this? She couldn't imagine drug counselling paid *that* well.

There didn't seem to be any lights on in the house but she couldn't be sure. The house across the street was lit up like Vegas with dozens of flashing Santas and reindeer, so much so that the houses on Ben's side probably didn't need to bother with their own lights throughout December.

She got out of the car, walked up the drive and knocked on the front door. After a minute or so a light came on in the hall and a figure emerged at the door. Freeman could hear a key turning in a lock and whoever was on the other side was

83

pulling on the door, trying to un-jam it. She considered pushing from her side to speed things up but instead stood and waited, hoping her feet wouldn't freeze completely.

The door finally opened and a man stood there with a tea towel slung over his shoulder and a pair of what Freeman called 'granddad slippers' on his feet. His hair, or what was left of it, was a reddish colour and it looked like he cut it himself. She had a sudden image in her head that this was what Brian would look like in fifteen years' time. The thought of her being there with him, in her own granny slippers, being run ragged by a herd of kids, made her feel ill.

'Yes?' he said.

'Ben Swales?'

'Yes.'

Freeman showed him her ID. 'I'm DS Freeman. Can I come in?'

Ben swallowed and nodded. He stepped back and allowed Freeman in before turning to the door and trying to coax it back into the door frame. He managed to get it closed and smiled nervously at Freeman. He showed her through to the kitchen and tossed the towel onto the table. He hadn't even asked why she was there.

'I'm sorry, I was just washing up.' He looked around and gathered two mugs from the drainer. 'Please, take a seat. Can I get you a drink?'

Freeman didn't usually bother with cups of tea when she went into people's homes, but she was so cold that she couldn't refuse the offer.

'Thank you, tea would be great,' she said and Ben turned away from her to boil the kettle. Freeman sat down and dropped her bag on the floor beside the table.

From upstairs a woman's voice called his name. Freeman turned towards the sound.

'I'm sorry,' he said. 'That's my mother. I'll be right back.'
He walked out of the kitchen and Freeman listened to him go
up the stairs. She could hear him moving around, the floor-
boards creaking, and the muffled sound of voices. A few
minutes later Ben walked back in and finished making the tea.

'I'm sorry,' he said. 'She's confined to bed. She can be
needy.'

'It must be difficult. Do you have any help to care for her?'

He shook his head. 'No, it's just me.'

'What about work?' Freeman asked.

'I gave up a couple of years ago when she took a turn for
the worse. I do the occasional day if I can get someone to
watch her but it's a rarity now.'

Ben poured the water and looked at Freeman over his
shoulder. She thought he was going to ask about milk and
sugar.

'Sorry, can I ask what this is about?' he said.

'Oh, sorry,' Freeman replied. 'I'm investigating a possible
murder. I'm just trying to speak to anyone who knew the
victim.' Ben's face was blank. 'Have you seen the news? A
body was found in Blyth.'

'No. I haven't seen anything.'

'Right. Well, I'm sorry to inform you, but we think it's probably Emma Thorley.'

She saw Ben stiffen, and waited. 'I'm sorry,' he said. 'I don't
know her.'

Freeman stared at Ben. Now this was interesting. She knew
for a fact he was lying. She just didn't know why. Ben waited.
His face remained impassive.

'You don't know her?' Freeman asked.

Ben shook his head. 'I don't recognise the name. Should I?'

Freeman suddenly felt like there was more to Ben Swales
than met the eye. He was hiding something.

'You don't know Emma Thorley?'

She saw him swallow but he still shook his head and smiled gently. 'I'm afraid not.'

Freeman acted surprised. 'Oh,' she said.

Ben let out a nervous laugh. 'Is something wrong?' He scratched his cheek, his face reddening again.

'Emma Thorley was an addict, went missing a couple of times. This is going back a bit. '99. Her father filed reports. Only the second time he retracted it after he was informed that his daughter was safe.'

Ben took a sip of his tea and Freeman noticed his hands shake slightly.

'Her father said that it was you who came to tell him she was okay,' Freeman said and stared at Ben.

'Me?' He shook his head and stumbled over his words. 'I don't recall that.' He swallowed again. 'He thought it was me?'

'Yes,' Freeman said.

Ben rubbed the side of his face and raised his eyebrows. 'Maybe I did. I don't remember it, but maybe.'

'He seemed to think you visited him on a couple of occasions. Surely you'd remember that? Also, another police officer questioned you after Emma Thorley disappeared for good. A couple of months after you'd visited her dad. You thought maybe she'd started using again and took off.'

Ben stared at Freeman like a rabbit caught in the headlights. 'I . . . yes.'

'Yes? Yes you remember now, or yes, you think you would remember?'

'Yes. I remember something about a girl. I helped a girl who was being abused. By her ex-boyfriend, I think? She left town and I passed on a message for her.'

Freeman tilted her head. 'It's all flooding back now,' she said.

'I remember saying I'd tell her father but I don't recall visiting him often. And her name. I don't remember that. It doesn't seem familiar. It was a long time ago.'

'Yes. Eleven years. You think you'd remember being questioned by the police, though.' Freeman watched Ben carefully. Why would he deny knowing Emma?

'I'm sorry,' Ben said. 'I can't believe I forgot about that.'

'No,' replied Freeman. 'You'd think it'd stick in your memory.'

If Ben caught the sarcasm he didn't show it. He swilled his tea, taking a moment, and then looked up at Freeman.

'I'm sorry, Detective Freeman, but I really didn't remember her name,' he said and looked down at the floor. She noticed him looking at her bag, realising it was open, the paper bag from the chemist's lurking at the top, sharing her secrets. She nudged the bag closed with her foot and Ben looked away, embarrassed.

Freeman watched Ben. Something was wrong here. The man clearly knew more than he was letting on; had clearly known Emma Thorley quite well. Freeman looked closely at Ben Swales. What did he know? What was his part in all this? He tried to hold her stare but after a few seconds his eyes dropped back to the table. He chewed his lip and Freeman could've sworn he was about to speak, but the call from upstairs stopped him.

'Ben!' his mother shouted. Ben blinked and looked at Freeman.

'Excuse me,' he said and scurried away.

Freeman listened to the muffled exchange and heard movement. She wondered who was really up there. She knew it was ridiculous but she couldn't help it. She walked out into the hall and listened at the bottom of the stairs. She couldn't quite make out what was being said. She climbed the stairs and stood in the doorway of the first room. Ben was helping an elderly lady out of bed, and being criticised for not doing it right. The old woman caught her eye and cried out. Ben spun around and Freeman felt her face burn.

'Sorry,' she said. 'Could I use your toilet?'

Ben stared at her for a little too long before nodding. 'Down there,' he said and pointed to the end of the hall.

Freeman heard Ben trying to placate his mother as she closed the bathroom door. She knew she wasn't going to get anything else from him. Not yet anyway. Besides, she was exhausted. She made use of the toilet while she was there and came out to find Ben waiting for her.

'I'm sorry, my mother needs her bath,' he said.

Freeman nodded. 'That's all right; I need to head back anyway.' She looked at Ben and the relief seemed to wash across his face. She pulled a card from her pocket and handed it over. 'If you think of anything you want to tell me, that's my number.'

Ben stared at the card and looked as if he might speak again but instead tucked it into his pocket and nodded at her. She waited, hoping he'd change his mind, but he turned and walked down the stairs to the front door. 'I'm sorry I couldn't be more helpful,' he said.

The rush of cold air hit Freeman and she was almost tempted to ask if she could bunk there for the night. But she stepped outside, shoved her hands into her pockets and turned back to Ben. 'I'll probably need to speak to you again,' she said. He just nodded.

Freeman walked to her car.

'Goodnight,' she heard Ben call after her and as she opened her car door Ben struggled to close his before turning off the light.

Freeman turned the heaters on. She knew she'd be back to

speak to Ben again. She just wasn't sure if time would make Ben more likely to talk or just give him a chance to sort out his story. At least one thing was certain. He wasn't a flight risk. Not with his mother up there.

Freeman waited until her hands warmed up and then pulled away, wishing she hadn't come to Alnwick. Partly because she barely had the energy to drive home, but mostly because it had given her more questions than answers.

Like why had Ben denied knowing Emma? What possible reason could he have? His old boss had suggested he was a bit too involved with some of his clients. But could he have had something to do with Emma's murder?

22

4 March 1999

Emma sat, knees to her chest, on the cold floor. He hadn't just locked her into the flat this time; he'd locked her into the bedroom. She shouldn't have said she wanted to leave, to go home. She'd pissed him off. More than ever.

She could've sat on the bed, could've tried to sleep, to pass the time unconsciously. But the sheets smelt of him and she knew she would never sleep. She rarely did these days. Always on guard, always waiting for the next time.

She could've moved to the other side of the room to where the radiator was, but what was the point? It was never on. And the window was useless. Too far up to climb out. Too far away for people to see her. As if anyone would care. As if anyone would help her. She wasn't Rapunzel.

Her legs ached from staying in one position so long. But she didn't dare move. She was cold. She needed the toilet. Every so often she wished he'd just come back so at least she could stop thinking about it, about what would happen when he did. At least it would be over for another day.

She could hear a TV next door. A laughter track. A dog barking. Maybe that was outside.

And then she heard the key in the door. The scrape of the door across whatever the postman had left. Probably more junk mail. Nothing good came here.

She pushed herself further into the corner. She could hear him in the kitchen. He'd bought more bottles, she could hear them clinking into the fridge. He was taking his time. She wondered what today would bring. It was giro day. Probably already spent. But money wasn't a problem for him. Never was. He'd told her they'd go away together when she first moved in. She knew that wasn't going to happen now. He'd never leave Blyth. Neither of them would.

The scrape of the bolt made her jump. He came in and lay down on the bed, didn't even acknowledge her. She waited for him to say something but he just lay there, staring at the ceiling. She waited, saw him close his eyes. She almost smiled. He's okay.

Emma stood up, her legs creaking. She walked out to the bathroom. Relief. And then she saw him standing there, watching. She felt embarrassed, vulnerable. She didn't know why. He'd seen her more intimately than this. She stood and washed her hands and he took her by the wrist, squeezing just a little too tightly.

She looked up at him and wondered if she should kiss him, if that was what he wanted. He lowered his face to hers and she knew. He didn't want that.

'Have you thought about what you said?' Lucas asked her. She nodded. 'And?'

'I'm sorry,' she said, feeling tears in the back of her throat, behind her eyes. She knew she wasn't sorry for wanting to go home, she was just sorry she'd told him.

He turned her away from him, pressing her against the filthy sink. The porcelain dug into her hips. He pulled her knickers down. She stood, waiting, while he unzipped his jeans. As he forced himself into her she could see her face reflected in the taps, distorted. She wasn't going to cry.

Sometimes she thought he liked it, other times he'd slap her, hard; tell her to shut up.

She would never win.

Not with Lucas.

23

14 December 2010

Freeman made her way up the stairs to her flat, dragging her feet, forcing her eyes to stay open for just a bit more time. It'd been a long day.

She was exhausted but knew that she was unlikely to sleep well. She wasn't any closer to finding out what had happened to Emma Thorley. Even saying definitively that it *was* Emma was proving tricky. They had the necklace and the ID, and the fact that the remains appeared approximately old enough for Emma to have been murdered when she disappeared the last time. But it wasn't enough. She was putting pressure on the lab to get back to her about the tracksuit but there were more pressing cases. Apparently. She knew there was no way to prove the blood was Emma's, but if they could find another person's blood – if Emma fought back – then maybe she'd be in business.

She was still pretty sure that Lucas Yates had to be the one who put her in the ground, but she had no evidence whatsoever – other than he was a little prick. She doubted that would stand up in court. She was desperate for his DNA to be on that tracksuit. At least it'd be something.

But then there was Ben Swales. She'd started the day thinking he was just another witness. Someone who could perhaps give her more details about Emma's last few months, maybe something about Lucas. But something was off there. *Maybe* he could've forgotten her name after all this time, but it just didn't ring true. And his old boss had also said something was off with him. Too involved with the girls, she'd said.

She listened to the sleet on the window and the sounds of the silent flat. For a split second she wished she hadn't told Brian to sod off, that he was there to keep her company, to talk about something other than dead girls. But she *had* told him to go, and for a good reason. She might not have been the most attentive girlfriend but that didn't give him the right to sleep with his yoga instructor. What kind of man *has* a yoga instructor anyway? She knew she'd have to speak to him eventually but as long as she kept ignoring it she could put it off. Having so much on her plate at work was a blessing. It kept her mind off her own shitty life. The only problem was there was a time limit on these things. She couldn't put it off forever. She dragged herself to the bedroom, promising to do something about it in the morning. Or the next day at the latest.

She couldn't stop thinking about Ben Swales. Why would he deny knowing Emma? She stared out of the window, watched a group of kids loitering in the car park. Maybe she should call DI Gardner again. See what he'd thought about Ben.

She'd barely closed her eyes when she heard the knock. She listened carefully and thought she could hear the sound of a game show. Freeman got up and went to the door. She could hear the TV louder now as her neighbour, Lady Clairville, stood there in her dressing gown and slippers, her little Jack Russell, Roy, yapping at her feet. She got the feeling the woman was in her seventies but you'd never know it to look at her. She dressed like she was attending a royal wedding every day, hence Freeman's nickname for her.

'Hey,' Freeman said. 'What's up?'

'Just thought I should tell you I saw *him* hanging around again. Don't know how he got in. One of them from upstairs must've done it. They'll let anyone in. Druggies, I think.'

Freeman didn't want to mention that he still had a key. Didn't want to admit she'd been stupid enough to give him one in the first place. 'Did he say anything?'

'Just that he wanted you to call him. I told him to bugger off,' Lady C said with a raised eyebrow. She didn't approve of Brian. She thought he looked homosexual.

'Thanks.'

'Why don't you come over? I was just watching a little telly.'

'No, I should get some sleep,' Freeman said. 'It's been a long day.'

'Suspicious death?' Lady Clairville asked. Freeman thought the reason her neighbour liked her company so much was because of her job. She was always fishing for gruesome details. She was a bit of a true crime buff.

'Something like that.' Freeman started to close the door.

'Just come over for a little tipple, then? It's nearly Christmas,' Lady Clairville said.

Freeman paused. She was tired. She had a lot on her mind. But maybe a drink with Lady C was what she needed.

'Give me two minutes. I just need to make a call,' Freeman said and closed the door to a disappointed-looking Lady C.

24

14 December 2010

Louise bit her nail and stared at Adam. He looked up from the laptop and smiled at her before turning his attention back to the screen. He'd already explained in great detail that there were two Johnny Cash live CDs he didn't have that were ending in thirty minutes but some bastard called Sexie69 kept outbidding him. Anyone who'd call themselves Sexie69 apparently shouldn't be allowed to buy Johnny Cash CDs. But she just wanted him to go. Actually she *wanted* him to stay. More than anything. But she *needed* him to go.

'What's up?' he asked her and she realised her foot was tapping.

'Nothing,' she said and looked past him to the clock on the table. 'What time's your bus?'

Adam half looked up from the screen and reached across the settee with his free hand to rub Louise's foot. 'Hmmm?' he muttered.

'Your bus? Aren't you going to miss it?' she said.

Adam tapped a few more keys and then looked at his watch despite the clock in the corner of the screen. He did a double take. 'Shit,' he said and closed the laptop. 'I'm going to miss my bus.'

He stood and ran out into the hall, grabbing his coat. He went back into the living room with his coat half on and pointed at the laptop. 'Make sure I win.' He kissed her on the top of her head. 'Won't be late,' he said and ran out the door.

Louise let out a breath she felt she'd been holding for days. She'd been like a madwoman – throwing herself at the TV to switch off the news, steering Adam away from newspapers in the corner shop. Every time she heard the name Emma Thorley she felt ill. Like she was being haunted by a ghost.

She got up and went upstairs to the spare room. She hoped it would still be there – the one thing to connect her to her old life. She peeled back the tape from the small cardboard box and looked at the contents. Everything she cared about was in there and most of it was from the last few years – the years she'd spent with Adam. At the bottom was the photo of her parents. She rarely looked at it any more, the memories too painful. What she'd done was too much.

The tears came without warning. In the empty house her cries seemed to echo. How could she have done it? How could she take someone's life?

'Bollocks,' Adam muttered and slowed down to a walk as the bus turned the corner. When he got to the bus stop he scanned the timetable. Another half an hour before the next one. He considered turning round and going home to his auction but he'd been looking forward to a night out with the lads. He walked down to the main road and looked for a taxi. Usually the place was swarming with them, the drivers all pulling in and offering their services like mobile hookers. But tonight – nothing.

Adam started walking in the direction of town but after a couple of minutes he stopped. If he just went home, the money he'd have spent on half a dozen pints and the obligatory pizza on the way home could pay for the Johnny Cash CDs. He turned around and headed back.

He threw his coat over the end of the banister and stuck his head round the door of the living room. His laptop was on the settee but there was no Louise. He checked his watch. The auction should've just finished. He opened the laptop to check how much he'd ended up paying and saw the email telling him he hadn't won.

'Lou?' he shouted, wondering why she hadn't upped his bid. He walked to the bottom of the stairs and noticed the light on in the spare room. Technically it was his study, where he was supposed to mark essays and write lectures but he usually did those things in front of the TV. Instead the room was used mainly to store stuff they hadn't found a home for. In the corner there were a few boxes that had never been unpacked despite the fact that they'd moved in over two years ago. Most of the boxes were Adam's – like most of the stuff in the house, in fact. Louise didn't have much, so what could she be looking for? Adam smiled. He'd bet she was trying to find her Christmas presents. She'd be lucky. He hadn't bought anything yet.

He started climbing the stairs, careful to miss the creaky step at the top. He walked to the doorway of the spare room, ready to catch her in the act.

He found her crouched over the single box labelled 'Louise's stuff'. It had never been opened since they'd moved in. All she kept in it was birthday and Valentine's cards, a few souvenirs from trips they'd taken. But now it was open, its contents spread across the floor.

Adam was about to say something but she was staring at a Christmas card he'd given her two years earlier. The one with the cartoon penguins. He remembered how funny he thought it was and how he'd tickled her into submission when she didn't agree with him. They'd gone out for a meal that night and he'd proposed. She said no. She'd tried to explain to him that she was scared, that her own parents' marriage had not been the best example and that maybe one day she'd be ready.

He accepted it in his usual manner, saying, 'Just let me know when you're ready and I'll get the ring back from the pawn shop.' And even though she'd said, 'One day,' they'd never spoken about it since. He couldn't take the rejection again.

He watched her brush her fingers over the card before putting it back in the box and picking up a small piece of paper.

'What're you up to?' Adam asked and Louise spun around. She shoved the paper in her pocket and started piling the cards and notes back into the box.

'I was just . . .' she said and turned away, moving the box into the corner. 'I was looking for a book. Thought it might've been in there. How come you're back?'

'Missed the bus,' he said. He wanted to ask her about the CDs but she looked like she had more on her mind than Johnny Cash.

Louise stood up straight and smiled at him, even though her face was red, as if she'd been crying. 'Do you want to watch a DVD instead, then?' she asked.

'Sure,' he said and they walked out of the study, turning off the light.

'Go and pick something and I'll be right down.' She kissed him on the cheek.

Halfway down the stairs Adam stopped and looked up as Louise went into their bedroom and pulled the piece of paper from her pocket. She stared at it for a second before tucking it inside her diary.

Adam turned, wondering what the big secret was. He waited for Louise to go into the bathroom before creeping back upstairs. Without turning on the bedroom light he opened her diary and the paper fluttered out. Adam picked it up. In a barely legible scrawl was an address in Alnwick.

He heard the toilet flush, shoved the paper back inside and headed downstairs.

25

25 March 1999

Ten days. Ten days since she'd walked out of the flat and back to her daddy. He'd called her bluff. She'd been whining for days. Weeks, really. After everything he'd done for her and she still wasn't happy. She wanted to go back to her dad, back to her miserable life. She wanted to leave him.

He wasn't having that. He'd kept her locked up, made sure she couldn't leave. Doped her up to the eyeballs and then left her hanging. Forced her to need him. And then one day she says she wants to stop. No more heroin. And he knows she means no more Lucas. She swears she still loves him, still wants to see him. She just has to go home. Her dad will be going out of his mind. Well boo-fucking-hoo. She should've thought of that before.

And then the tears start. He can't fucking bear the water-works. He tells her to shut up but she keeps going. On and on. So he hit her. Hard. Not for the first time, but this time it took her longer to get up. At least it shut her up for a while.

And then she told him she hated him. She screamed in his face. Maybe he'd knocked some spirit into her. It almost excited him. He was ready for a brawl. Ready to make her understand how things were going to be. But she walked away. Slammed the bedroom door. He thought about locking her in. Give her time to think about it. Instead he called her bluff. He unlocked the front door, left it wide open. Told her to piss off out of his flat if that's what she wanted.

Turns out that was what she wanted. She just walked out. By the time he'd realised, she was halfway down the street. He went after her, wasn't just going to let it go, but there were coppers hanging about. So she just walked away. Thought it was over. But she was wrong.

He walked to the window at the front of her daddy's house and looked in. There was no one in the front room but that didn't mean she wasn't home. He'd been following her for days. Waited outside the school gates. Came to the house, trying to rattle her. Sat on the wall across the street, for hours at a time, watching her watching him. Daring her to come out or to call the police. Instead she cowered inside. He was going to be in her life one way or another.

A couple of kids played on bikes in the middle of the street, driving round and round in circles. He ignored one of them asking him for a fag and walked around the back of the house. It was getting dark. Not that it mattered much. Street like this, no one gives a shit what's going on.

He'd never been round the back of the house before. The kitchen jutted out beneath her bedroom window. Perfect for lovers sneaking out in the night. Or sneaking in during the day. Lucas stood on the bin and pulled himself onto the flat roof. He cracked the window with his elbow and reached in to open it. Inside he felt a surge of warmth. The heating was on. He climbed inside and pulled the curtain closed. Someone might've seen him break in, that didn't worry him too much, but he'd rather they didn't see what he was going to do next.

Lucas took a deep breath, inhaling her smell. There was still a hint of her at home – he hadn't changed his sheets. But this was different. Pure. He lay back on the bed and thought about her, remembering the feel of her skin against his, the taste of her. He unzipped his jeans. He'd thought about leaving her a note so she'd know he'd been. So she'd know he wasn't going to stop until she came back to him. But a note was so impersonal. Instead, his hand drifted down and he thought about the last time as he touched himself.

He would leave something much more intimate.

26

14 December 2010

Lucas pulled up his hood, as much to keep warm as to cover his face. He walked alongside the clinic to scope it out. There weren't any shutters or bars. They probably wouldn't even notice he'd been there. The library had been a bust. No trace of Ben online. And the old bag who worked there said they didn't keep phone books any more. So it was back to plan A.

He walked around the back, into the alley, making sure no one was around. In this part of town it was unlikely. Or at least it was unlikely to find anyone who was willing to talk to the police. The main attractions were a parade of closed-down shops and a pub where all the windows were permanently boarded up. He found a window high up and tried to work out where it'd lead to. He dragged the wheelie bin over and climbed on top. With a gloved hand he punched the window through and waited for the sound of an alarm. Nothing. Jesus, these people were practically inviting thieves. Why not just leave the doors open and save the junkies the trouble.

Climbing down onto a desk, he cursed as he slipped on a pile of papers, and looked around the darkness of the office. He walked to the door and found himself in the reception area where he climbed over the desk and glanced around, turning his attention to the office door. He tried the handle. Locked. He raised his fist, ready to punch through the glass in the door but stopped and turned back to the reception desk. In the dim light he noticed a couple of drawers and tried them. In the first was nothing but stationery. He tried the one beneath. A few Cup a Soups, some tea bags and a mug with 'Hot Stuff' written across it. Course you are, Catherine, he thought. He wouldn't if she were the last woman on earth.

Lucas pushed aside the packets of biscuits and was about to close the drawer when something caught his eye. He pulled out a set of keys and shook his head. These were supposed to be the people making the world a better place. Fucking idiots.

Lucas swung the door open and walked into the office. He noticed there was no window and felt around the wall next to the door, flipping on the light switch. The warm light revealed a depressingly sparse room. He pulled at the top drawer in the filing cabinet. Locked. He turned to a desk and rummaged about in the drawers. Nothing but chocolate biscuits and a newspaper from the week before. He scanned the desk looking for a hidey-hole where someone might stash keys. Coming up empty-handed, Lucas kicked the bottom of the filing cabinet. He tried the other drawers, knowing it wouldn't help.

He stood in the middle of the room and considered his options. He could nick the computer, maybe make a bit of cash if nothing else. But that wasn't what he wanted. He came for information and he was going to get it.

'Fuck,' he muttered. He booted a wicker waste-paper basket across the room, causing debris to scatter. He should just trash the place out of fucking spite. He walked to the door and then stopped and pulled it away from the wall, noticing a small cabinet tucked away in the corner, buried under pots full of dying plants. He bent down and tried the keys again. Finally he got the right one and pulled open the drawer. Several files were stacked inside and a small metal box was placed on top. As Lucas lifted the box out he heard the clatter of loose change. He put it aside and pulled out the files. He opened the first few and recognised the names Catherine and Andrea. Bingo. He threw aside the ones belonging to current staff and kept looking. No Ben Swales.

'Fuck,' he muttered again and threw the files across the floor. There was no information on Ben. No clues to where he'd gone. Lucas leaned against the wall. The blonde said Ben had gone home to look after his mum. What else would he have told her? Lucas scanned the scattered pile of records. Andrea Round. He pulled the file out and scanned the information for what he wanted. If her records were up to date, Andrea Round lived a fag-end flick away from The Fox and Hounds, not far from the bedsit. It wasn't the kind of establishment he frequented himself. But he knew from passing on his way into town that Tuesday was quiz night and that it was populated by middle-aged losers with nothing better to do and no one to do it with. If he couldn't find Ben Swales he was willing to bet he'd be able to find Andrea.

Lucas grabbed the metal money box, smiling as he made his way back to the window. He was one step closer to finding Ben. And to finding out what he knew.

27

14 December 2010

Gardner tried to decide if the flat looked even sadder *with* the four-foot Christmas tree than it had without. Maybe Tom Waits playing in the background was making things worse. He hadn't put decorations up for years, didn't much see the point. More often than not he chose to work Christmas. Let the people with lives have the time off.

The tree and accompanying decorations were an impulse buy from Tesco on his way home. He'd only gone in for something for his tea. But the thought that there could be a message waiting for him at home from the dating site had spurred a sudden desire to get into the Christmas spirit. He didn't want anyone he brought home to think he was a miserable git. So he'd grabbed the last Christmas tree left on the shelf and gathered up a selection of mismatched baubles and tinsel. On the drive home he realised he was decorating the place for an imaginary woman. He hadn't even been in touch with anyone yet. He wondered if he could get any lower.

He remembered the tree he'd bought with Annie for their first Christmas as a married couple. They'd barely managed to get it through the door. They spent hours decorating it. Every bauble he put on she'd moved somewhere else. This time he'd do it his own way.

The ping from the laptop perked him up. One new message.

Gardner clicked onto his emails, deflated when he saw the message from B&Q offering him a discount on power tools. Was this who he was now? He was going to be forty-six next month and he was reduced to scouring the internet for dates and getting emails from DIY stores.

He clicked onto the dating site and logged in. No new messages. Maybe give it a week or so and people would start getting desperate about being alone for Christmas. He scrolled through a list of women who met his basic requirements. He didn't think he was being that fussy. He didn't care about things like hair colour or height. He was fairly open about age, although he didn't want anyone too old or too young. He didn't want to be *that* guy. Most of them looked pretty normal. But how did you know? They could all be complete lunatics. Maybe they felt the same about him. He thought he was pretty normal.

He sighed. Maybe he needed to start sending messages to them instead of waiting for someone to land in his inbox. Isn't that what women wanted? For the man to do the chasing? But it all felt so desperate. He couldn't face all the time it'd take to write a message (and he knew it would take forever to get it right) for them to then decline his offer – or worse, ignore him altogether. He felt a stab of guilt at the message he'd ignored himself. But really? Hats for cats?

Gardner logged out and closed the laptop. Maybe tomorrow. He got up, turned the light off and switched the Christmas lights on. It almost made the room look cosy. Gardner's fingers tapped on the computer lid and Tom Waits started singing 'Please Call Me, Baby'. Tomorrow he'd do something. He'd make a move.

He checked his voicemail. One new message from DS Freeman in Blyth, wanting more information on Ben Swales. Could he give her a call back? He pushed his phone across the table. He didn't want to get involved in this again.

He looked around him at the sad Christmas tree. At the sad little life he'd made for himself. He couldn't hide from the world forever.

28

25 October 1999

'DS Gardner? A word, please.'

Gardner followed his boss through the office, past the prying eyes of his colleagues. He knew he was being paranoid. But it bothered him more than he cared to admit. He didn't know how many of them had known about the affair *before* he did. But every last one of them knew about it now. Threatening to castrate Wallace in front of the whole team probably hadn't helped with keeping it under wraps. DC Bob McIlroy smirked as he walked past. He hated McIlroy almost as much as he hated Wallace, if that were possible. McIlroy was Wallace's lap-dog. Wallace said jump, McIlroy said thanks for the opportunity to jump. Gardner had no doubt in his mind that McIlroy had known about Wallace and Annie long before he had, and that bothered him almost as much as the affair itself.

DCI Clarkson ushered him into her office and Gardner gritted his teeth as McIlroy muttered something under his breath.

Clarkson closed her office door and pointed to the seat in front of her desk. 'Take a seat, DS Gardner,' she said. She always referred to people by their rank, maybe to keep the lower ranks in their place. Gardner didn't mind. He hadn't quite got used to being a DS yet. He was beyond surprised that he'd managed to pass the exam, with everything that'd been going on. He'd only just scraped a 2:2 for his degree, but to be fair he'd put a lot less effort into studying at university than he had for the sergeant's exam. When you're twenty-one and living in London, there are better things to do than read Chaucer.

'How's your relationship with DS Wallace these days?' she asked.

At first Gardner thought she was taking the piss, though Clarkson wasn't known for her humour. She knew what had happened as well as the rest of the team. She'd been the one to pull them apart when he'd threatened Wallace's family jewels. She may have been almost a foot shorter than they were, with the build of a malnourished sparrow, but she still managed to drag them off each other and Gardner into her office for a bollocking. Which was kind of what he'd been threatening Wallace with.

'Let me put it this way,' Clarkson continued. 'If I asked if you could work together on something, what would you say? Do you think you could manage it without killing one another?'

Gardner's stomach churned. She wanted him to work with Wallace? He could barely manage to pass him in the corridor without wanting to punch his face in. He wasn't even going to go to the Christmas party, which he usually never missed, in order to avoid him. And now she thought it'd be a good idea for them to work together. She was more sadistic than he'd thought.

'What did Wallace say?' Gardner asked.

Clarkson almost cracked a smile. 'He asked what you'd said.' She stood up, indicating he should do the same. 'It's a big case. Think about it. Let me know.'

Gardner's foot tapped under her desk. 'I'm in,' he said. He

wasn't going to let Wallace be the bigger man. He just hoped Wallace would decline the offer.

'Good. I'll see you both in the briefing at three,' she said and showed him out.

Gardner sloped back to his desk. This wasn't going to end well. He hadn't seen Wallace for weeks; they'd somehow managed to keep out of each other's way. He'd long since passed the stalking phase: following Annie home to her love nest; waiting to see her outside her office. He'd never actually approached her. He wasn't sure what was more pathetic. He hadn't even wreaked the revenge on Wallace he'd been so adamant about, other than tossing some tacks under his tyres one night.

Gardner grabbed his coat and headed out for some lunch. The shops already had Christmas decorations in stock. It was depressing. He wasn't going to bother putting the tree up at home. What was the point? He'd be spending Christmas alone this year. Facing his parents was too much to bear. Or rather, facing his dad would be. No doubt he'd find some way of making it all Gardner's fault. Norman Gardner had quite the knack of making *everything* his son's fault.

Plus Gardner's brother, David, would be bringing his girl-friend, who was six months pregnant. He didn't think he could take their smugness. He'd rather sit by himself with a takeaway watching *Only Fools and Horses*. Failing that, he could always go to work.

As he walked out of Greggs, pasty in hand, he saw a famil-iar face across the road. Ray Thorley appeared to have aged years in the last few months. The investigation into his daughter's disappearance had come to a standstill. Although this had been the longest she'd stayed away, there was no evidence that anything had happened to her. She was just another runaway.

He watched as Ray trudged by, shopping bags full of meals for one, and wondered how he'd be spending Christmas. Gardner couldn't help but wonder if he'd done enough for him and his daughter.

29

14 December 2010

Freeman stared into the glass of sherry Lady Clairville had handed her. She hated sherry but didn't want to offend her host.

'So, I take it things are over with you and your fella,' Lady Clairville said, settling back into her recliner chair.

'Yep,' Freeman said and took a sip, cringing at the taste.

'So you're going to your parents for Christmas, then?'

Freeman shook her head and then thought about it. Her dad said they'd be going to her older brother Mark's family down in Wales. She was welcome to go but it was unlikely. She had too much work to do. Things to sort out. Plus she didn't think she could face a day, never mind a week, with four screaming kids going into overdrive after too many selection boxes. She loved her nieces and nephew but only in very small, highly controlled doses. And Christmas wasn't a small dose no matter how brief your stay. Plus, she doubted her mum really wanted her there.

'No, they're off to see my brother and his family,' she said.

'You're not going?'

'Nah,' Freeman said.

'Have you just the one sibling?'

Freeman took another sip of sherry. She wondered if Darren counted now. If someone you hadn't spoken to, who refused to speak to you, for eight years counted. Did someone who was dead for all you knew count?

'Yeah, just one,' she said and left it at that.

'So it'll just be you for Christmas, then?'

She wondered if Lady C was angling for an invite for Christmas dinner. She'd regret it if she was. Freeman had no idea where to start with making a proper roast. She could barely boil an egg. She watched as Lady C topped up her glass and wondered if that would be her in forty years. Sitting watching *Family Fortunes* with just a small dog to keep her company.

'You?' Freeman asked, just to be polite.

'Oh, I've got no family now, dear. It'll just be me, Roy, and the telly. A few glasses of sherry. You're welcome to come.'

Freeman stared at the old lady and it clicked. The lonely old lady felt sorry for her. She was being offered charity, a place to go. She didn't even have a dog to keep her company.

'Is that you, dear?' said Lady C and Freeman glanced up before realising her phone was ringing. She pulled it out of her pocket and answered.

'Freeman.'

'DS Freeman, it's Michael Gardner.'

'Oh,' she said and stood up, indicating to Lady C she'd be back in a minute, and returned to her flat.

'Is this a bad time?' Gardner asked.

'No, no, it's fine. I just didn't expect you to call back tonight.'

'Yeah . . . well,' Gardner said and the line buzzed with quiet for a moment. 'So, Ben Swales. To be honest, I don't remember a huge amount about him. I think I only met him once.'

'Yeah,' Freeman said. 'And that probably answers my question. It's just, I went to see him today about Emma. He denied knowing her.'

'Really?'

'Yeah. He backtracked when I mentioned him going to see her dad, but he still didn't have much to say about her. I got more from your report. Hang on . . .' she said and found the notes from Gardner's interview with Ben. 'She first went to the clinic in March '99. Wanted help getting off heroin. But then she disappeared again in April, which was when Ben visited her dad. From your notes he admits to that, said, "I did visit Mr Thorley on a couple of occasions. But Emma and I didn't have a relationship. Emma trusted me. She'd been having problems with an ex-boyfriend." You asked if it was Yates and he said, "I believe so. I didn't really know any details. I just knew that she wanted to get away for a while. She came to me and asked if I'd go to her father's house and give him a note. She knew he'd been upset when she left before." Thing is, he'd only known her a month. In which case, yes, you might forget someone eleven years later. But he admitted going to Ray Thorley's when he talked to you.'

'So?'

'So, doesn't it seem weird that he'd go to all that trouble for someone he'd known a month? A little bit creepy?'

'I don't know. He was just trying to help her. That was his job.'

'His job was to help her off the drugs, not to help her leave town and act as a go-between.' Freeman sighed. Maybe she was being too hard on Swales. Maybe Gardner was right. 'But why lie about knowing her? He can't have forgotten her. Plus his boss reckoned he was overfriendly with some of his clients. The girls.'

'I didn't speak to his boss,' Gardner said, and Freeman caught a hint of something in his voice. Regret, maybe. 'Remind me, did he just go to her dad's once?'

'No,' Freeman said. 'He took another note later on but claimed he didn't see Emma. She posted it to the clinic and he took it to Ray. Then she came back and Ben didn't see her again. Or so he claimed. He did suggest she was still using, though.'

'Yeah, I remember. He thought she'd just taken off again.'

'Said, "No doubt she'll turn up sooner or later."'

'Guess we were both wrong,' Gardner said.

They let that thought hang between them for a moment. 'It's possible he had forgotten about her,' Gardner said after a while. 'If he saw a lot of people through his work.'

'But you remembered her.'

Gardner didn't reply for a moment, then just said, 'I did.'

'And you didn't get any bad feeling about him? Nothing bothered you?'

'I don't remember having *any* feelings about him. He was someone who'd known Emma. Someone who had an insight into her state of mind. His professional opinion was that she was unstable.'

'Yeah. I'm just wondering how professional he really was,' Freeman said, more to herself. 'Well, sorry to disturb you again.'

'No problem. Just let me know if there's anything else you need.' Gardner cleared his throat.

'Thanks,' Freeman said. 'Night.'

She went to her neighbour's and said goodnight to Lady C before going back home, feeling like shit. She wanted to believe it was Gardner's call that'd lowered her mood, because he'd had no answers for her. But she knew it was seeing her neighbour, seeing her future. She wondered about calling Brian, but knew it would be a huge mistake. She took the cardboard box from her bag and carried it to the bathroom, thinking it didn't matter either way.

The night before, she'd drifted off thinking about the possibility of having a family but woke in a hot sweat, dreaming of screaming babies. She knew it was the thought of being old and alone that was making her waver, seeing Lady C without anyone to care for her. But she wasn't going to let it get to her. She didn't *want* to be a mother. Nothing would change that. Besides, as far as she could tell, having kids caused nothing but trouble. Imagine the grief, the years of pain Ray Thorley had been through. That her own parents had been through.

And shit, maybe she wasn't even pregnant anyway and all this headfucking was for nothing.

30

14 December 2010

Lucas watched as Andrea tried to wipe away the lager she'd spilt down her chin without anyone noticing. It was hardly subtle but as she appeared to be the soberest person in the pub – staff included – it worked. It was apparent that the quiz had been won, the winnings had been drunk and now those still upright were singing along to Slade.

Lucas made his way to the bar and stood a few feet away from Andrea, waiting for her to stop draping herself across some pensioner in a trilby and notice him. She was hardly Marilyn Monroe but she was making an effort with her low-cut jeans and high-rise thong. She could do better than the old bloke, and tonight she might just get lucky.

'Pint of lager, please,' Lucas said and the barman roused himself and found an almost clean glass from beneath the bar. Lucas wasn't going to put it anywhere near his mouth but a few quid wasted was a small price to pay for getting what he wanted.

'Don't I know you?'

Lucas looked across at Andrea. She was squinting at him the way only drunks do. He smiled at her. 'I don't think I've had the pleasure.'

She giggled. 'No. I definitely know you from somewhere.' She slid off her stool and staggered towards him, tits first. 'Do you work in the offy on the high street?'

Lucas waited. She'd get there in the end. Maybe he should've left his suit on.

'No, I know,' she said, slapping him on the chest. 'You came to work earlier. You were looking for Ben.'

Lucas raised his eyebrows. 'Oh, yeah. That was you.' He clicked his fingers as if trying to remember her name.

'Andrea,' she said, her hand still on his chest. 'But you can call me Anders.'

'Well, Anders,' he replied and slid the filthy pint glass towards her. 'Can I get you a drink?'

Lucas untangled himself from the dead weight of Andrea's arms. She'd been snoring for twenty minutes and he was starting to think it hadn't been worth it. Especially as she hadn't told him any-fucking-thing. To be fair, she wasn't bad in bed, but he didn't have time for this bullshit. He needed to get what he came for and get out. He'd already given her his sob story about how sick he'd been and how much he'd turned his life around thanks to Ben. Ben, Ben, fucking Ben. He'd been talking about him all night and still she hadn't told him anything.

Lucas looked at his watch. He was losing the will to live. And he needed to piss. He tried shoving her a little but she was in a booze coma. 'Fuck's sake,' he muttered and looked around the room. Beside the bed was a small chest of drawers. He reached over and opened a drawer before slamming it shut. Andrea jumped and rolled away from him. She brushed the matted hair back from her face and wiped the drool from the corner of her mouth.

'What time is it?' she asked.

'Half six.'

'In the morning?' Andrea rolled onto her side of the bed and grabbed her cigarettes from a pocket in the pile of clothes on the floor. She lit one and held the pack out for Lucas.

After he'd lit his he lay back, staring at the ceiling. 'I should quit these next,' he said.

'I'll never quit smoking,' Andrea said. 'My nana smoked every day from age fourteen to eighty-four. Never did her any harm.' She took a long, deep drag. 'Died of lung cancer. But she was eighty-four.'

Lucas took a drag and then stamped the fag out on the bedside table. Why wouldn't she just shut up? Why did she keep bringing everything back to herself?

He rolled onto his side and faced her. 'I wish I could've thanked Ben. I liked him.'

'Yeah, he was nice.'

'How come I never saw you about when I went to the clinic?'

She shrugged. 'Dunno. I just do admin stuff.'

'Were you friends with him?'

'Yeah. Sort of. He was a bit weird, though. Never wanted to do anything with us. Never came on work nights out or anything. But canny enough.' She put out her cigarette. 'We've got our Christmas do coming up soon. You could come with me if you like.'

Lucas stared at her. He wanted to punch her in the face. Instead he sat up, swung his legs out of bed and started getting dressed. 'Don't know about that.'

Andrea sat up in bed. 'How come you're just coming to see Ben now? How long have you been clean?'

Lucas turned around. Maybe she wasn't as stupid as she looked. 'Long time,' he said, eventually. She sat looking at him, waiting for him to say more. 'I moved away, got a job down south. Just came back a few months ago. Felt like I should come and say thanks.'

Andrea shrugged. 'Well, Ben's long gone. Got a call about his mum one day and he just dropped everything and went back to Alnwick.'

Lucas stopped, belt in hand. Finally. Alnwick. Would he still be there? He started looping his belt through his jeans. 'How long ago was that?'

'I don't know. Ages,' she said. 'Ten, eleven years maybe.'

'Eleven years,' Lucas murmured, thinking of the last time he'd seen Emma. He could feel Andrea staring at him. 'Eleven years,' he said again. 'Have I been clean that long? I should get some sort of badge.' He smiled, sat down on the edge of the bed and tied up his laces. 'You didn't keep in touch, then?'

'Nah,' she said. 'He reckoned he was going to come back when his mum was better but he never did.' She lit another cigarette. 'Be a darling and get us a glass of water, would you?'

Lucas grinned at her and walked out of the room. He picked up his coat from the floor in the hallway and let himself out. She could get her own fucking water.

31

17 April 1999

Emma slumped down to the bathroom floor. She'd prepared herself for it, knew it was a possibility. A big possibility. She wasn't stupid. The odds were that it'd be positive considering how careless they'd been. How careless *she'd* been. But seeing it, confirming it was true, some things you're never ready for.

She pressed her face into her hands, knowing her dad was downstairs, that he could hear her as soon as there was a quiet moment in whatever TV show he was pretending to watch. She didn't want him to know anything was wrong, especially this, but she couldn't stop it. The tears came hard. She gulped for air, hiccupping between sobs. Her chest ached and she could barely breathe. She wanted her mam. She might've been angry but she'd have known what to do. Would have told her everything was going to be okay.

But thinking about her just made it worse, made her chest tighten even more. If her mam were still here none of it would've happened. She never would've met Lucas. Never would've let him do what he'd done.

Maybe she *should* tell her dad. There was a chance he'd understand, know what to do. But she just couldn't do it to him. He knew she'd been with Lucas, knew she'd taken drugs, but he never mentioned it. Never asked her what'd happened, what she was going through. He couldn't comprehend that his little girl had done those things. Or didn't want to. She'd told him she was seeing someone to help her get off the drugs, help her get her life back on track. He'd even given her a lift so she wouldn't run into Lucas but he never asked for details, never tried to understand. If he didn't acknowledge it, it'd go away.

She wondered if she could tell Diane. But she'd pushed her friend away. Things weren't the same between them any more. Besides, Diane was even more naive than she was. How would she know what to do?

'Em?'

Emma jumped at the tap on the door. She wiped her eyes as if her dad could see through the wood.

'Are you okay?' he asked.

'Yes, I'll just be a second,' she said and tried to find somewhere to hide the plastic pregnancy test. She slid it into the waist of her jeans, tore the packet into pieces and shoved them into her pocket, pulling her jumper down to cover it all. She looked in the mirror at her red, swollen face. There was no way she could disguise the fact she'd been crying. Lucky she had so many reasons to cry.

She opened the door and her dad looked at her with concern. 'Em?'

'I was just thinking about Mam,' she said and her dad's eyes welled up before he put his arms around her, smothering her. She could feel the plastic digging into her skin but he didn't seem to notice.

'I'm okay,' she said and pulled back.

'You want to come and watch TV for a while?'

Emma shook her head. 'No, I'm just going to go to bed.' Her dad nodded and she gave the best smile she could summon before closing her bedroom door. She wasn't going to tell him. He didn't need more problems. But she needed someone to help her. She couldn't do this alone. She wondered if someone at the clinic could help. Ben had been so kind to her. Never judged her for what she'd done. Maybe he could help her again. Tell her what to do.

She went to the window, wondering if she could go there now, if he'd still be working. She pulled back the curtain and yelped. Lucas was out there, watching. She let go of the curtain and moved away from the window. She didn't want him to see her.

She shouldn't have been surprised to see him there. Since she'd left him he'd been everywhere she went; every step she took, he was there, haunting her. He'd even been in her room. She came home one day and found the window broken and his cum in the bed. She had to tell her dad about the window, convinced him that maybe kids had done it, that it must've been, because nothing had been taken. But she'd stripped off the sheets, put them in a rubbish bag and dumped them in a bin behind the pizza shop. It made her sick every time she thought about it. Or perhaps that was the baby.

She touched her stomach. There was a baby growing in there. *His* baby. She wondered what he'd do if he found out. If he'd be pleased or if he'd be angry that she was so careless. Didn't matter. He was never going to find out. Not over her dead body.

32

15 December 2010

Freeman was waiting for Diane Royle to arrive. They'd agreed to meet in a cafe down the street from where Diane worked. Freeman had got there early, keen to have a seat and a hot drink.

She recognised Diane as soon as she walked in. She hadn't seen a picture of her but she could tell from the slightly worried, sad look on the woman's face. This was a woman who didn't make a habit of talking to the police.

Freeman stood. 'Diane?' she asked and the woman turned and smiled at her, coming over to shake her hand. 'Can I get you a drink?'

Diane shook her head. 'No thanks. I've had too much coffee this morning already.'

They took a seat and Diane removed her gloves but left her coat on. Freeman wrapped her hands around the mug of hot chocolate. After the first sip she'd decided it was too sickly but the warmth on her hands was worth the disagreeable taste.

'Thanks for meeting me,' Freeman said, and watched the woman twist her gloves on her lap. 'I won't keep you too long.'

Diane's eyes shifted around the small cafe as if she shouldn't be there. 'You wanted to talk about Emma?'

'Yes.'

'So it *is* her, then?'

'We haven't positively identified her yet, but we have reason to believe it's her, yes.'

Diane nodded, tears in her eyes.

'Emma's dad said you'd been friends since you were little. When did you stop hanging around with her?'

'I suppose it was after her mum died,' Diane said. 'Emma didn't come to school for a while afterwards. I went round to see her but she didn't want to talk. She came back after a few weeks but then she started skipping lessons and she'd ask me to cover for her. She stopped talking to her dad and then stopped talking to me, and she'd just go and hang about in the town during the day.' Diane shrugged. 'I think her dad thought she just needed a bit of time and then she'd be okay.'

'Did you know Lucas Yates? How did she get involved with him?' Freeman asked and saw Diane stiffen.

'I didn't know him. Not really,' she said and glanced over her shoulder as the door opened and a gust of cold air followed a couple of pensioners in. 'I hadn't seen Emma for a while. She was barely coming to school. And then one day I saw her in the town with this gang. They all looked older than Emma. I started to go over but then this lad put his arm around her and she turned away.'

'Lucas?'

Diane nodded. 'Yeah. That was the first time I'd seen them together. I'd seen him waiting outside school before then. I guess he was waiting for her. She seemed kind of happy but he made my skin crawl.'

'In what way?'

'I don't know. He was quite good-looking but there was something about him that just wasn't right. I told her that Lucas was trouble. She said I didn't know what I was talking about. A few days later her dad reported her missing.'

'And this was the first time?' Freeman asked, the mug cooling in her hands. 'In February?'

'Yes,' Diane agreed. 'She was gone a few weeks, maybe a month. I knew he had something to do with it.'

'Did you tell the police?'

Diane nodded again. 'I told them she'd been seeing Lucas. They said they'd speak to him but I don't know if they ever did. Nothing happened and then Emma just came back.'

'Did you speak to her when she came home?'

'Yeah, but she was weird when she came back. Distant. She'd always been quiet but this was different. She told me she'd stopped taking drugs and hanging around with those people. She was seeing someone, getting help. She wanted to change. But he wouldn't let it go.

'She came to my house in tears one day. She was too scared to go home because Lucas was waiting outside for her. She didn't tell me everything. I could tell she was keeping stuff back but she said he'd been violent with her. That he was following her. He'd broken into her house. He told her he'd hurt her dad if she told him anything or if she went to the police. She said when she'd left with Lucas she'd wanted to go, but after a few days she'd seen a different side to him and wanted to come home. He wouldn't let her. She was terrified of him. And then a week or so later she disappeared again.'

'And you thought she was back with Lucas?'

'I did at first. I thought she was being stupid. That he'd sucked her back in. But I saw Lucas around while Emma was gone. He was with someone else. And then Emma came back again because she couldn't stay away from her dad any more.'

Freeman sat back. The chill in her bones had been replaced by anger. What kind of animal takes advantage of a teenage girl, a girl who's just lost her mother? Drives her away from her own home?

'I kept telling her to go to the police but she was too scared. She hadn't spoken to Lucas since she came back, somehow managed to avoid him. But one day he showed up at my house, looking for her. We were watching him out of the window, trying to see what he was up to, and then my brother went out to chase him off.' Diane looked at the floor. 'He battered him, black and blue, right in our front garden. I rang the police but by the time they got there Lucas had run off and my brother wouldn't tell them anything. He was frightened of him. Emma stopped coming after that.'

'You never saw her again?' Freeman asked. 'Do you remember when that was?'

Diane frowned. 'I'm not really sure. I guess it was the end of June. School hadn't finished, but I couldn't tell you the date.'

'Okay,' Freeman said. 'What about what Emma was wearing that day? Do you remember that?'

Diane shook her head. 'I'm sorry.'

Freeman slid a picture of the necklace they'd found on the body towards Diane. 'Do you recognise that?'

Diane picked it up. 'It was her mum's. She gave her it when she got ill. Emma loved that necklace. Always had it on.'

'What about this?' Freeman asked and handed her a picture of the tracksuit top found in the grave.

Diane stared at it for a long time, then shook her head. 'I don't think so,' she said. 'I can't really remember her wearing anything like this. She didn't really dress like the rest of them.' She shrugged. 'But I'm not sure. Sorry.'

'That's okay,' Freeman said. 'But you're sure that was the last time you saw her. When Lucas attacked your brother?'

'I think so. I remember calling her a couple of days in a row but she wouldn't talk to me. And to be honest, I was scared of getting involved,' Diane said, unable to look at Freeman.

'That's understandable.'

'I know it wasn't long before her dad reported her missing because I felt guilty for not going to see if she was okay. And I know the police looked for her but I think everyone thought she'd just gone off, like before. They didn't seem too worried.'

'What about you? What did you think had happened? The police spoke to you again, didn't they?'

'Someone came to my house once but they didn't seem too concerned. I thought Lucas had done something to her. They said they'd look into it but I don't know if they did. I think maybe Lucas left after that. I didn't see him around any more. Part of me wondered if she'd gone with him.' Diane looked directly at Freeman, her eyes welling. 'Do you think he killed her?' She wiped the tears that slid down her cheeks and Free-man handed her a napkin.

'That's what I'm trying to find out.' Freeman looked at her notes and wondered what else she could get from Diane Royle. 'So you didn't hang around with that group at all? Didn't know any of them?'

Diane shook her head. 'Not really. I knew some of their faces but that's it. Most of them were older than us.'

Freeman took some photos out of her bag and put them on the table. 'Does this man look familiar?' Diane looked at the picture. 'That's Christian Morton,' Freeman said. 'He was friends with Lucas.'

Diane bit her lip. 'I don't recognise him. Sorry.'

'What about Jenny Taylor?' she said.

'The name rings a bell. I think Emma mentioned her. Didn't like her.' Freeman passed her a picture and Diane almost did a double take. 'This is the girl,' she said, holding up the photo.

'Which girl?'

'The one I saw with Lucas when Emma was gone.'

'You're sure?' Freeman said.

'Positive. I saw him with her a few times. I think maybe they were going out after Emma broke up with him. And I'd seen her with them before, too. The day I saw them all hanging around in the town, drinking, making a load of noise, shouting at people. That one,' she said, pointing at Jenny, 'was showing off for Lucas but then Lucas started grabbing Emma.' Diane leaned closer to Freeman and lowered her voice. 'He was trying to put his hand down her jeans but she was pulling away. So he grabbed hold of her arm and shoved her against the wall. I wanted to go over and do something but there was a big group of them.' Diane sighed. 'I went round to her house the next day and tried to talk to her but she wouldn't listen. She could barely move her arm, she had—'

'Wait,' Freeman said. 'Had she broken her arm?'

'I'm not sure. It looked bad but I don't know that it was broken. Why?'

'Was it her left or right?'

Diane shook her head. 'I'm sorry. I can't remember.'

33
15 December 2010

Freeman stood with her head against the scratched veneer of the toilet door. She stared down at the piece of plastic in her hand and wondered how long it had been. She was meant to be updating Routledge.

The test had been in her bag for a couple of days. She'd told herself that she just hadn't done it because she hadn't had time to take a breath, never mind pee on a stick. But truth be told she was just putting it off because she didn't want to deal with it. She didn't want to deal with Brian either. She'd hoped it would just go away. That *he'd* go away. She'd finally done it at home the night before but hadn't trusted the results. Stupid pound-shop test. So she'd bought another one on the way back to the station this morning. Just to be thorough.

Freeman looked at the stick again. Why was it taking so long? *Was* it taking so long? She checked the box again. Two minutes, it claimed.

She looked down at the stick again and felt a shockwave right through her body. 'Fucking, fucking, fuck,' she said, loud enough for anyone else in the ladies' to hear. She'd been expecting it, but it was still a shock to the system to see it in front of her again in black and white. Or in blue, rather. She'd been telling herself it didn't matter what the stick said because she'd made up her mind anyway. But now it was real. Now it was a real decision, not a hypothetical one. She felt tears stinging the backs of her eyes and pressed her fingers into them to stop them from coming.

She stuffed the test, along with the packaging, into the sanitary bin and then kicked it for good measure. Brian could go fuck himself. This was none of his business. Nothing was going to change.

Routledge was sitting on her desk as she walked in. Arms folded, foot tapping. He gave her the look.

'I know, I'm late,' she said. 'I was speaking to a witness.'

'Who?'

'Diane Royle. A friend of Emma's.'

'And did you learn anything useful?'

'Lucas Yates might've broken Emma's arm.'

'Might've?' Routledge said. 'Have you spoken to Ben Swales yet?'

'Yes,' Freeman said. 'Yesterday.'

'And? What did the creepy little bastard have to say for himself?' He'd seen Ben's picture on his driving licence and had made a snap decision that he was creepy. She was glad to see such stellar police work in action.

Freeman sighed. 'He denied knowing her.'

Routledge's eyes lit up. 'Really?' he said. 'Now that doesn't sound like the response of an innocent man, does it?'

'Well, he changed his mind when I reminded him about Emma's dad—'

'I bet he did.'

'Said he'd forgotten about her.'

Routledge snorted. 'Perhaps you should bring him in.'

'On what grounds?'

'The same grounds you had for bringing in Yates. He knew Emma. At least Yates isn't denying it.'

'No, but why would Ben Swales kill Emma? What reason would he have?'

'They don't always need a motive,' Routledge said and stood up. 'Speak to him again. Speak to the people he used to work with. Anything else?'

'There was another girl. Jenny Taylor. Knew Emma and Lucas. I'm hoping to speak to her as soon as we trace her. Lloyd's on it,' she said before Routledge could ask.

Routledge glanced over at Lloyd throwing peanuts into his mouth like a trained monkey and gave her the look again before walking back to his lair.

'Lloyd,' Freeman shouted across the room and the DC turned around before slapping McIlroy on the shoulder. Everybody's mate. He headed in Freeman's direction and she wanted to smack him in his stupid jolly face.

'Boss?' Lloyd said.

'Jenny Taylor.'

'Ah yes, Jenny Taylor,' he said. 'I found her.'

'Really?'

'Don't act so surprised. I do have my uses.'

'That's debateable. So, where is she?'

'You have to say the magic word, now you've insulted my amazingness.'

'Tell me or I'll break your legs,' Freeman said.

'That'll do. Okay, I couldn't find her through the DVLA and there was nothing on our system since all the fun and games in that pub. But I checked her NI number and discovered she was claiming benefits from 2000 to 2003 in Sheffield. Then she got a job, bless her little cotton socks, and then—'

'Where is she now, Lloyd?'

'Middlesbrough.'

'Middlesbrough?'

'Yep. Sunny Middlesbrough.'

'Okay,' Freeman said, 'give me the address and phone number.'

'No phone number, I'm afraid.'

'Okay. Give me the address.'

Lloyd scuttled back to his desk, rummaged around the mess and came up with a piece of paper, the corner torn off.

She thanked Lloyd and checked the time. She really wanted to speak to Ben Swales again, but not because Routledge said so. Alnwick was forty-five minutes away. Middlesbrough over an hour. Unfortunately they were in completely different directions. She also wanted to speak to Ben's old colleagues at the clinic again.

Freeman plonked herself down on the edge of her desk and dialled. He answered after three rings.

'Gardner.'

34

19 April 1999

Emma sat on the edge of Diane's bed, an uncomfortable silence hanging between them. Diane had been so excited when she'd opened the door to find Emma standing there. She'd hugged her, told her she was so glad she was back to normal. And then Emma had burst into tears. She knew she couldn't tell Diane about the baby, no matter how much she needed to tell someone. But she had to get away from her house, from Lucas.

'So . . .' Diane said. 'You want to tell me what's up?'

She didn't realise she was crying again until Diane looked like she was going to burst into tears herself. She came and sat beside Emma, draping her arm around her.

'Is it *him*?' Diane said.

Diane hated Lucas even though they'd barely met, even though she didn't know half of what'd gone on. Maybe she wasn't as naive as Emma thought. Maybe she would understand.

Emma nodded. 'He won't leave me alone. He stands outside the house, just staring, waiting for me to come out. And if I do come out he says things, threatens me. He follows me everywhere. I daren't go out most of the time. And I'm scared in case he does something to my dad. He broke in, too. He—' Emma caught herself. She couldn't share that with Diane. 'I know it was him,' she said.

'You have to call the police,' Diane told her.

'I can't. They won't do anything. They'll just tell him to leave me alone and then he'll get even more pissed off. I don't know what to do.'

She waited for Diane to say something, to give her an answer to all her problems, but she just sat there, her forehead creased with concern. She shouldn't have come. Diane couldn't help her. She was on her own.

35

15 December 2010

Freeman wondered if she'd be better spending her time speaking to Jenny Taylor. The girl had known Emma, hadn't liked her, but knew her. And, according to Diane Royle, was intimately acquainted with Lucas Yates. If anyone knew anything, it was likely to be her.

Instead she drove through town, past the clinic Ben had worked at. She swung the wheel and turned into the back alley, causing the car behind to honk its horn. Ben's memory of Emma Thorley was a little cloudy, to say the least. Maybe his boss would recall something that had slipped Ben's mind.

Freeman walked past a group of teenagers blowing smoke into the clinic and went into the relative warmth. The manager, Jessie, was standing beside the reception desk, speaking to a young girl, her hand on her shoulder. Jessie looked up as Freeman walked in and handed the girl over to a colleague. There was no sign of Catherine. Perhaps she'd been fired for losing the letters.

'Oh, are you here about the break-in?' Jessie said. 'I was beginning to think no one was coming.' She walked around the desk, coming to a stop in front of Freeman.

'I'm not here about a break-in,' Freeman said.

'Oh. Then why are you here?' Jessie asked. 'We called about this first thing.'

'I'm sure someone will be here as soon as they can, but I wanted to ask you something else.'

Jessie seemed to bristle at this but led Freeman to a small room down the hall. She closed the door behind them.

Jessie indicated the hard plastic chairs and sat down. Freeman noticed the broken window, covered up with cardboard and Sellotape.

'Was anything taken?' she asked Jessie.

'Just the petty cash box, I think, but we get it a lot. Usually people looking for drugs. Why they think we'd have any is beyond me. We're in the business of getting them off drugs, not supplying them.' She looked around the room and then turned her attention back to Freeman. 'You asked about Ben Swales.'

'Actually, I wanted to know about him and Emma Thorley,' Freeman said and saw Jessie's brow twitch. 'You said something last time about seeing Ben with a girl. Was this her?' She showed Jessie a photo of Emma.

'Yes,' Jessie said. 'That was her.'

'Do you remember anything else about her?'

'Not really. I never worked with her. But I remember her. Quiet. Different to most of the young people we get in here. She seemed . . .'

'What?'

'I think there was something going on with her and Ben.'

'Going on?' Freeman said. 'They were seeing each other?'

Jessie shook her head. 'I don't know that for sure. But it was odd. I saw him leave with her several times.'

'When was this?'

'Oh, I don't know. Not long before he left.' Jessie looked up as someone came to the door. 'Do you need something, Andrea?' Jessie asked. The blonde woman stared at Freeman before turning back to Jessie.

'Someone's here about the break-in,' she said.

'Excuse me,' Jessie said and got up. Freeman followed her into the office behind Catherine's desk. A uniformed officer she didn't recognise was looking at something behind the door. She edged around and saw the mess in front of a small filing cabinet. The contents had been pulled out and left all over the floor. Freeman looked to Jessie for an explanation.

'We haven't touched anything,' Jessie said, not knowing who to address any more. 'I guess our night-time intruder thought we might have something of value in there.'

'And did you?' Freeman asked.

'No. Like I said, we don't keep drugs or money on the property, other than the petty cash box with a small amount of tea money. They took the tea money. All three pounds forty.'

Freeman showed the officer her ID and bent down and scanned the files.

'Personnel files?' she said and looked up at Jessie.

Jessie nodded. 'Yes. They found the keys and went through all the drawers. Clearly they found nothing they wanted.'

She looked down at the files. 'Have you checked to see if anything is missing?'

'No. I was waiting for the police,' she said and crossed her arms. 'But why would anyone want paperwork?'

Freeman noticed Andrea staring through the small window in the door and took a pair of latex gloves from her pocket, pulled them on. She started flicking through the files. 'Would Ben Swales' file have been in here?' she asked.

'No. He left a long time ago,' Jessie said. 'It would just be current staff.'

Freeman got to the bottom of the pile. She sighed and peered into the empty drawer. 'Can you take a look? See if anyone's is missing?'

Jessie bent over and looked through the files, shaking her

head. Freeman stood back and the officer called it in, requesting someone to come and take prints.

Freeman turned, looking around the office at the other drawers. 'Do you keep records of clients?'

'Yes,' Jessie said.

'For how long?'

'Usually ten years after their last treatment. But . . .'

'But?' Freeman prompted.

'But anything not from the last couple of years would be in the store cupboard.' Jessie led Freeman down the corridor to a small, windowless room. There were dozens of boxes of paperwork.

'Emma Thorley's file could still be there?' Freeman said.

'You're welcome to take a look.'

'Any tips on where to start?'

Jessie shrugged and closed the door.

Freeman turned to the boxes and opened the first one. Hundreds of sheets of paper were stuffed in but she couldn't make out how it was ordered.

Several boxes later she still hadn't found Emma's records. But something else had caught her attention. Jenny Taylor had apparently sought out help too. She flicked through the file and noticed a signature on several of the sheets. B. Swales.

It looked like Lucas Yates wasn't the only one to know both girls.

36

15 December 2010

As Gardner walked out of the station, wondering why he was doing DS Freeman's donkeywork, he saw Lawton standing outside with a man. His arm was resting on her shoulder, hand around her neck, possessive. Gardner stopped and watched. Was this the boyfriend? Lee, the infamous motivational speaker. From where Gardner stood he looked like a bit of a dick. Not what he was expecting at all, not from Lawton.

He watched as Lawton shrugged away from the man, her head down. Lee took hold of her chin, forcing her to look at him. They were clearly having a serious, personal conversation, although he was doing most of the talking. Gardner wondered if he should leave them to it. Probably. But when did that ever stop him.

He extended his hand as he walked towards them. 'You must be Lee,' he said and Lawton looked at him as though she'd been caught having a sneaky fag behind the bike sheds. Lee looked from Lawton to Gardner and reluctantly held out his hand.

'Michael Gardner,' he said and shook Lee's hand. All of a sudden the other man sprung into life, a smile spreading across his tanned face.

'So you're DI Gardner,' Lee said. 'Dawn never shuts up about you.'

Gardner glanced at Lawton and saw a slight flush spread across her face. He let go of Lee's hand and Lee smiled. It almost reached his eyes. 'So what brings you to our neck of the woods? Been doing some motivational speaking?'

Lee did the almost-smile again, struggling even more this time. 'No. I don't do that any more. Obviously you don't talk about me that much,' he said to Lawton and put his arm around her shoulder, pulling her towards him. 'I work in the town now. Phones Galore.'

'Phones Galore?' Gardner said. 'Well. Everyone needs phones.'

The three of them stood there in silence for a moment and Gardner wished he hadn't come over. He probably wasn't alone.

'Anyway, I should get back to it,' Gardner said. 'Nice to meet you, Lee.' He didn't bother with another handshake. He started to walk away and then turned back. 'You coming, Lawton?'

Lawton looked up at him, surprised, but nodded. 'Give me a minute?' she said.

Gardner left them to it and went to his car, the sudden warmth making his cheeks burn. He turned and saw Lee talking again as Lawton listened with her head down. Lee bent down and said something, close to her face. He looked up and saw Gardner watching. He kissed Lawton on the cheek and walked away, looking back over his shoulder. Gardner waited for Lawton to come over as Lee disappeared down the street. She walked towards the car, head down, face red. She slid into the passenger seat.

'Where're we going?' she asked and fastened her seatbelt, never looking at him once.

Gardner and Lawton turned into Ayresome Street and looked for the right house. The sleet was really coming down now and you could barely see out of the windscreen. Gardner didn't even know why he was there, what business it was of his, but he'd promised. He hadn't been much use to DS Freeman so far and he *had* said if she needed anything else . . . Famous last words.

He pulled up outside the house and looked for any signs of life. There was a Christmas tree in the window, lights flashing on and off. No other lights on in the house, though.

'Wait here,' he said to Lawton. 'No point us both getting wet.'

He got out and ran towards the door, hoping someone would answer quickly. He wasn't even sure what he'd say when they did answer. Freeman had told him this Jenny Taylor was an associate of Emma's, could possibly know something about her murder. She hadn't said much else; he hadn't asked. Freeman just wanted to speak to her but hadn't been able to find a number, and as he was in Middlesbrough . . .

Obviously Taylor wasn't a suspect or Freeman would've made the effort to drive down herself. Instead she was going to visit Ben Swales again. Although Gardner only vaguely recalled Ben, Taylor didn't ring *any* bells. Didn't think she'd come up in his investigation. He hoped that hadn't been another oversight on his part.

Gardner knocked again and squinted through the sleet into the living room window. There was no one in.

He turned to leave and then pulled out his notebook. He scrawled his name and number and a note for Jenny to call him. The ink ran as soon as it hit the paper, making his name illegible. He screwed the note up. He didn't want Jenny calling him anyway. It wasn't his case. He found Freeman's number in his phone, scribbled it down and then stopped, wondering what he'd want Freeman to do if their roles were reversed. Who knew what Taylor had to do with all this? Freeman had mentioned she was a junkie, had been in trouble with the police more than once. Maybe a note would make her skittish.

'Fuck it,' Gardner muttered as he ran back to the car, the sleet biting down on his face.

Lawton looked at him but said nothing, as always. Always trusting, never questioning him.

He'd had no doubt at the time that Emma Thorley would show up sooner or later like she always had done. But she hadn't. And there had obviously been a good reason for it.

What if he'd tried harder? He'd spent five years searching for Abby Henshaw's daughter. Why hadn't he done the same for Emma? What if he'd found her back then and saved her father years of heartache? He knew he'd failed her, knew it was too late to make it right. All he could do was make sure it never happened again.

He found the slightly soggy note with Freeman's number on and ran back out to the door, sliding the note through the letterbox. Freeman wanted him to find Jenny, get her to contact her. That's what he'd done. If she could help find Emma's killer, he'd done his part.

But now he needed to stop thinking about Blyth. About the past. He'd had the dream again the night before. He hadn't had it in years. But there she was. Heather Wallace, with her red hair and freckles, asking why he'd killed her dad. Gardner blinked away the image of her face. What had become of her? Was she another lost girl?

'What time on Friday?' he said to Lawton, the words falling from his mouth before his brain changed its mind.

A smile spread across Lawton's face before she caught herself and regained some professional impassivity. 'About eight, sir,' she said.

'All right, excellent,' Gardner said and Lawton smiled again.

Gardner started the car and opened the window a fraction, needing some fresh air. He had a feeling he'd live to regret this.

37

30 April 1999

Emma sat on the narrow single bed in the tiny, magnolia-walled room. This had been her home for a week but it felt like a prison cell. She'd barely spoken to anyone since she'd arrived, since Ben had dropped her off and promised that Jasmine would take good care of her. But that was fine. Not many people in there were big on conversation. There were a lot of secrets under that roof. And now hers was one of them.

She'd gone to Ben when it finally became too much to deal with by herself. She knew that if she didn't do something soon, that if Lucas kept hanging around, her secret would get out. So she'd gone to Ben and he'd found somewhere for her to go. A friend of his ran a women's shelter and would let her stay for a while, as long as there was room. She also helped Emma organise an abortion. Went with her to doctor's appointments, listened while Emma talked about how badly she needed to go through with it even though she felt terrible. Jasmine had heard it all before.

But it was Ben who went with her that morning. Ben whose hand she held as she went into the hospital. And Ben who'd brought her back again, promising her it'd be okay.

He'd already done so much for her. He'd been to see her dad, convinced him that she was okay, that she'd be back soon.

She didn't know how she'd ever repay him. Just another thing to feel guilty about.

Emma rolled onto her side and brought her knees up to her chest. The doctor had said this would probably happen. There'd be cramps and bleeding. She guessed that was her punishment. It didn't seem that severe, considering.

Outside her room she could hear a muted conversation: two voices, one muffled by tears. The woman was scared for her son, scared in case her husband found them. Emma closed her eyes. She didn't need to talk to the other women there to understand them. They were all the same in the end. They were frightened of someone they'd loved. Maybe still loved.

She knew that she couldn't stay there forever. That someone would come and take her place and she'd have to go home. But as she lay there on the lumpy mattress, in the room chilled by ghosts, she wished she could stay there forever.

38

15 December 2010

Freeman knocked at the door for the third time before walking back to the car, phone already ringing in her hand. She yawned as it continued to ring on the other end. She was tired even though she'd slept like the dead for a change. She hung up and wondered if she should be concerned about Ben Swales. His car wasn't there but she was trying to be optimistic.

She'd been searching for anything on Ben, anything that'd suggest he was somehow involved in Emma's death, but had found nothing. The man was a saint. Though that was as suspicious as anything. He had no criminal record. He'd never been questioned – other than after Emma disappeared. Not even so much as a parking fine, a speeding ticket. Nothing.

Freeman tried Ben once more and gave up, wondering if she could get local police to keep an eye on him. She couldn't hang around Alnwick all day.

She called Alnwick police station and asked to be put through to DS Janet Williams. They'd worked together a few years back and got on well. Maybe she'd be open to doing a favour. After being on hold for a few minutes, Williams finally answered.

'Well, well, well, if it isn't Strawberry Shortcake,' Williams said, and cackled down the phone.

All of a sudden Freeman wished she hadn't bothered. She'd

forgotten how annoying Williams could be. The woman came up with nicknames for everyone she met, usually based on the person's appearance. Unfortunately at the time they'd worked together, Freeman'd had a bad dye job, red gone wrong. Mix this with her height, or lack thereof, and Williams was onto a winner.

'Hi, Janet,' she said. 'How's things?'

After Williams had covered all aspects of her life since the last time they'd seen each other, Freeman got to the point. She told her colleague about her case and how Ben Swales fitted in.

'So, you think you could organise some eyes on him?' Freeman asked.

Williams sighed. 'We're a little stretched. I could maybe swing by in a while. Check if he's still around. I can try and get one of our newbies to watch the place, but I doubt it.'

'Whatever you can do. Thanks, Janet.'

Freeman hung up and hoped that she wasn't too late. That Swales hadn't disappeared. Maybe she should stop being so bothered about him and think about herself. She'd been sick again this morning. She knew she had to do something but it was easier to just ignore it and hope it went away.

Freeman pulled out and headed back, hoping Gardner had had more luck with Jenny Taylor. Everywhere she went, Jenny Taylor kept coming up. She knew Emma, Lucas *and* Ben. And her gut was telling her that maybe this girl was the key.

Freeman stuffed the last piece of Mars Bar into her mouth and brushed the stray bits of chocolate off the file in front of her. It was well known in the station that if a report had some kind of food stain on it then it had probably been in her hands at some point. But right now she didn't care.

There'd been no answer at Jenny Taylor's house in

Middlesbrough but she'd got Lloyd to work his magic and found an address for Jenny's parents. Maybe they had a number.

Jenny's parents lived in Morpeth – less than half an hour away. Freeman pulled up to their house and wondered if she should've just called. But it was too late. She'd come now. And the longer she was out doing this, the less she'd be sitting still, thinking.

The door opened and a woman answered. She was dressed in an unbelievably short skirt and vest top despite the weather. At first Freeman wondered if it was Jenny. But closer inspection revealed the woman was much older.

'Yeah?' the woman said.

'I'm DS Freeman,' she said, showing her ID. 'Are you Angela Taylor?'

'Angie,' she said and stepped forward, arms wrapped around herself. Freeman couldn't decide whether it was a defensive gesture or just that she was, understandably, freezing. 'Why?'

'It's about your daughter, Jenny.' Freeman saw Angie stiffen. From behind her a man appeared, hunched over slightly.

'This is my husband, Malcolm,' Angie said. 'She's here about Jenny,' she said over her shoulder to her husband.

'Oh God,' Malcolm moaned.

'Don't worry, nothing's happened. I was just wondering if you had a number for her. I need to speak to her regarding Emma Thorley, someone she used to know in Blyth.'

'Blyth?' Angie said.

'Yes,' Freeman replied, wishing they'd invite her in. 'It's going back a bit. About eleven years.'

'Well, we wouldn't know anything about that. Haven't seen her since she was sixteen.'

39

15 December 2010

Angie walked through into the living room and Freeman followed as Malcolm shuffled between them. As he got close she saw that he wasn't much older than his wife, maybe mid-fifties, but whatever condition he was suffering from made him appear frail. Mrs Taylor, on the other hand, was fighting the ageing process with spades of make-up and inappropriate clothes.

Malcolm made it to a seat next to Angie and Freeman sat down opposite them.

'So you haven't seen Jenny for . . . twelve years?' Freeman said, trying to recall how old Jenny was.

'Almost thirteen,' Malcolm said.

'Can I ask what happened?'

Angie Taylor cleared her throat and looked at her husband. He sat with his head down.

'She just buggered off one day. Never came back,' Angie said and lit a cigarette. Freeman didn't want to say anything but thought she might puke all over their shag pile carpet.

'She was always a bit of a troublemaker,' Angie went on, and Malcolm let out a breath that made Freeman turn her attention to him. 'She *was*, Mal. You know she was. Always in trouble right from when she was a little girl.'

'That's our daughter you're talking about. It's no bloody wonder she left,' Malcolm said.

Angie pursed her lips and looked back at Freeman. 'She was expelled from school twice. She got into fights with other kids. Girls *and* boys. She never did well at school, she wasn't the brightest kid—'

'For God's sake, Angie,' Malcolm said.

'Anyway,' Angie said, looking pointedly at Malcolm, 'she'd run away a few times before, always for a few days and then she'd be back. She'd make promises that she'd be good but she just couldn't do it. It wasn't in her nature. She started doing drugs when she was thirteen.' Angie sat forward and stared at Freeman. 'Thirteen. Can you imagine?'

Freeman said nothing. But she could imagine. She could imagine far worse because she'd seen it for herself. Darren had been younger when he started drinking.

'She started lying. I mean she always told lies, but not like this. She stole from us. Her own parents. She took my credit card, ran it right up to the limit buying God knows what and then sold it all for drugs. She was shoplifting, sleeping with anyone who'd have her—'

'Angie!' Malcolm shouted and his wife looked at him, eyes wide as if he'd dare raise his voice to her.

Freeman took a breath and put her hands up to try and placate them. 'I'm sorry,' she said, 'but when was her disappearance reported?'

Malcolm let out a bitter laugh that turned into a cough. Angie reached over and rubbed her husband's back until he calmed down. When he was composed again he looked up at Freeman. 'That's the thing,' he said. 'We never reported her missing.'

Freeman's eyebrows rose. She couldn't help it. 'You never reported your daughter missing?'

Malcolm looked at the floor again and Angie sucked in her cheeks and stared at the wall above Freeman's head.

'And when did she disappear?'

'1997. May. We tried to help her, time and time again,' Angie said. 'We did. But she didn't want help. All she wanted was money and drugs.' Finally she looked Freeman in the eye. 'Before she went for the last time she did something.' Angie pulled a tissue from her handbag and wiped her nose. 'I was at home one day. I'd come home from work with flu. I was in bed and I heard the door and then all these voices. Three or four of them, another one sat out in the car, waiting for them. I went downstairs and she was there with three boys. Or three men, I suppose. They were taking everything. The TV, the stereo, everything.

'We didn't have a lot. I don't even know that they would've got much money for it but they were taking it anyway. I screamed at her to stop but she wouldn't. Two of the boys pushed past me, carrying the TV out to a car. I knew one of them, his dad lived round the corner. Little bastard he was. Chris something.'

'Christian Morton?' Freeman asked.

'Yeah. That's him. His dad was a right one as well. Anyway, I told them I was calling the police and went into the kitchen to the phone. I could hear the other boy shouting, telling her to hurry up but she came in the kitchen after me. I picked up the phone and was about to dial when she had this knife in my face. My own daughter standing there, threatening me with a knife.' Angie shook her head and Malcolm put his hand over hers.

'I put the phone down. I was shaking so much but I begged her to put the knife down and go. I said she could have the TV, have whatever she wanted. And she just looked at me with such hatred. I've never seen anything like that before. The boy came back in and told her they were leaving so she stepped back and I thought that was it. But as the boy walked out she came forward again and pressed the knife into my face.' Angie swept her hair back and turned towards Freeman. An inch long scar ran along Angie's face, parallel to her ear. 'She did this to me.' Angie sat back and sucked in her cheeks again. 'I didn't want her back.'

Freeman frowned. 'You didn't report it to the police?'

Angie shook her head. 'No. I thought it'd make things worse. And when she didn't come back after a week I knew she was gone for good.' Angie shrugged. 'Maybe she thought I'd called the police and thought better of coming back. Or maybe she'd already decided to go and that was her final fuck you, Mother.'

Freeman cringed, thinking about the difficult relationship she had with her own mother. In the aftermath of Darren's arrest, she'd barely spoken to her. Blamed her for everything that'd happened. And in some ways she *was* to blame. Freeman was the one who'd told the police where they could find him. But she hadn't forced him to do what he did. And after a couple of years inside even her mum had to admit that maybe Freeman had done what was best for Darren. Got him the help he needed. It was only once he got out and things turned to shit again that her relationship with her mum soured once more. At the memorial service they held for him, her mum didn't even look at her, never mind speak. But that was five years ago and in the intervening years Lorraine Freeman had softened slightly. Was willing to admit it wasn't *all* her daughter's fault.

'We did look for her, eventually.'

Freeman glanced at Angie and from her expression she guessed that the search had been her husband's idea. 'Three years ago I was diagnosed with cancer,' he said. 'It was a difficult decision but I wanted to make amends, wanted to see her again. We hired this private detective. We figured it was a bit late to file a missing persons report with the police so we got this private eye type. He looked for a while but he didn't find her. We thought she probably didn't want to be found. We gave up after that.'

40

20 May 1999

Emma watched as Ben drove away, leaving her on the door-step, scared to go inside her own home. He'd asked if she wanted him to go in with her but she'd said no. He'd done enough for her. She was on her own now.

Jasmine had told her the night before that she was really sorry but they needed the bed. A woman with a three-month-old baby was coming in. Emma had begged her to let her stay but it was no good. So sorry, Jasmine said. So she'd called Ben and he promised to pick her up in the morning. She'd cried all the way home, begged him to let her stay with him, or to find somewhere else to go. Hell, she would've settled for a lift to the bus station. Anything but go home.

But here she was. Home.

Someone told Ben he'd seen Lucas around with another girl. Maybe it meant Lucas had moved on. That he'd got bored of torturing her and had found another plaything. She felt bad for the girl, whoever she was. But she had to think of herself. As long as Lucas was out of her life, maybe things really would be okay.

Emma took a deep breath and opened the door. Her dad looked over his shoulder from his seat in the living room as if he were expecting someone to come home any time. She wondered if he was still expecting her mam to come in. She wondered if she was a disappointment.

'Em?' He jumped up and grabbed her, pulling her towards him. 'You're back.'

'Hi, Dad,' she said.

He stepped back and looked her over, a smile spreading across his face as if she'd just come back from a jolly holiday instead of disappearing again. 'I wish you'd told me you were coming. I'd have got something in for tea.'

'I didn't know until last night,' she said and stood there listening to the clock ticking. 'I'm sorry, Dad.'

He just shook his head. 'Don't be silly. You're back now. That's all that matters.' He walked out to the kitchen and started making two cups of tea. 'Did Ben bring you? He's a nice chap. I'm so glad you got him to come. I would've been so worried otherwise.' He turned to her as the kettle boiled, suddenly sad. 'You are going to stay this time, aren't you?'

Emma felt a twist in her guts. How could she keep doing these things to him? How could she think it was okay to just walk away from him? From now on things would be different. She would make things right with him. She wouldn't leave him again.

'I promise,' she said.

41

15 December 2010

Adam was waffling on about the film and Louise made noises agreeing with him but if anyone had asked her what the film was about she wouldn't have had a clue where to start. The whole thing was a blur, same as the rest of the world over the last few days. Since hearing the news about the body in Blyth she'd been unable to focus on anything else.

Adam took the shopping bags through to the kitchen and Louise closed the front door. She noticed the scrap of paper sticking out of the letterbox. She pulled it out, tearing it where the paper was soggy.

She opened the note, tried to make out the scrawl. *Please can you call DS Nicola Freeman in Blyth on . . .*

Louise crumpled up the note as Adam came up behind her. 'What's that?' he said.

'Nothing,' Louise replied. 'Junk mail.'

Adam kissed the back of her head. 'I'm going to get changed,' he told her. 'Do you want to eat now?'

Louise squeezed her hand around the note. How did they know where she was? Did they know that she was involved?

'Lou?' Adam said.

She looked up at him. He was waiting for her to answer him. She didn't even know what the question was.

'What?' she said.

'Do you want to eat now?'

Louise nodded and Adam headed upstairs. 'Stick the oven on, then. I'll just be a minute.'

Louise watched him go upstairs. He had no idea. No idea that she'd been keeping secrets from him all this time. No idea what kind of person she'd been – an addict, a whore. If he knew the things she'd done, he would hate her. And he'd have every right. She couldn't bear it if he found out what she'd done in a past life.

42

11 November 1999

The man was in intensive care. Gardner couldn't stop thinking about him. He checked the time again. Almost 4 a.m.

He rolled over, desperate to sleep. He could hear the neighbour putting his bin out. God only knew why he did it at four in the morning. Maybe he couldn't sleep either. He closed his eyes, tried thinking of anything else. Tried counting backwards from a thousand. But all he could see was Wallace, the bloke on the floor, the blood pooling around him.

Gardner got up and went to the bathroom. Without turning on the light he splashed his face with cold water, gulping it down from his cupped hands. In less than four hours he'd be in front of a panel telling them what'd happened. It wasn't a thought he relished. And despite what anyone else thought, he wasn't doing it because it was Wallace. He was doing it because it was the right thing to do. Unfortunately no one else agreed. Out of every copper who was there that day, not one person saw what Gardner had. Course they didn't. They had the 'us against them' mentality. You don't grass up another copper. To be fair, he never thought *he'd* grass up another copper. But this was different.

Gardner leaned against the cold mirror. Maybe he should call in sick. Maybe he should just let it go. Who was going to believe him anyway? The only witness happens to be the one guy who hates Wallace's guts. There'd be a dozen guys in the office who'd make a statement saying he was out to get Stuart Wallace. Why was he putting himself through it?

He scrabbled around the bathroom cabinet in the dark, searching for some paracetamol. He thought about the guy in ICU, the pain he must be enduring. He was a kid. Barely twenty-one. And he might've been a dealer, might've been a scumbag selling drugs to school kids, but he didn't deserve what Wallace did to him. The law would've dealt with him. It wasn't Wallace's place. The guy had been so stoned he could barely walk.

Gardner slammed the cabinet door and stared at himself in the dark. He was doing this for the right reasons. Wallace was out of control.

He needed to pay for what he'd done.

43

15 December 2010

Lucas came out of the pub, fag already lit by the time he was on the pavement. They'd put a heater out there for the smokers but there was more heat coming from the cigarettes. To be honest, he'd rather freeze his bollocks off than listen to Christmas songs any more.

He'd been wondering how to track down Ben Swales all day. The slapper from the clinic said he'd gone back to Alnwick but Lucas hadn't found any trace so far. Nothing in the phone book, nothing online. He couldn't just rock up to Alnwick and expect to find him. But he *needed* to find him. Needed to find out how much Ben knew. If he'd really left the past behind.

Lucas stubbed out the cigarette on the wall and tried to decide whether to call it a night when he saw someone staggering up the road, face red from the cold and too much Brown Ale. He didn't seem to notice Lucas as he walked past.

'Oi, fat fuck,' Lucas shouted after him and DC Bob McIlroy turned, his eyes finally focusing on Lucas.

'Hey, Lucas,' McIlroy said, grinning the way only the inebriated can. 'How's it going, mate?'

'Not bad. Apart from one of yours giving me stick.'

McIlroy started laughing. 'Oh, yeah. You've been a naughty boy, haven't you? Freeman's got a proper hard-on for you.'

'Yeah, well, she's got nothing 'cos I haven't done anything.'

McIlroy laughed again and slapped Lucas on the back. 'Pull the other one. It's got bells on. Christmas bells.' He turned to walk away, still laughing to himself.

'Hang on,' Lucas said. 'I need you to do me a favour.'

McIlroy shook his head. ''Fraid not, mate. That ship has sailed. I'm retiring in a few years. Don't need none of your problems messing with my pension.'

'It's just an address,' Lucas said. 'Ben Swales.'

McIlroy kept shaking his head. 'Not going to happen.'

Lucas wanted to tell the stupid fat prick that he'd be dead within a year if he didn't give up the burgers and beer, but he bit his tongue.

'Come on, mate,' he said.

McIlroy turned away again. 'Forget it. Anyway, you said yourself, she's got nothing. It'll blow over in a couple of weeks. She's too busy looking into that other cunt you used to knock about with. Jenny whatshername.'

'Jenny Taylor?' Lucas said, wondering if McIlroy had noticed the look of panic on his face. Why the fuck were they looking at her too? 'What's she got to do with it?'

McIlroy shrugged. 'Dunno. Had someone looking for her. Heard her on the phone to that prick Gardner in Middlesbrough.'

Middlesbrough? A million thoughts ran through his head. Something was almost clicking but he couldn't quite get it.

Lucas felt a chill go through him that had nothing to do with the weather. He didn't want Freeman looking for Jenny Taylor. That would only lead to bad things. Maybe he needed to get to Middlesbrough first. But that'd be like finding Ben in Alnwick. A needle in a haystack.

McIlroy had started walking away, staggering about, stumbling off the kerb. 'Happy Christmas, arsehole,' he shouted over his shoulder.

Lucas caught up with him and threw an arm around his neck, dragging him into a headlock. McIlroy tried to pull away, eventually pushing Lucas off him. But it'd given him plenty of time to take what he needed. Who knew when a police ID would come in useful?

44

16 December 2010

Freeman locked the car and walked towards Ben's house. She was in a particularly foul mood and didn't need Ben messing her around again. The case was getting to her. And her dick of a boss was getting to her too, talking to her like she had no idea what she was doing. She may have lacked some focus in the last couple of days but she knew what she was doing. But it wasn't that that'd caused her mood. When she'd got home the night before she'd found Brian loitering in the doorway.

'What do you want?' she asked and dug out her keys from her bag.

'You haven't returned my calls,' Brian said, coming towards her, gym bag thrown over his shoulder.

'Well, there's a reason for that, Brian. I don't like you.' She swiped her key fob and pushed open the heavy door, blocking the way so he couldn't follow.

'We need to talk,' he said, pushing his blond hair behind his ear.

'Are you stupid?' she snapped, spinning around to face him. 'I told you to leave me alone.'

Brian grabbed hold of her arm as she tried to walk away. 'I know you're pregnant, Nic.'

Freeman froze, nausea rising again. 'Excuse me?'

Brian held up the spare keys she'd given him when she still

thought he was worth her time. 'I went in to get my stuff. You wouldn't speak to me, so I thought I'd just get my things and go. I saw the pregnancy test in the bin.'

She didn't know whether to cry or punch him in the face. 'You keep a lot of your stuff in the bin, do you?'

'Come on, Nic. Let's talk about it,' he said, touching her face. 'This could be good. For both of us.'

She removed his hand. 'You have to be fucking kidding.'

'Nic—'

'Anyway, I'm not pregnant,' she said. 'I've been to the doctor. The test was wrong.'

Brian's face dropped.

'Please don't come round any more. We're done,' Freeman said, and taking the key from him, she slammed the door.

Freeman kicked the gravel from the path as she approached Ben's door. Luckily, for both their sakes, he answered straight away. She followed him into the kitchen as she had done a couple of days earlier. She'd started to think he'd skipped town but Williams had called first thing to say she'd driven past and spotted Ben helping his mother into the house. Freeman had relaxed a bit but decided to pay him another visit. His memory had let him down with Emma; she wondered if he recalled Jenny Taylor any better.

'Tea?' Ben asked as Freeman sat down. She nodded and let him get on with it, wanting his full attention when she asked him about Jenny. He turned back and looked into the mugs as if he'd forgotten what he was doing. Freeman watched him for a few seconds and then intervened. 'Milk, no sugar,' she said.

'Yes,' he said. 'Yes, of course.' He opened the fridge and pulled out the milk and poured it into both mugs, then put the mugs on the table in front of her and sat down. 'It's cold,' he said. 'I thought it might snow again.'

'Yes,' Freeman said and watched him. He seemed nervous

but sat still, now staring into his tea. 'I wanted to ask you about someone else who came to the clinic. Jenny Taylor.'

She thought she saw something, a reaction, but Ben kept his head down. He started to lift the mug of tea to his lips but his hand trembled.

'Does that name ring a bell?' Freeman asked.

Ben put the mug down and finally looked at her. 'Yes.'

She was almost surprised. Thought he might've denied knowing her too. Although he'd have to be pretty stupid to do that. And why would he need to, anyway? Jenny hadn't been murdered and left in a shallow grave.

'You worked with her, tried to help her get off the drugs. Is that right?'

'Yes. For a short time.'

She waited for him to elaborate.

'I'm sorry,' he said. 'What does she have to do with Emma? That's what you're investigating, isn't it?'

Freeman nodded. 'I'm trying to find anyone who knew Emma. Who might be able to help me find out what happened. Jenny and Emma were . . . not friends, I suppose, but they knew the same people, hung around together for a while.'

'I didn't know that,' Ben said.

'Can you tell me what you do know about Jenny?'

Ben cleared his throat. 'She came to the clinic asking for help but she was . . . difficult,' he said and scratched his ear.

'How do you mean?' Freeman asked.

'Well, she was . . .' Ben frowned and looked past Freeman. 'There were kids who came in who *wanted* to get clean. Sometimes they hadn't been using very long, sometimes they'd had something bad happen to them and they wanted out of that world. Usually they were the ones who succeeded.' He looked back at Freeman. 'Don't get me wrong, it was always hard. For all of them. And most of them needed a few attempts before they finally got clean but some of them, some like Jenny, they just seemed wired to be that way. No matter what she said she never seemed to really want out. She'd come to a session and I'd ask why she was there and she didn't have an answer. You could tell that she'd already made her mind up that that was her life.'

Freeman shrugged. 'So why would she bother to go to the clinic in the first place?'

'Who knows? Sometimes they find themselves in terrible situations. They get hurt, see others get hurt. They want out but it doesn't last. The addiction's too strong. It wasn't just Jenny; there were lots of kids, lots of people who'd do the same. The general consensus is that once an addict, always an addict. Whether it's drugs or alcohol or gambling, whatever. Once you're in, you're in. Many people can quit if they work at it but there's always that temptation, always a chance of relapse.' He shrugged again. 'Sometimes people would ask, "Why bother?"'

'And what do you say to those people?' Freeman asked, her mind drifting to Darren again. He'd sobered up in prison. Fat lot of good it did him in the end.

'Why not?' He smiled, but Freeman could see the sadness behind it.

'Were you an addict?'

He gave a sad laugh. 'No. No I wasn't. And a lot of people were wary of that, believe me. They'd ask how I could say I understood, how I could know how they felt if I hadn't been there myself.'

'And how do you?'

He turned the mug around in his hands. 'My sister was an addict. I know that doesn't make me an expert but it gave me an inside perspective. Made me want to help others.'

Freeman watched him carefully, waited for him to expand.

When he was quiet she asked, 'What happened to her? Your sister. Did she get clean?'

Ben shook his head. 'No. She overdosed when she was nineteen.'

Freeman gave him a gentle smile. Maybe that'd explain his need to help other teenage girls. 'I'm sorry,' she said. Ben just nodded and looked into his tea.

'A lot of people who do this job, or who volunteer, are ex-addicts. Often the kids will respond to them more, but I don't think it's necessary. Doctors don't know what it's like to suffer from all the diseases they heal,' Ben said.

'Is that how you see yourself? As a healer? Like a doctor?'

Ben shook his head. 'No, not really. I'm sorry, that sounded very pretentious, didn't it? I just meant that you don't have to have been through an experience to want to help. You don't need—' Ben stopped and seemed to struggle with finding the right words.

Freeman decided to help him. 'I understand,' she said, wanting to move on. 'Let's get back to Jenny. You said she was difficult, but how was your relationship with her? Did you know her well?'

'No,' Ben said. 'I didn't get to know any of them well. I'm not there to be their friend.'

'Not any of them?' Freeman asked, thinking about Emma.

'No,' Ben repeated. 'You can't get involved. I don't think it would end well. There's a certain intimacy involved some-times if the client divulges information about their personal life. Some of them see you as a sounding board, often the only person they can talk to . . . but a lot of the time it's lies.'

Freeman watched Ben turn his mug in his hands, his tea swilling about. She didn't like the way he was steering all her questions, making them into generalisations rather than discussing Jenny directly. She wondered if it was a habit borne of his profession – keep things impersonal, don't discuss the client – or whether he had something to hide. 'So Jenny told lies?' she asked.

He nodded. 'Yes, I think so. Like I said, she wasn't really ready for help. She couldn't be honest with me because she didn't want to be there.'

Freeman took out her notebook. 'Jenny was arrested a couple of times. One was a drugs charge, amphetamines, and the other was for soliciting.' She looked up at Ben as she said this. He swallowed and gave an almost imperceptible nod. 'On that second charge, she asked for you to come and pick her up.'

She watched the muscles in Ben's jaw work and waited. He nodded again, this time more certain. 'Yes,' was all he said.

'Was that usual? For a client to do that? Especially one that you weren't friends with?'

Ben shook his head and opened his mouth to speak when his mother shouted from upstairs. 'Excuse me,' Ben said and hurried away.

Freeman sighed. Did his mother have some kind of radar that picked up when Ben was uncomfortable? She could hear muffled voices, movement. She stood up and walked out into the hallway. The place was run-down, hadn't seen a paint-brush in years. She stuck her head into the living room. There were pictures of angels on the walls, crystals on the mantel-piece. She wondered if they were Ben's or his mother's. She guessed at the former. He had the look of an ageing hippie.

On top of the ancient TV was a framed photo of a teenage girl. His sister, she presumed. Freeman picked up the picture and saw a pretty blonde girl, maybe twelve years old. Before the drugs got her.

She put the photo back and returned to the kitchen. An image of Darren sprang to mind, playing Nintendo, jumping up and down on the settee, pissed off she was beating him. Ordering a massive pizza when their parents were out. Him eating most of it, far more than a boy of his size should've rightfully been able to manage. His short, skinny body, made worse by drink and drugs. She wondered if Darren had come across someone like Ben in prison. Her brother would've hated him. Would've called him a stupid bloody hippie. She almost laughed. She missed him. Wished things had been different. That she'd made different choices. That *he'd* made different choices.

'Sorry about that,' Ben said, interrupting her thoughts.

Freeman nodded, almost smiled at him. 'So, we were talking about Jenny and her arrest.'

Ben's face reddened and he stared down at the table. 'It wasn't something I made a habit of. I never did it before or after Jenny. I can't say most of the people who came through the clinic would even *think* of me to come and get them. I'm not sure why she asked for me. Or why I went.'

'But?' Freeman said, wishing he'd get to the point.

'But Jenny seemed to think I was, I don't know,' he said and threw up his hands. 'I think she thought I was a soft touch. And maybe I was. Am. But I think she thought that I could somehow get her out of things. That that was what I was there for. If she had trouble with the police I could sort it. If she needed money I could get her it.'

'You gave her money?'

'No, of course not.' Ben stood and tipped his drink down the sink. He picked up her mug and did the same, switching the kettle back on. 'Maybe that's why she went to the clinic in the first place. Maybe she was under the impression that it was a place that handed out drugs or gave addicts money so they wouldn't have to rob pensioners.' He shrugged and turned back to Freeman. 'When they called me to go and get her I didn't know what to do. All they said was she'd asked them to call me. Like I say, maybe I am a soft touch. I got the impression she didn't have anyone else. She hadn't mentioned her family much but I figured they weren't in the picture any more.' He sighed. 'I suppose I thought, what if it was Kerry?'

'Your sister?' Freeman guessed.

'Yes. I suppose it always came down to that. What if Kerry was in that situation? What would I do? What would I want other people to do? I couldn't just ignore Jenny.'

'So what happened?'

Ben stirred the milk into the tea and came back to the table. 'I went to the station. Picked her up. I tried to talk to her but she wouldn't say much. I dropped her off at a friend's and left.'

'That was it?' Freeman asked.

'That was it.'

'And that was June 1999?'

Ben shrugged. 'I couldn't say for sure.'

'So did she come back to the clinic after that?'

'Yes, she came a few times over the next couple of weeks. She was quite aggressive to start with.'

'In what way?'

Ben seemed to consider his answer. 'I think she was embarrassed about that night, about calling me for help. That was hard for her, asking for help. So she put up a front, was abusive.' He caught Freeman's eye. 'Not physically. She just shouted and screamed for a while, called us names.'

'Us?'

'Me and the other people at the clinic, the police, anyone who was in the vicinity.'

'And then what?'

'I let her get it out of her system and then asked her what she wanted. She told me she wanted to get off the drugs for good.'

'Did you believe her? You said you thought she was wired to be that way, a user.'

Ben sighed and rested his hands on the table in front of him. 'It was the first time I'd seen real emotion from her. I thought maybe she was ready but again maybe *I* just wanted her to be ready. I made her appointments, pencilled her in regularly. I thought if I showed confidence in her she might stick with it.'

'But she didn't?' Freeman asked.

'She did. For a while.'

'And she was clean?'

Ben smiled. 'Not totally,' he said. 'But that's how it works. We didn't do cold turkey. We couldn't be with clients twenty-four-seven, we weren't a rehab centre. It was a longer process for us. But she seemed to be trying.'

'And then?'

'And then she stopped coming.'

'So when was the last time you saw her?'

Ben looked up at the ceiling. 'I can't say for sure. Late June, maybe.'

Freeman nodded. She'd checked Jenny's file. The last appointment Jenny had attended was 28 June.

Ben looked at Freeman. 'I'm sorry,' he said again. 'I'm afraid I can't be more helpful.'

Freeman shook her head. 'No, that's fine. So the last time you saw her was June. Can you remember the last time you saw Emma?'

Ben's face darkened. 'I told you, I don't really remember.'

'Okay,' Freeman said, making a note. 'And then you left in what, July?'

'What's that got to do with it?' Ben snapped.

'Just trying to establish a time frame. Find out who saw Emma last.'

'I'm sorry,' he said. 'But I have no idea what happened to her.'

45

10 June 1999

Lucas closed his eyes again. He couldn't look at her as she went down on him. Couldn't think about how low he'd sunk. He could've done much better. But she was there. And she was desperate. She'd do whatever he wanted her to. Do anything she was told. But he still couldn't look at her. She disgusted him. He could focus on the hair, pretend she was Emma. But it didn't work. Emma was gone.

It was taking forever. He wanted to stop. Shove her away. Tell her to get the fuck out of his flat. But he'd started. Might as well finish. Might as well get something out of having her filthy mouth on him.

He barely made a sound as he finished. She sat back and wiped her mouth, smiling. So fucking pleased with herself. Lucas zipped up his jeans. She tried to grab him, probably wanted him to return the favour. Not in a fucking million years. He pushed her away and went to the settee, turning on the telly.

She was standing in the doorway, half-naked, trying to get his attention. He kept his eyes on the screen. Something about antiques.

'That it, then?' Jenny said. He ignored her, flicked through the channels. 'You can fuck me if you like,' she said, coming up behind him. Wrapping her arms around his neck. He shrugged her off.

173

'No thanks,' he said and got up, heading to the kitchen. 'You can get your clothes on and piss off.'

Jenny slid onto the settee instead. 'What? You scared you'll get *me* up the duff as well?'

Lucas got a lager from the fridge. 'With all the diseases you've got? You'd be lucky.' He walked back in to find her sprawled on the settee. He stood over her.

'Come on, Lucas,' she said, spreading her legs. 'I wouldn't kill your baby.'

'What the fuck are you talking about?'

Jenny sat up straight, a grin spreading across her face. 'Didn't she even tell you? What a little cow.'

Lucas strode towards her and she backed off, into the corner of the settee. 'What are you talking about?' he repeated.

'That little slapper, Emma. She had an abortion.'

Lucas felt his stomach drop. She was lying. Emma wasn't even pregnant.

'Liar,' he said.

'I aren't. Stacey saw her at the hospital weeks ago. Same place I went to before. Said she saw her coming out. Crying like she was the first person to ever kill her fucking baby.'

Lucas could feel his lungs pressing against his ribs. She had to be lying. Emma wouldn't do that. She wouldn't fucking dare. Would she? He knew she'd gone off again. Had been gone a while. So long he'd got sick of hanging about, waiting for her to show up. Thought maybe she'd gone for good. He'd been keeping his eyes open but wasn't holding his breath.

Lucas's fists tightened and he leaned over Jenny, his face an inch from hers. 'If you're lying to me, I'm going to hurt you.'

'I'm not lying,' Jenny said, her voice shrill. 'Ask Stacey. She told me she saw her. She was with that freak from the drugs clinic.'

Lucas threw his can of lager at the wall and grabbed his

coat. He was going to find that faggot and break his fucking legs.

Lucas waited around the corner for Ben. Wanted to show him what a mistake he'd made by fucking with him, getting involved in other people's business.

He'd found Jenny's mate, Stacey, in the pub where she always was – draped over some loser who couldn't see past the tits to the money-grabbing little bitch she was. She was slurping a cocktail through a straw when he pulled her off the old bloke's lap.

'Oi,' she said. 'What're you doing?'

'Tell me what you told Jenny,' Lucas said.

'What?' she said, staring at him like *he* was the piece of shit in this situation.

'Tell me what you told Jenny. About Emma.'

Stacey screwed her face up. 'I never said nothing about Emma.'

Lucas snorted a laugh and let go of her. 'Lying little cunt,' he said and started to walk away. He'd find Jenny and teach her a lesson she wouldn't soon forget.

'What'd she say, like?' Stacey shouted after him.

Lucas walked back to her and she swayed on her heels. 'You wanna be careful who you knock about with, love,' Lucas said. 'She's been telling lies. Said you told her Emma had an abortion. That you saw her.'

'Oh, that,' Stacey said, her face like a shrug. 'No, that's true. I thought you were on about something else.'

Lucas felt his anger surge again.

'She was with that fella from the drug clinic. Proper weirdo, he is.'

Lucas turned, slamming the door into the wall as he left. And now he was waiting. Someone was locking the door to the clinic. Not Ben, some fat woman. So where was he? Lucas looked up and down the street and saw him walking out of the alley that ran behind the clinic. He must've been locking up the back. The fat woman disappeared down the street and Ben dug about in his pockets for keys. Lucas moved quickly, hood covering his face. It wasn't quite dark yet, the streets not quite empty.

Ben looked up as Lucas came up behind him but he wasn't fast enough to respond to the punch in the gut. He buckled and Lucas grabbed him, dragging him into the alley.

'Where's Emma?' Lucas said and threw Ben to the ground. Ben tried to tell him he didn't know her and Lucas slammed his fist into his face. 'Where is she?' he said again, his fists tight around the collars of Ben's jacket.

'I don't know,' Ben said, shaking.

Lucas pressed Ben into the pavement, hands now around his neck. 'I know what you did,' he said.

The sound of the glass bottle smashing at the other end of the alley made them both look up and Lucas loosened his grip. A group of kids threw another, laughing as it shattered into pieces. Ben wriggled away from Lucas and started running. Lucas was almost on him when he saw the cop car parked across the road. He slowed down and watched as Ben crossed the street. Lucas turned the other way, glancing over his shoulder before he walked around the corner. Ben walked straight past the police car, didn't even pause.

Lucas considered going back, finishing what he started. But he knew he'd get another chance. He'd find Ben again.

46

16 December 2010

Louise sat on the settee, her arms hugging her knees. The TV was playing to itself in the corner but she couldn't recall anything that had been on in the last few hours. She'd barely slept. Adam had looked worried when he left that morning but she'd just said she didn't feel too good again. That was true. He'd offered to stay but it was half-hearted. He had to go on a trip with the students. An overnight stay in Leeds. He denied it but he'd been looking forward to it.

Part of her hadn't wanted him to go but the other part felt relief. What if the police showed up again? What if he'd seen them? Maybe she should just go, leave. He'd be better off without her anyway.

She looked at the Christmas card she'd received. It was from Karen, who worked in the local shop. That was about as far as her social circle went. She didn't let people in. Didn't make friends. There was only Adam she was close to and in reality he was a million miles away. He knew nothing about her. She wondered how much longer it could last.

She knew she should just go. Leave before the police came knocking again and she'd have to tell Adam everything. How could she look at him and tell him she'd lied? Tell him what she'd done? She wished it would all go away but she knew it would catch up with her eventually. She'd always known that.

The phone rang, making her jump. She checked the caller ID before answering, taking a breath, ready to get into character.

'Hello,' she said. 'Aren't you supposed to be herding teenagers around Leeds?'

'Yes. But this is more important. I was thinking maybe we could go out tomorrow night. Maybe to Al Forno's or somewhere like that.'

'Won't it be full of work Christmas parties?' The thought of going out, being surrounded by people, made her sick.

'I suppose,' he said. 'Well, maybe I could pick something up on the way home, something fancy.'

'Fancy?' She forced a laugh. 'Like what? Caviar? Oysters? The fanciest we ever get is burgers made with actual beef.'

'All right,' he said. 'I'll surprise you. I *can* do fancy, you know. I'll swing by the shops on the way home. I should be back by lunchtime.'

'Okay,' she said. 'See you tomorrow.'

She hung up and squeezed her eyes tightly shut, trying not to cry. That was why she hadn't left. Why she hadn't kept running. He was always so sweet, always trying to make things better for her. And what did he get in return? A liar. A fake. A criminal.

47

16 December 2010

Lucas stared out of the window as the streets whizzed by in a blur. Hearing McIlroy saying Jenny's name had been like a punch in the gut. He didn't know why Freeman was suddenly looking at Jenny, but it made him nervous. He needed to stay ahead of the game.

He stepped off the bus and looked up and down the street. He remembered the area fairly well. Things hadn't changed much. He just hoped Jenny's parents still lived in the same shitty house.

He started walking, checking the numbers on the houses. He remembered coming here all those years ago, helping Jenny nick her parents' stuff. Driving her back to Blyth where she became a permanent pain in his arse. Thankfully he'd had the sense to stay in the car, out of the way. Didn't want Mr and Mrs Taylor identifying him to the cops.

Lucas walked up to the door and rang the bell. He wanted to know what Freeman had told them, if anything. Find out what they knew about their daughter.

Angie Taylor answered the door and stopped short. She looked at Lucas. Lucas looked at her chest. 'Mrs Taylor?' he said.

'Yeah?' She crossed her arms.

'Hello. I was just wondering if I could talk to you about Jenny.'

179

'Who're you?' Angie asked.

'DC McIlroy,' he said, sliding the ID back into his pocket before she could look too closely. 'Can I come in?' he asked and Angie stood up straight but didn't move to let him in. 'DS Freeman asked me to come.'

Lucas sat down in the unwelcoming home of the Taylors. They didn't offer him anything, no tea or coffee, not a sausage, the stingy bastards. He sat forward in the cheap fabric armchair and looked between Angie and Malcolm.

'Who did you say you were?' Malcolm said, more to Angie than to Lucas.

'Another copper. Here about Jenny,' Angie told him.

'Bob McIlroy.' Lucas leaned closer to Malcolm, extending his hand. Malcolm looked down and hesitated before shaking.

'We already told the other one we don't know where she is,' Angie said and lit up a cigarette, causing Malcolm to cough and give her a dirty look. Angie rolled her eyes and stood up, walking to the window which she opened barely a crack. She stood in front of it, still facing into the room, blowing smoke towards the two men. 'You lot have as much idea as we do.'

'Sure,' Lucas said, trying not to smile. Obviously Freeman didn't know a thing but he couldn't just up and leave now. Besides, maybe they could fill in some blanks. 'She ran away from home, correct, in ninety . . .'

'Seven,' Malcolm said.

'Right. And then she was in Blyth for a few years. But then she dropped off the radar. She never contacted you again, after she left?'

'Nope. Not a thing,' Angie said. 'For all we know, she's dead. Overdosed on whatever shit she was taking.'

Malcolm gave his wife a look that could kill and Lucas wondered if he should just leave. 'You don't know that,' Malcolm said, sadly. 'She could've changed. Stopped all that.'

Angie finished her cigarette and opened the window further in order to throw the butt out. As she walked back to the settee she looked to her husband. 'So why hasn't she shown her face, then?'

'Why would she come back here?' Malcolm said, raising his voice. 'Why would she come back to you?'

'You think she would've come back? If she was okay, that is?' Lucas asked.

Angie and Malcolm looked at each other, a moment of sadness before Angie caught herself. 'I don't think she'll ever be okay.' Angie crossed her arms and her fingers dug into her flesh, leaving a mark on already goose-pimpled skin.

Lucas waited a few moments before continuing. 'Well, maybe the fact she's disappeared from our radar is a good thing. Maybe she's moved on. Found something better,' he said, playing the good cop better than McIlroy ever could. He was about to stand, ready to go, when Angie spoke again.

'We did look for her. Eventually,' she said. 'Told your mate that.'

It took a few seconds before Lucas noticed it was his line, and after a brief pause he leaned forward. 'When was that again?'

'Couple of years back. I was diagnosed with cancer. Wanted to see her,' Malcolm said. 'Hired a private investigator.'

'But he didn't find her?'

Angie and Malcolm looked at each other and Lucas saw a flash of anger in Malcolm's eyes. He didn't want to push too hard. But if there was any chance of finding out what he needed to know, he had to try.

'Bloody cowboy,' Malcolm said. 'Paid him a fortune for him to piss about, driving around the country finding any old girl called Jenny Taylor. Some of them weren't even the right age. One was a bloody pensioner, virtually.'

Angie looked like she was going to argue with that point but thought better of it. She turned her attention back to Lucas.

'He wasn't very good,' she said. 'But to be fair, he did find a few Jennys with the right date of birth. Just not our Jenny.'

'Who was the investigator?' Lucas asked.

Malcolm shook his head. 'Johnny Bloody Cowboy,' he said and Angie rolled her eyes.

'He was called Lawrence. I can't remember his first name,' she said.

Lucas nodded. 'How did you get hold of him? Did someone recommend him? The police?'

Malcolm snorted. 'No one in their right mind would recommend that idiot. Least of all the police, if they were any good at their jobs.'

'We never went to the police,' Angie said. 'It was too late by then. She'd been gone so long you lot wouldn't have listened.'

Lucas caught the look out of the corner of his eye. In one brief second all the blame and hatred Malcolm seemed to have stored up was directed at his wife. It was her fault they hadn't looked for Jenny sooner. Lucas almost smiled; they reminded him of his own parents. Lovely couple.

'You still have his number?' Lucas asked.

'No,' Angie said and Lucas wondered what was the point of coming. True, he knew that Freeman didn't get anything from them, but then neither had he.

'Show him the folder,' Malcolm said.

Lucas watched as Angie stood and smoothed down her skirt. She walked over to a low cabinet and slid open a door, pulling out a flimsy folder. As she took her seat across from Lucas she opened the file and handed him the loose papers from inside. As he took them, a photo fluttered to the floor. Lucas bent and picked it up. It showed a young woman maybe in her early twenties, though it was hard to say. You could barely make out her features as the photo was taken from a distance.

Malcolm leaned over. 'That's what we were paying for,' he said and slumped back into his chair.

Lucas looked back at the sheets of paper in his hand and his heart raced. Suddenly he was back in the game.

'Did you show this to DS Freeman?' Lucas asked, crossing his fingers and toes.

'No,' Angie said. 'She never asked.'

Lucas nodded and his eyes skimmed the sheets of paper. He knew he'd struck gold.

48

16 December 2010

'I lied to you yesterday,' Ben admitted. 'When I said I didn't know Emma.'

'I know that already,' Freeman told him.

Ben sighed. 'It was only because I was trying to protect her.'

'Whatever it is you know, you have to tell me. Do you know what happened to Emma?'

'No,' Ben said. He stared at her as if he was weighing up whether to spill.

Freeman listened to the noise of the TV upstairs. 'What would happen to your mother if you went to prison, Ben?'

'What do you mean?' Ben said, his voice unsteady.

'Well, you're acting like someone with something to hide and if you don't start telling me everything you know I'm going to assume it's because you're involved in this somehow. So again I ask: what would happen to your mother if you went to prison?' It was a low trick. She didn't have anything on him. But he was pissing her off.

She heard him let out a long sigh. 'Emma came to me one day. She'd been to the clinic, she'd stopped using. But she came to me for help with something else.' He paused, knotting his hands together. 'She was pregnant. She didn't know where else to go. She asked me to help her. I took her to a friend who ran a shelter. She stayed there for a while after she had an abortion.'

Freeman let out her own long breath. 'How old was she?'

'Sixteen. Just. She didn't want her dad to know but she asked me to go and tell him she was okay. I told him she was getting help getting clean and that she wanted to stay away until she was.'

'I'm guessing it was Lucas Yates' baby,' Freeman said.

'Yes.'

'Did he know?'

Ben paused. 'She didn't tell him. I didn't think she told anyone else. But somehow he found out. He went ballistic.'

Freeman was quiet. Imagine being pregnant with Lucas Yates' kid. It'd probably come out with a '666' birthmark. No wonder she got rid of it. She fought the urge to touch her belly, to think of her situation in the same breath as Emma's. Things were different for Emma. She'd been a sixteen-year-old girl, a drug addict. She'd been abused by her boyfriend. Brian was a dick but he wasn't abusive. She should've been able to handle this so much better than Emma but she still felt out of control.

Emma hadn't told Lucas Yates about the baby but he'd found out and gone apeshit. She wondered what Brian would say if he found out the truth. She wondered if she would even tell him the truth. She should. But that didn't mean she would. She'd cross that bridge when she came to it.

'I know I should've mentioned this earlier but I swore to Emma I wouldn't tell anyone. I know it probably doesn't matter now but I gave her my word.'

'Do you think Yates could've killed her?'

Ben didn't say anything for a moment. 'Yes,' he said, eventually. 'I think he did kill her.'

'And the last time you saw her alive was when you took her to the shelter?'

'Yes.'

Freeman left Ben's house and wondered if he was telling the truth this time. Something was off about him but she couldn't put her finger on it. If what he'd said was true, then Emma Thorley had clearly trusted him more than anyone else in her life. And he'd been the person Jenny Taylor had called, too. So was he a protector of these girls, a knight to save them from the likes of Lucas Yates? Or was there more to it?

49

17 June 1999

He thought it was *her*. He thought he'd finally found her. And then she'd turned and he realised. It was Jenny. He was going to walk away. He couldn't do much now, not with all these people about. All the dole scum and old biddies with nothing better to do than hang around the town centre, spending their cash on fish fingers and fruit machines. But he just couldn't do it. Couldn't let Ben get away with it again. Couldn't let Ben take another one from him.

'Oi!' Lucas shouted and Jenny and Ben both turned. Ben looked like he'd shit himself but Jenny just glared. She was pissed off at him because of last time. Suddenly decided that she was too good for him.

Lucas caught up to them and shouldered his way past Ben, grabbing Jenny by the arm. 'What're you doing?'

'What's it gotta do with you, like?' Jenny said and squirmed out of his grasp.

'You're not going with him.'

Ben stepped forward but Lucas stared him into silence.

'Says who?' Jenny said. 'You don't tell me what to do. I'm not Emma, you know.'

Lucas slapped her hard across the face and she staggered backwards. Ben grabbed Lucas's arm. 'Leave her alone,' he said.

'Or what?' Lucas asked, stepping up to Ben, who dropped

his arm. 'What're you gonna do? Eh?' Lucas pressed his forehead to Ben's, pushing him back. 'You keep your fucking nose out of this.'

Jenny pushed Lucas away from Ben. 'Fuck off, Lucas,' she said.

'What? You think you're gonna get clean? I fucking doubt that.'

'I am,' Jenny said.

'Yeah, good luck with that, Jen.'

'Piss off,' Jenny said and started to walk away, Ben following behind like a little obedient dog.

'You'll be back at my door tomorrow, begging me for some shit.'

Jenny gave him the finger.

Lucas started walking away too, but turned one last time. 'Some people are born losers and they'll die that way.'

50

16 December 2010

Freeman was almost home when the phone rang. She wanted nothing more than to ignore it and go inside to bed and stay there for a week. Instead, she picked up but before she could speak she heard, 'Is that DS Freeman?'

Now Freeman really wished she hadn't answered the phone. Angie Taylor sounded pissed off.

'Speaking,' she said.

'Are you lot in the habit of thieving stuff from people's homes?'

'What?' Freeman asked. She already had plenty on her plate. She didn't need to be accused of stealing from witnesses too.

'That bloke you sent round. He took the file we showed him. Never said a bloody word. If you lot wanted the information—'

'Hang on,' Freeman said. 'Which bloke are you on about?' Freeman could hear the TV blaring in the background but Angie made no attempt to turn it down.

'McEwan,' she said and then Freeman heard Malcolm shout 'McIlroy' in the background. 'Whatever,' Angie said. 'McIlroy, McEwan, same bloody difference.'

'McIlroy?' Why was Bob McIlroy at the Taylors'? He had nothing to do with the investigation. Not unless Routledge had been interfering.

'Yes,' Angie said. 'Clearly the arse doesn't know what the elbow's up to.'

'What did he want?'

'Same as you. Asking about Jenny.'

'And you're sure it was DC McIlroy?'

'Yes, McIlroy. Young fella,' Angie said.

Freeman swerved slightly on the road. She hadn't been expecting that. 'Wait, what?' Freeman's mind was racing. She looked in her rear-view mirror and if there hadn't been a stream of traffic behind she might well have stopped right there in the middle of the road.

Angie sighed down the phone. 'Look. I don't know what you lot are up to but—'

'When was he there? What time did he leave?' Freeman said, her heart thumping.

'This afternoon sometime. He left, what . . .' She could hear a muffled conversation and guessed Angie was conferring with her husband. 'A couple of hours ago. Maybe four-ish.'

Freeman's hands gripped the wheel. 'What did he look like? Height, hair colour, anything like that.'

Angie sighed. 'He was about average height I'd say.'

'So what, five-eight, five-ten?'

Another sigh. 'I suppose. Brown hair, looked like a lot of gel or something in it. Sort of sexy too. For a copper.'

That proved it. Bob McIlroy was not what anyone would call sexy. Even Angie Taylor. Lucas Yates, on the other hand, was a walking hair-product ad.

Freeman wanted to put the wheels in motion for a warrant for Lucas's arrest but first she needed to prove it had been him at the Taylors'. The little shit wasn't going to get away with it. She'd already asked someone to find McIlroy to ask why

Lucas had chosen to impersonate him. Perhaps when he sobered up they'd get an answer.

She pulled up, leaving the car at an angle on the kerb, and walked to the door of the bedsits. There was a speaker system and a main door that was supposed to be locked but in all the times she'd visited it'd never worked. She pulled the door open and went inside. It was almost as cold inside as it was out. There was no one at the desk or in the front room despite the TV playing quietly in the corner. Freeman was relieved; she didn't want to speak to the old crone unless she had to.

She started climbing the stairs. Lucas's room was on the first floor, according to his probation officer. She could hear the sound of TVs and radios playing. As she got to the first floor she could hear someone snoring. It was ridiculously loud. She wouldn't be surprised if they were called in to a homicide there shortly. If she had to sleep next door to that guy she'd kill him within minutes. Brian was a snorer. Just one more reason she was glad he was gone.

She reached the door to Lucas's room and knocked. She waited about ten seconds before knocking again, harder, but there was still no answer. Freeman muttered under her breath. Great, now she'd have to go and speak to the old witch. She headed back down the stairs and stood at reception. There was a bell on the desk like it was an old-fashioned hotel. Freeman was about to ring it when the old woman came out of the room behind her. She stopped short when she saw Freeman.

'We're full.'

'Excuse me?' Freeman said.

'We're full. No rooms,' the old woman said and pushed past with her laundry basket.

Freeman sighed. She knew she didn't exactly look like a copper but come on – she hardly looked like one of the reprobates that stayed in this shithole. She pulled out her ID and the old woman snatched it to inspect it two inches from her face. Satisfied, she handed it back. 'Which one is it?' she asked, without so much as a mutter of apology. 'Which one of the little bastards has done something now?'

'Lucas Yates.'

'Little prick,' she said. 'Thinks he's something special, that one. Thinks the rules don't apply to him. Always smoking in his room. Brings little whores back with him. He thinks I don't know but I do. And when I tell him he acts like butter wouldn't melt. Prick.'

Freeman tried not to smile. The old woman's dislike made Freeman warm to her.

'Is he here?' Freeman asked and the woman eyed her up.

'What's he done?'

'I just need to speak to him,' Freeman said but she knew she'd have to give the woman something if she was going to talk any more. 'He could be a witness to a serious incident.'

The old woman laughed, a high-pitched cackle. 'A witness? More bloody likely he did it.' She pulled a set of keys out of her apron and started up the stairs. 'I gather you've tried the door,' she said but didn't wait for Freeman to reply.

They stopped outside Lucas's room and the old woman bent to unlock it. She pushed the door open and stepped into the room. 'It's all yours,' she said. 'Let me know when you're done.' She moved past Freeman and as she walked back towards the stairs she hammered on the door of the snorer. 'Shut up,' she shouted and then disappeared downstairs.

Freeman pushed the door closed and looked around. The bed was made and there wasn't a thing out of place. No clothes scattered across the floor, no takeaway boxes piled up or lager cans crushed and abandoned. She wondered if it was a legacy from his stay in prison or if he'd always been a neat freak. There was a small sink with a toothbrush, toothpaste and a razor on it. In the small cupboard were some clothes, all hung up or folded neatly, mostly designer or knock-off designer stuff. A couple of books on the table next to the bed – Jim Thompson and Elmore Leonard.

She walked to the window and noticed some cigarette ash on the windowsill. The only real sign of life.

She turned around and was about to leave. She didn't know what she'd expected to find. She was only looking for the man himself. She was halfway to the door when her phone rang.

'Freeman,' she said, still looking around, sure she'd find something.

'It's Gardner. You rang?'

Freeman tried to ignore the sarcasm in his voice. She knew she was pushing her luck a little, but needs must. 'Thanks for getting back to me,' she said. 'I need you to try Jenny Taylor again.'

'She still hasn't called?' he said.

'No. And I'm starting to think she's avoiding me.'

'You think she has something to do with Emma's murder?'

'I don't know,' Freeman sighed. 'But Lucas Yates has been creeping around, visited her parents, trying to find out where she is. I don't know if she's involved or in danger.'

'All right, I'll see what I can do,' Gardner said.

'Thanks. Just make sure things look all right. I'm going to try and come down in the morning, speak to her myself.'

'Okay. If you like, I could meet you at the station. Take you over there.'

'Great,' Freeman said.

'In the meantime I'll head over, see what's happening.'

'Thanks. I'll see you tomorrow.'

She hung up and flicked through Lucas's wardrobe, wondering how an arsehole like Yates could smell so nice.

51

16 December 2010

Lucas stood on the platform, shivering. He shoved his hands into his pockets and looked down at the few passengers scattered about at the other end of the platform, all studiously ignoring each other. None of them were carrying any proper luggage. Nothing he could lift, no chance of a better coat or another fucking jumper. Maybe when he got into Newcastle.

He didn't have any money yet. He reckoned he could get away with no ticket from Morpeth to Newcastle but they were starting to get picky once you got on the major lines. That didn't bother him. A station the size of Newcastle always had plenty of opportunities for snatching a wallet.

He watched his breath fog in front of him and looked at his watch. The train was due three minutes ago. He reached in his pocket and took out the picture. It hadn't been hard to swipe the file. A quick nudge of the cold cup of tea on the table next to him and Angie Taylor was shrieking about her good carpet. Took what he needed, the rest went in the bin.

He stared at the photo. She hadn't changed that much. Brown hair instead of blonde but other than that she was the same girl. Anyone else might not have recognised her between the disguise and the shoddy photography. But he did.

He heard the train approach and tucked the photo away. He got on and moved to the far end of the carriage. He was watching the ticket inspector. Sometimes they tried to catch you out by starting at the other end.

Lucas sat down low in the chair and closed his eyes. He could hear a kid yammering a few seats behind him. After a couple of minutes he felt the presence of someone standing over him.

'Ticket.'

Lucas opened his eyes. The sleeping passenger ploy never worked. He sat up and dug into his pocket.

'Newcastle, please,' he said.

The ticket guy pressed buttons on his machine and the ticket spewed out. 'Four-ten,' he said.

Lucas continued to search his pockets, giving the inspector a smile. He made a show of it, patting himself down.

'It's in here somewhere,' Lucas said and the inspector just stared, unimpressed. Lucas stood and frowned. 'Shit,' he muttered. 'I've lost my wallet.'

The inspector raised one eyebrow and leaned one arm on the back of the seat. 'It's four-ten or you'll have to get off at the next station.'

Lucas shrugged. 'I'm sorry. I've lost my wallet.' He looked on the floor around him. The inspector just shrugged back.

'Get off next station then,' he said and turned to the old woman on the seat opposite him.

'Newcastle,' she said and looked at Lucas. 'And for the young man.' She smiled at Lucas like old people do.

'Oh no, I couldn't,' Lucas said.

'Don't be silly. Two to Newcastle,' she said to the inspector, who just shook his head. As he walked away Lucas returned the smile.

'Thank you,' he said and thought maybe his luck was turning. If he'd known beforehand that he could rely on the kindness of strangers he would've asked for the fare all the way to Middlesbrough. Still, it was better than nothing.

'That's all right. Where're you off to?'

'I'm going to see an old friend.'

'Oh, that'll be lovely,' she said and Lucas grinned.

If only you knew.

52

16 December 2010

Freeman stood against the reception desk, waiting for someone to come out. She needed to go back to Morpeth, make sure it was Lucas who'd been at the Taylors', but something had made her stop as she drove through the town. Someone had broken into the clinic. They might've been looking at the personnel files. *Might've.* Maybe it was just a junkie searching for anything worth money. But it didn't feel right.

'DS Freeman? Back again?'

Freeman looked up as Jessie came out into the reception area, pointedly looking at her watch. Clearly Jessie was nearly done for the day. Lucky her. Another woman, the blonde she'd seen last time, followed, looking nervous.

'I'm not sure what else I can tell you about Ben.'

'I'm not here about Ben this time. I was just wondering if you recognised this man,' she said and slid a picture of Lucas across the desk.

Jessie shook her head but the other woman let out a breath.

'Andrea?' Jessie said.

'You recognise him?' Freeman said. 'He's been here?'

Andrea nodded and burst into tears. Freeman looked to Jessie, who just shrugged.

'What's the matter?' Jessie asked.

'I'm sorry,' Andrea said. 'I know I should've told you before but I didn't tell him anything. I swear.'

'Excuse me,' Freeman said, taking the picture back.

'He came here looking for Ben a few days ago. We never told him anything. But then I saw him in the pub. I recognised him and started talking to him and then the next thing . . . he'd sweet-talked me into bed with him.'

'Lucas Yates did?' Freeman asked, pointing at the photo, her brain struggling to keep up with Andrea's teary confession.

'Wanker,' Andrea said. 'He kept asking about Ben. I didn't think. I thought he liked me and then the next thing he just buggers off.' She wiped her eyes, her mascara crawling down her cheeks.

'What did you tell him?'

'Nothing. He wanted to know where Ben was.'

'And did you tell him?'

'No. I don't *know* where he is. I haven't talked to him since he left. I just said he went back to Alnwick to look after his mum.' Andrea looked at Freeman. 'I'm so sorry.'

Freeman ignored her. So Lucas was looking for Jenny *and* Ben. Why? Did they both know what'd happened to Emma? Was he trying to get to any witnesses before they could tell her what'd happened?

She walked out, trying Ben's number. 'Why would Lucas Yates be trying to find you?' she said as soon as Ben picked up.

'I don't know,' he said, his voice a whisper.

'Mr Swales? You did know Lucas Yates, didn't you?'

'Yes,' Ben said. 'Well, no, not really. More by reputation.'

'So why would he be trying to find you?' She waited for Ben to talk but all she heard was a faint buzz on the line. 'Ben?' Freeman said. 'You clearly know a lot more about this than you're telling me. So, I'll ask again. Why is Lucas Yates looking for you?'

'I don't know. Maybe he found out what I did for Emma. I don't know.'

'Well, he obviously knows something. He's going to great lengths to find you.' Freeman sighed. 'Look, I don't think Yates knows exactly where you are yet but he'll probably keep trying. So just be careful.'

'Thank you,' Ben said and hung up.

She had no idea why Lucas wanted to find Ben or how he was involved. But whatever was going on, she knew it couldn't be good.

'Excuse me,' Angie said, hand on hip, drink in the other hand. 'I've had enough of you lot. I've got nothing else to say to you.'

Freeman stomped past Angie, through to the Taylors' living room. She was already in a bad mood without Angie Taylor's attitude problem. She was sick and fucking tired of this case.

'This won't take long,' Freeman said. She took out a picture of Lucas Yates and held it up in front of Angie. 'Recognise him?'

'Yes. It's your mate, McIlroy,' Angie said.

'Wrong.' Freeman shoved the picture into her pocket. 'It's Lucas Yates.'

Angie was about to argue but instead turned to her husband who was sitting quietly on the settee. Angie turned back to Freeman.

'Lucas Yates was an acquaintance of both Jenny and Emma Thorley. I believe he had something to do with Emma's death and I think Jenny knows something about it. So I need you to tell me everything that was said earlier. What he wanted, what you told him, everything.'

Freeman looked from Angie to Malcolm and back. Angie stood gawping, almost as if she were going to cry. Freeman let out a breath. Maybe she'd been too harsh. Angie Taylor was a pain in the arse but she obviously had some shred of feeling left, and now she'd come bounding in telling her that she'd probably been entertaining a killer. Perhaps she could've been gentler.

'Why would he pretend to be someone else?' Angie said, her voice softer than before. 'What's he want Jenny for?'

Freeman sighed. 'I don't know, to be honest. Maybe Jenny knows something about Emma's death, knows that Lucas killed her. That's why I need you to tell me everything.'

Freeman listened to Angie and Malcolm tell their tale, overlapping and interrupting each other. When they'd finished she asked how much they remembered from the file Yates took. Not a great deal – the locations of some of the girls this investigator had found, little else. But clearly he hadn't traced their daughter, so what else was in the file that Lucas found so interesting?

'Was there an address in Middlesbrough in there?' Freeman asked.

'Yes,' Malcolm said. 'I think so. Why?'

'I found an address for Jenny in Middlesbrough,' Freeman said, watching as the Taylors' faces changed in unison.

'You knew where she lived and didn't tell us?' Malcolm said.

'I had someone drop by but there was no answer.'

'I don't bloody believe this,' Malcolm said, animated for the first time.

'Look, it's starting to look like she's not even there any more. But,' Freeman continued, trying to placate them, 'you said there were photos in the file. Obviously your daughter wasn't one of the girls but is it possible this guy got it wrong? How much do you know about him? Was he legit? Maybe took pictures of the wrong girl?'

Angie and Malcolm exchanged glances. 'It's possible,' Malcolm said. 'Bloody cowboy.'

53

16 December 2010

Lucas stepped off the train and looked around the station. So this was Middlesbrough. Unfortunately he'd found no sweet old ladies to con at Newcastle Central station so instead he'd had to lift a couple of wallets. But that was fine. One paid for his ticket. The other, well, the owner of that one wouldn't miss it. Anyone who carried two hundred quid around with them didn't need it that much. He wondered if he should find somewhere to stay for the night but he needed to make his move. If Freeman was on the same track he needed to get it done fast.

He walked down the steps, through the subway. He had no idea where he was going so he followed the small crowd who'd got off the train with him and found himself on the other side of the platform. He walked out into the cold night air and tried to decide what to do. There was no chance he'd be able to find the address by himself so a taxi was in order. He walked across the gravel, found one idling and climbed in the back.

'Ayresome Street,' Lucas said and slammed the door. The driver grunted and pulled away, saying nothing. Lucas was grateful for that at least. He hated chatty taxi drivers.

He watched the grimy streets pass by. Groups of Ben Sherman'd chavs and their slappers piled out of pubs and staggered up the street to the next bar, already unable to stand properly. Several had Santa hats or flashing reindeer antlers on. God, he hated Christmas.

The taxi turned a corner into a residential area. The driver glanced back at Lucas. 'What number?' he said.

'Here's fine, mate.'

The driver pulled over at the side of the road and turned. Lucas looked at the meter. Three pounds sixty. He didn't have enough change. He wanted to make a show of counting out the exact money. Instead he pulled a fiver out of his pocket and gave it to the driver.

The driver nodded. 'Thanks.'

Lucas sat and waited for his change. The driver looked back at him and seemed indignant. He made a show of his own, rummaging around and finding the right coins. He slapped them into Lucas's palm and Lucas grinned and got out.

'Have a good night,' he said and slammed the door. Through the window he could see the driver saying something not altogether flattering as he drove off.

Lucas turned and looked back up the road. It was freezing. Colder than it had been at home, if that was possible. He kept his eyes on the house numbers and came to a stop as he saw the one he was looking for. He could see the shape of a Christmas tree behind the curtain and he wondered if she was there, anticipating a happy Christmas, and what she'd say when she saw his face. The ghost of Christmas past.

Lucas walked up to the house. There was no one around, no one else on the street. He raised his hand and knocked.

No answer.

He moved closer to the window, listening for movement or the sound of the TV.

Nothing.

Lucas tried the door. Locked. He stepped back and looked along the street. The houses were terraced; eight, maybe ten in a row. He shoved his hands in his pockets and stepped back. He started walking to the end of the row. There had to be a way in at the back. Probably a better way, less conspicuous. He turned the corner and found himself staring at the backs of the houses, small yards behind each. A narrow alley ran along the back, but a blue metal gate restricted access. Lucas glanced behind him. The street was empty so he made a run for the gate and climbed over.

When he worked out which one was hers, he opened the back gate and stepped into the yard. It was empty except for a couple of wheelie bins. He tried the back door. Locked as well. He looked around, spotting a brick outside the gate. He picked it up and smashed it into the door's narrow windowpane. He didn't wait to see if anyone was watching, or if anyone had heard. He quickly unlocked the door and went inside.

Lucas stuck his head in the first room. There was a dining table and four chairs but it looked like it was rarely used. Instead of place mats and salt and pepper shakers the table was covered in books and papers. He walked into the living room where the light had been left on and a Christmas tree stood in the window. Lucas looked around. There were some letters on the table. He bent down to look at the name on the labels. Adam Quinn. Adam Quinn. Adam Quinn.

Lucas stood up and went to the mantelpiece. Not even a photograph. He picked up a Christmas card. It was just signed 'best wishes from Karen'. He put it down just as car lights shone in on him. He went to the window and watched someone get out of a taxi across the road. He turned and started up the stairs.

He walked into the bedroom. The double bed took up most of the room. He could see that, but it was too dark to make out anything else. He flicked on the light using his elbow. He still couldn't see any photos, nothing to give him any certainty. He scanned the room. It was a mess. And then he noticed it on the bedside cabinet. A diary.

Lucas sat on the edge of the bed. He picked it up, flipping to the first page where personal details should've been.

Empty. He flicked through. Most of the pages were blank. Whoever the diary belonged to didn't have much of a life. He stopped when he saw writing. *Adam's birthday*. He flicked further, past more empty pages. And then something fell out, fluttering to the floor. Lucas bent to pick it up. It was an address. He was about to shove it back in when he stopped. The address was in Alnwick. A smile started to spread across his face.

He slid the paper into his pocket and stood up. He wondered if she could've gone there already. He turned off the light as he walked out of the room and then froze as he heard the door.

54

6 July 1999

Lucas pushed his way out, not caring whose drinks he knocked over in the process. Some fat cow with a Tango tan screeched after him that he owed her a drink. Any other time he would've stopped, had a word with her, but he didn't have time now. The sound of Robbie Williams faded as the door slammed behind him.

He made his way outside, walking into the road to see better. He knew it was her. Could tell her hair from a mile away. Blonde. The colour of butter. Lurpak, Tomo said one night. He was off his face, thought he was being poetic. He was just being a dick.

A car beeped at him and Lucas gave the driver the finger without turning. He could see her at the end of the street. She was walking with her head down. He started to run after her.

'Emma!'

She almost stopped but instead looked over her shoulder before speeding up. She dodged a group of old folk with small, yappy dogs and turned the corner. Lucas picked up his pace. By the time he reached her he was almost out of breath but he knew it wasn't from the running.

He moved in front of her, blocking her path. She didn't look at him, just kept trying to get round him.

'I was shouting you,' he said. She ignored him and turned to walk back the way she'd come. 'Oi,' he said. 'I'm talking to you.' He grabbed her shoulder and spun her around.

'Leave me alone,' Emma said and tried to pull away. Lucas gripped harder and pushed her against the window of the bookies. No one batted an eyelid. All eyes on the race.

'Where've you been?' he asked her, pressing himself into her body. 'Eh? Answer me. Where've you been? I've been looking for you. I know you were at your mate's house when I came round. I know you saw what I did to her brother. None of that would've happened if you'd just come out and talked to me.'

Emma looked up and down the street. If she thought anyone was going to interfere she had another think coming. People knew better than to bother him.

Lucas ducked his head, trying to force her to look him in the eye. He knew what she'd done. He just wanted her to say it. He pressed himself harder into her.

'Stop it,' she said.

Lucas grabbed her by the throat and shoved her into the wall. 'I know what you did,' he said and watched her eyes fill up. 'I know you went behind my back, Emma. Got rid of it.' She tried to shake her head but his grip was too tight. 'I know what you did and you're going to pay for it.' The tears were really coming now. He could feel them, hot and wet, trickling onto his hand. 'You think you can do that without telling me and get away with it?' He punched her in the stomach and she crumpled. 'I don't think so, Em.'

He started to pull her up. 'You think you've had it bad up to now. You haven't seen nothing, darling. Better keep your eyes open, Em, or else you and your daddy are gonna both be sorry.'

The door to the bookies opened and a group of

disappointed punters streamed out. One broke away from the gang and stopped to light a fag. 'All right, Lucas,' he said.

Lucas pulled Emma towards him, his hand around her neck. 'You better watch out, Emma, 'cause you and your fucking poof of a mate are both dead.'

Emma wriggled out of his grasp as Mikey approached him. 'I'll be seeing you,' he said and let her go.

As Mikey started spouting off about losing all his giro in one go, Lucas tried to control himself. His blood was boiling. He looked over his shoulder as Emma ran down the street.

He'd see her later. She could bet on it.

55

16 December 2010

Louise walked into the house, glad to be out of the cold. She closed the door behind her and stood for a moment, thinking the place was too quiet without Adam. Without him coming to the door to greet her. Maybe she should get used to it.

She'd been out, walking around for hours. She couldn't bear being in there. Alone with her thoughts. It was driving her crazy. Every time she heard a car outside, every time she saw a shadow, she thought it was the police. Thought they'd figured it out. What she'd done. She couldn't take it any more. She'd considered leaving. Just disappearing. Becoming someone new. Someone without a past. But she knew she couldn't leave Adam. He was the best thing in her life. The *only* thing in her life. She could be a real person with him, a different person. Almost.

She shrugged off her coat and draped it over the banister. Adam would be back the next day. And maybe things would be okay. Maybe the police would leave her alone.

She turned towards the living room and then stopped. She thought she heard something upstairs. She stood still, listening. All she could hear was her heart beating and the gentle pitter-patter of drizzle on the windows.

She took a step and stopped again. She definitely heard something. A creaky floorboard.

Someone was upstairs.

'Adam?' she said, turning towards the stairs. Maybe he'd come home early. She hoped so. 'Adam?' she said again, putting one foot on the stair.

A shadow moved on the landing. She paused. And then the shadow moved and became a person and her heart stopped.

'Hello, Emma,' said Lucas.

56

16 December 2010

Lucas took a moment to watch the fear spread over her face. It was like the last eleven years had never happened. When he'd first heard the news about her death he'd felt something. Not sadness. Pity, maybe. Disappointment someone else had got to her before he had. And then DS Freeman had shown him the picture of the trackie top and he knew. Knew it wasn't her who'd been buried in the woods after all. Thing was, he knew who it really was, only he couldn't work out how she'd got there.

He watched Emma. She was shaking. Maybe she thought she'd got away with it. That she'd never see him again. He wondered if she'd just stand there all night, staring. And then she answered his question by bolting.

He took the stairs three at a time and grabbed hold of her arm before she'd even got the door open. She tried to pull away, screaming and clawing at him. She'd grown a spine since the last time he'd seen her.

Lucas flinched as her nails scraped the side of his face and he shoved her into the door. Her head smacked into it hard and she finally stopped screaming. He pulled her up straight and dragged her into the living room, pushing her down onto the settee. She tried to move but he straddled her, keeping her down.

'I reckon it's time we had a chat, don't you?' Lucas said, watching her eyes dart around the room. 'But maybe we can get to that in a minute.' He grinned at her, pushing himself against her. He liked that she struggled.

He leaned into her, his mouth against her ear. 'I've missed this,' he said and unzipped his jeans. Emma wriggled beneath him and he sat back to see her face. He laughed as she reached over the side of the settee, searching for something. What was she going to do? Call the police? She wasn't that stupid.

He didn't see it coming until it was too late. The laptop smacked the side of his head and he fell backwards onto the floor. He reached out as she fled from the room, blinking as blood dripped onto his eyelashes.

'Emma.'

He heard the door open and scrambled to his feet. He felt his head spin as he stood and grabbed the door frame to steady himself. He wiped the blood away and staggered towards the open door.

He couldn't see her but she couldn't have got far. He tried to recall which way was the town centre. He didn't know what was in the other direction but she'd surely head towards people. He pushed himself away from the wall, the door slamming behind him and started jogging up the street. His head was pounding.

He looked around. There were little streets going off in all directions. She could've gone down any of them. He stopped and listened for signs of life. For any echo of footsteps. But there was nothing except the sound of a distant siren.

Lucas kicked over a wheelie bin, scattering its contents along the road. He had to think. He hadn't seen a car outside the house, hadn't heard one starting up after she'd escaped. She had to be on foot. He doubted she'd still be there, waiting for him to go. She'd keep running. It's what she did best.

He put a hand to his pocket. Ben. Would she go there? Run to him again? She knew where he lived. Thing was, so did he.

57

17 December 2010

Freeman leaned against Gardner's desk. The guy she'd spoken to when she came in had disappeared to find the DI and said he'd be right back, but after fifteen minutes she was beginning to doubt he was coming at all.

She'd set off early and it was still dark when she'd arrived in Middlesbrough. So much for a good, long sleep.

'Can I help you?'

Freeman looked up at the young uniformed officer who was giving her the once over.

'No thanks. I'm just waiting for DI Gardner,' Freeman said and looked at the clock. Seven-fifteen. Her stomach was rumbling; she should've eaten something before racing out of the house. She wondered if there was a vending machine around and felt in her pocket for some change.

'It's his day off,' the PC said. 'Is he expecting you?' She walked over, putting herself between Freeman and Gardner's desk. She looked the kind that shined her shoes every night before bed. Freeman looked down at her own battered DMs and wondered why no one ever took her seriously.

'He should be. I'm DS Freeman. We spoke last night,' Freeman said and extended her hand to the blushing PC.

'Oh. PC Dawn Lawton,' she said and pushed her hair back behind her ears. 'It's his day off.'

'So you said. But he told me to meet him here.'

'DS Freeman?'

Freeman turned and saw someone coming towards her. 'Sorry for keeping you,' he said, dumping a paper bag on the desk before extending his hand. 'I'm Michael Gardner.'

Freeman shook his hand and realised she'd been expecting someone older, maybe fatter, maybe with a moustache. She didn't know why. Maybe because every DI she knew was older and fatter and had a moustache. As DIs went he was pretty hot. And PC Lawton clearly thought so too.

'No problem,' she said and noticed that Lawton was still lurking.

'Shall we?' he said.

'Sure.' Freeman turned her attention to the paper bag on his desk. There was something in there that was making her stomach growl. Gardner followed her gaze and opened the bag.

'Coffee and croissants,' he said and offered the bag to her. Freeman took her share and dug into the croissant, dropping crumbs all over his desk. Lawton shuffled her feet beside her.

'Thanks,' Freeman said. He didn't seem like the arsehole McIlroy had made him out to be. Freeman took a gulp of coffee, stuffed the croissant into her mouth and pulled her coat back on.

Gardner collected his things. 'You all right, Lawton?'

Lawton nodded, started to walk away before turning and saying, 'See you tonight?'

Gardner cleared his throat and muttered a quick 'Yep' before leading Freeman down the stairs.

'DI Gardner. What a lovely surprise. Coming in on your day off. Such commitment.'

Freeman saw Gardner's eyes roll before he turned around. She followed his gaze to a short man with a General Melchett moustache. He stood with his hands behind his back, a smirk on his face. Freeman wondered if he realised how ridiculous he looked.

'Just helping a colleague,' Gardner said. 'This is DS Freeman from Blyth. DS Freeman, this is DCI Atherton.'

Atherton looked Freeman up and down and then gave the briefest of smiles. 'Helping with what, may I ask?'

'A possible homicide. Girl in Blyth. I worked on the case when I was based up there. And there's a possible witness living here.'

Atherton raised an eyebrow and Freeman thought this guy made Routledge look like the world's best boss.

'Meeting's about to start, sir.'

Atherton turned to the perky young woman who'd stuck her head out of a room at the end of the corridor and nodded in her direction. 'I'll be there in a minute,' he said and she disappeared. 'Well, I hope this doesn't interfere with your *actual* work,' he said and stalked away.

Gardner waited until the door had slammed before muttering, 'Prick,' and walking back towards the stairs. 'Your car or mine?' he asked and Freeman shrugged.

'I don't mind driving,' she said.

As they exited the car park Gardner gave her directions and she nodded, taking a left.

'So,' Gardner said. 'You think she's going to be in this time?'

Freeman almost laughed. 'Let's hope so.' She shook her head. 'Jenny's parents hired someone to look for her. Apparently the guy wasn't exactly Magnum PI, but he did find a few Jenny Taylors. One of whom lived in Middlesbrough.'

Gardner frowned. 'But they didn't try and contact her?'

'They say the picture he gave them wasn't their daughter.'

'Was it the same address?'

'Don't know. They didn't pay much attention to the exact

address once they'd ruled it out. And now Lucas Yates has disappeared with the file so we'll never know.'

'But if Yates was interested enough to steal the file, surely it must've been her. Right?'

Freeman nodded. 'That's what I thought. But something's off.'

'Like why would Yates bother if none of the photos were of Jenny?'

'Exactly. Maybe he's grasping at straws, trying all the addresses. Or maybe he knows something we don't. Maybe he's been in contact with her before now.'

'Have you tried contacting the PI? Check what was in there?'

'The Taylors don't remember his first name, just his surname: Lawrence. I've checked and can't find anyone with that name. I doubt he was legit.'

Gardner went quiet, probably trying to answer the same questions she'd thought of on the journey down. She wished him luck with that.

'But Yates is definitely looking for Taylor,' Gardner said. 'You think he'll come here?'

Freeman shrugged. 'Maybe.'

Gardner directed her round a corner and indicated a house across the road. She pulled into a tight space.

'But he's also looking for Ben Swales. I don't know where he's likely to try first,' Freeman said.

'He knows where Swales is?'

'He knows he's in Alnwick. Other than that, I don't have a clue.'

'You got eyes on him?' Gardner asked.

'I asked a friend to keep an eye on him. I doubt it's round the clock.'

'All right.' Gardner opened the car door. 'Let's see if

Jenny's home. And then we can go and see if Ben Swales gets a visitor.'

'Isn't it your day off?'

'What else am I going to do?'

58

17 December 2010

Lucas woke up as a car door slammed. For a second he didn't know where he was until he saw the photograph he'd torn from the frame the night before – he'd finally found one in the spare room, buried beneath a pile of folders. Emma and this new boyfriend – Adam Quinn, he assumed – playing at happy families, as if she'd never been a junkie slag.

He'd made his way back to the train station after she'd bolted. Figured she'd probably go running to Ben. But it was late and there were no more trains north. Last one was eleven p.m. It was nearly eleven when she'd come home and found him. So if Emma wasn't going to Ben's, neither was he. He decided the best thing to do was go back, wait and see if she showed up.

He had approached the house with caution. There were no cops about, no flashing lights. He'd gone round the back again. Let himself in. She wasn't there. But his head was pounding so he'd settled in for the night. Found something to eat, watched her TV, eventually fell asleep in her bed. A proper little Goldilocks.

Now, Lucas got up and went to the window, wondering if she'd returned. He pushed the curtain back an inch and stared down at the street. He saw a familiar face – just not the one he was expecting.

DS Fucking Freeman was walking towards the house. Lucas dropped the curtain and ran out, down the stairs. He ran through the kitchen, shoes crunching over the broken glass from the door, and out into the alley. He stopped, trying to work out which way to go.

He heard a noise at the end of the alley and turned and ran. She wasn't going to catch him. Not now. Not until this was finished.

Emma stepped onto the train, checking Lucas wasn't there amongst the early-morning commuters. She'd kept on running the night before despite not knowing where she was going. Despite her lungs burning. Despite Adam.

She just knew she had to get away from Lucas and maybe that meant leaving everything behind. Again.

But she had no coat, no phone, no money. How far was she going to get? She'd found herself running into the station, thinking she'd just jump on the first train that came. But nothing did. She'd stood there on the cold platform, the drizzle spraying her face, mixing with her tears. She knew there was only one place she could go but she couldn't get there until morning. So she'd left, found a doorway, and prayed for the night to end quickly.

As she made her way back for the first train, she felt bad for Adam. Felt sorry for herself. She wished he were there with her. Wished she hadn't run away. But she knew she couldn't stay. Maybe she'd always known that.

She got on the train, soaked to the skin. The women in front of her had left their handbags on the floor, pushed back under their seats. They'd barely stopped talking so didn't notice as she slid one towards her and took out the purse. She took what she needed and put the rest back before moving to another carriage. She felt sick. The irony of her using one of

Lucas's tricks was too much. She wanted to get off. Wanted to stop it all and go back to Adam. If she went home now maybe Adam would never know she'd been gone.

But each station came and went and she stayed where she was. She ignored the conductor when he asked if she was okay and just asked for a ticket. One way.

59

17 December 2010

Adam tried to juggle the shopping bags whilst unlocking the front door. As he opened it, the box of fancy French dessert fell out and landed on the floor. Adam cursed and put down the rest of the bags to inspect the chocolate tarte. It was still in one piece; just about. He nudged the other bags further into the hall and closed the door behind him.

'Louise?' he shouted, thinking how impressed she was going to be with his choices. Okay, so he hadn't got caviar and oysters but it was still pretty good. 'Lou?'

He listened for the TV playing in the front room, wondering if she'd moved from the settee at all. The house was freezing.

Adam carried the bags through to the kitchen. He opened the fridge door and pulled out a can of Pepsi, noticing it was colder in the kitchen than it was in the fridge. As he turned around he realised why. The back door was open, glass smashed all over the floor.

'What the fuck?' he said and spun around, trying to see if anything was missing. He ran through to the living room. The TV was still there. His laptop was on the settee. The Christmas lights were still flickering.

He stood at the bottom of the stairs. 'Lou?' he called up. He frowned and went upstairs. 'Louise?' He stuck his head into each room.

He waited at the top of the stairs and pulled his mobile out of his pocket. After a few seconds the phone at the other end of the line started to ring. He pulled the phone from his ear and realised it was ringing downstairs. He went down and found her phone in her bag in the hallway where she always left it. He picked it up and scrolled through the call log. The last call was from him, the one before was from him. They were pretty much all from him. So she hadn't got a call from anyone else, seemingly no emergency to make her go out without leaving a note.

He went back into the kitchen and let out a breath. It was probably just kids pissing about. He'd seen a window boarded up a few houses down the other day. It was probably the latest hobby for local kids. Smash a window, impress your friends.

But where was Louise?

Adam sat down. He wasn't going to panic. Maybe she just ran out to get something for tonight. Maybe the back door had been broken while she was gone.

Adam tapped her phone on his knee. He wished she'd left a note.

For a moment he thought about calling the police. But how would that go? My girlfriend wasn't here when I got home. It's the middle of the day and she's a grown-up.

He'd wait a little while. She'd be back soon.

He got up and stood at the window, pulling the curtain back to look up and down the street. After a couple of minutes he dropped the curtain and grabbed his keys.

60

17 December 2010

Freeman headed north again. Going to Jenny's had been a waste of time. She knew it would be but had to check for herself. Now she was really starting to doubt Jenny was still there. Maybe the note had spooked her. Maybe she knew more about Emma's murder than they thought. Maybe Lloyd was right and Jenny *had* killed her.

'You okay?' Gardner asked.

'Just thinking,' she said. 'You reckon someone like Jenny could be capable of murder?'

Gardner pulled a face. 'I don't know anything about her. But we're all capable of extremes when we're pushed into a corner.'

Freeman stared at him, thinking about what McIlroy had said – *he killed another copper*.

The sound of her phone shook her from her thoughts. 'Freeman,' she answered.

'Nic, it's Mike Rogen.'

'Hi, Mike, what can I do for you?' she asked.

'We picked up a guy last night. Possession and drunk and disorderly. He claims to know something about your case. Or your "skelington in the woods", as he put it. Not the sharpest tool.'

'What does he claim to know?' she asked and Gardner

222

turned and looked at her, questioning. She knew that whatever this guy said would probably be bollocks.

'I don't know,' Mike said with a sigh. She could hear shouting in the background, banging on cell doors. She didn't envy Mike and his team spending all day and night down there in the cells. 'He was paralytic last night, couldn't string a sentence together. And to be honest he's not much better this morning. Said he saw something.'

'But he didn't elaborate?'

'He claims he saw something suspicious. Could've been a body being moved. He wouldn't tell me anything else. He wanted to speak to someone important. Not a uniformed monkey. Apparently.'

Freeman smiled. She liked Mike Rogen and his dry sense of humour. He put up with all sorts of crap but never let it get to him. He even spoke about some of his 'regular customers', as he called them, with affection. He probably knew a lot of them better than most of his friends and family, he spent that much time with them.

'Is there anyone else who can speak to him? I'm heading to Alnwick.'

'Rang upstairs. They told me to call you. I can try again but they said they were swamped.'

Freeman looked at Gardner. 'All right. We'll be there as soon as we can,' she said.

'I'll be waiting,' Mike said and hung up.

'What's up?' Gardner asked.

'Some guy who was arrested last night wants to speak to me about Emma Thorley.' From Gardner's lack of expression Freeman guessed he'd had the same experience with these chancer-witnesses. 'He claims he saw something suspicious. A body. Won't say anything else yet.'

'Probably full of it,' he said and then pulled a face. 'But then you never know.'

Freeman blew out her cheeks. 'All right, looks like we're going home then.'

Gardner frowned at her. 'We?' he said. 'What about Swales?'

She shrugged. 'I don't think he'll be going anywhere. Not with his mother upstairs,' Freeman said. 'Plus, we won't be long.'

'But what if Lucas is headed there now?'

Freeman sighed. 'I'll give Williams another call, see what's happening.'

'You could just drop me off,' he said. 'I'll meet you there later.'

'Blyth's on the way,' she said and made a turning. 'We'll be half an hour. Tops.'

Gardner didn't say anything. He wasn't at all interested in going to Blyth. She just wished she knew why.

Freeman got back into the car and hoped Gardner wouldn't say anything. Pulling over at the side of the road to vomit was hardly professional. He probably thought she'd been out the night before, had a skinful. She supposed that would be better than the truth. She wished it *was* the truth. She put her seatbelt on and pulled away. 'Sorry about that,' she said. 'Must be something I ate.'

Gardner glanced at her but said nothing. She suddenly thought about the breakfast he'd so kindly provided that morning and started to apologise, but thought better of it. She didn't want to talk about it any more.

Freeman pulled up at the lights and hoped that this drunk would have something useful to say. Anything as long as it was useful. As long as it meant driving back to Blyth had been worth it. That postponing going to Ben Swales' had been worth it. She was just hoping Williams was true to her word and was going to head back over to Ben's house. Williams claimed Ben and his mother had been safely tucked up inside under the beady eye of a green PC earlier on. Unfortunately, PC Green had been called away to a fight in the town centre and no one had checked on Ben since. For all they knew Ben could've packed up his mother in his shitty car and be halfway to Scotland by now. Williams swore she'd go over herself as soon as she got five minutes. Freeman hoped she could trust her. And that it wasn't too late.

She looked at Gardner. Maybe he'd been right. The closer she got to Blyth the more she started to think that talking to Ben would've been a better use of their time than coming to talk to some drunk looking for a deal. Plus Gardner had barely said a word the whole journey. He'd made a few comments about the case, made a little small-talk when she instigated it. But other than that he'd been quiet. She thought about what McIlroy had told her. There was obviously more to it. You don't just kill someone and keep on working, whether it's in another town or not. Maybe he'd messed up and got someone killed. She'd tried Googling his name and the word murder but all that came up were articles about cases he'd worked.

She glanced over at him. He sat slumped in his seat, his jaw clenched. He clearly didn't want to be going back to Blyth and who could blame him if something that bad was hanging over his head. And yet he *was* going. Did that mean McIlroy had over-dramatised it?

'Mint?'

Freeman stared at Gardner for a second before realising he'd asked a question. He raised his eyebrows and waved the packet of Polos at her.

'No,' she said. 'Thanks.' She wondered if he was hinting she had vomit breath. He popped one into his mouth and slid the packet back into his pocket. 'You don't sound like you're from Blyth,' she said, realising as she said it that trying to subtly get information out of another detective probably wasn't going to work.

'You've just noticed that,' he said and smiled. 'Nice detective work.'

'No. I noticed your accent before, but I hadn't given it any thought until just now. Where are you from?'

'Coventry,' he said. 'Originally.'

'I wouldn't have guessed that.'

'Spent a lot of time in London too. Maybe there's a hint of that in there.'

Freeman nodded. She could pick up little bits of a London accent now that he'd mentioned it. 'So what made you move up north?'

Gardner cleared his throat and then paused. She thought he wasn't going to answer.

'My wife,' he said eventually and Freeman automatically looked at his left hand. Something he noticed. 'Divorced,' he said and Freeman nodded. 'A long time ago.'

'Was it because she made you move to Blyth?'

Gardner laughed. 'That's where her family lived. She'd been working in London when we met but she wanted to go home. I came with her and we got married six months later.'

'But it didn't work out?' Freeman said. 'How come?'

Gardner gave her a sideways glance. 'Sometimes it just doesn't work,' he said.

'So you left when you got divorced? Too many memories?'

'Something like that.'

There was another silence in the car and Freeman wondered if she'd pushed him too far. She hadn't asked anything too personal. She hadn't asked him who he'd killed.

'So, you keep in touch with any of your old workmates?' she asked, and Gardner turned and looked at her.

'What is it you want to know, Detective Freeman?'

She shook her head. 'Just making conversation.'

'Right. I gather you've already been talking to someone. I can't blame you for that. But I wouldn't believe everything you're told. You know that. You're a detective.'

'So why don't you just tell me what happened?' she asked.

'Because it's irrelevant,' he said. 'And none of your business.'

They sat in silence for the rest of the journey, which was thankfully not very long. She knew she shouldn't have pushed him. And he was right, it *was* irrelevant and none of her business. It wasn't as if he'd asked a million questions about her vomiting at the side of the road.

61

29 November 1999

Gardner pulled in and sat there wondering what the day would bring. For the first time in his life he hated coming to work. As he'd left the night before he'd found dog shit on his windscreen again. He barely blinked before retrieving one of the doggy bags from the boot. After the third time he'd decided there had to be a better way to get rid of it than with the sports section of the *Guardian*. He was starting to think maybe he should get an actual dog to go with the bags. At least he'd have someone to talk to. At least someone would listen when he told them about his crappy life.

He picked up the shit and located McIlroy's car, returning the crap to its rightful owner. Emptying the contents onto the windscreen, he threw the bag aside. Then he got into his car, put his wipers on to get rid of the remains of the dog turd, and sat watching as people came and went. He didn't want to go home. The house felt too big, too empty.

But he couldn't stay at work either. Things were worse than ever. Worse even than in the aftermath of Annie's announcement. At least then he'd got some pity. Now it was pure scorn. DS Gardner the grass. It made him sick to think about it. He never thought he'd be that person.

The cases he was getting were nearly as shit as the stuff on his windscreen. It wasn't that DCI Clarkson had it in for him. She was practically the only person to stand by him through the whole thing. It was just that no one wanted to work with him and no matter what was said from on high, if your colleagues haven't got your back you're not going to get far. So he was wasting his time on bullshit cases and spending his nights alone.

Maybe he should've taken comfort in the knowledge that at least Wallace was going to get his comeuppance. He was now awaiting trial and would hopefully find himself serving at Her Majesty's Pleasure, though not completely thanks to Gardner. He'd been right in thinking his word wouldn't exactly be treated as gospel. But when the dealer's elderly neighbours had come forward and confirmed Gardner's story suddenly things started being taken seriously. A few too many coppers had been getting away with stuff recently and the media was whipping up a storm of outrage. The top brass decided Wallace would be their poster boy for justice. They didn't give a monkey's about the kid who ended up with a brain injury and went blind in one eye. Collateral damage. It was the image of the police force that was at stake and someone had to be the sacrificial pig.

Gardner couldn't pretend he hadn't felt anything when Wallace realised he wasn't getting away with it. But in the end was it all worth it? It didn't get Annie back – she swore she'd never speak to him again. And it sure as hell didn't make his own life any easier. He was starting to think he should move, transfer somewhere new. But he didn't want pricks like Bob McIlroy thinking he'd won. He'd rather spend the rest of his life in misery.

He watched as McIlroy strode towards his car, chest puffed out. Gardner craned his neck to watch his approach and smiled when he noticed the crap. McIlroy spun around, searching for Gardner, who obliged by flashing his lights. McIlroy gave him the finger and Gardner drove away.

And now he was here again for another day in paradise.

A hush fell over the room as Gardner walked into the office. For a second he kept walking to his desk. Awkward silences as he walked in were nothing new. But this time there was something different. The lights on the mini Christmas tree sitting on top of the fridge weren't flashing. He looked for DC Carol Smith. She always turned them on as soon as she came in. Having the Christmas lights on was more important to her than any crime. Not having them on *was* a crime in her eyes. He located Carol at McIlroy's desk, drying her eyes with a tissue. Every other eye was on him.

He didn't bother asking what was wrong. He doubted anyone would respond. Not even Carol. Carol who used to flirt outrageously with him at every work do despite being fifteen years his senior, who'd bring cakes in for the office and always made sure he got one before the rest of the team. He'd always liked her. He was the one who'd started calling her Smithlet. He didn't call her that any more. She barely spoke to him these days.

'DS Gardner?'

Gardner turned and found DCI Clarkson in the doorway of her office. She nodded for him to join her. All eyes followed him. Clarkson closed the door gently and pulled out the leather seat for him to sit down.

'What's going on?' Gardner asked.

'Please,' she said. 'Take a seat.'

Gardner did as he was told and waited for Clarkson to tell him. Instead she sat gazing out at the rest of the team. McIlroy was standing staring in at them, his arms crossed, his face red.

'What's wrong with Carol?'

Clarkson let out a deep breath and licked her lips. She looked tired. Before she spoke she spread her hands out on her desk as if to steady herself. 'I was informed this morning about the death of DS Stuart Wallace,' she said.

Gardner felt like he'd been hit in the chest with a griddle pan. Wallace was dead? He looked over his shoulder and saw McIlroy was still watching him. He turned back to Clarkson; a thousand thoughts went through his mind. 'What happened?'

'It appears that DS Wallace took his own life,' she said.

Gardner felt the thud against his chest again. He hadn't been expecting that.

'Slit his wrists. He wasn't found until it was too late. He was pronounced dead at the scene.'

Gardner couldn't get his head around it. Wallace was dead. Killed himself. He'd never have imagined he was the kind of man who'd do that.

'Jesus. They probably would've just given him a slap on the wrist,' Gardner said.

Clarkson raised an eyebrow and he quickly regretted his choice of words. 'Probably,' she said. 'But clearly he didn't see it that way.'

Gardner thought he was going to puke. He could feel his pulse in his neck. There was comeuppance and then there was fucking stupid. The stupid bastard. Gardner put his hand over his mouth. He hoped Clarkson didn't notice the shake.

'What about Annie?' he said, more to himself than to Clarkson. 'Did she find him?'

'No, but I believe she's been informed. As has his wife.'

'His daughter?'

Clarkson shrugged. 'I imagine her mother would do that,' she said. 'She's how old?'

'Twelve,' Gardner said. He almost looked over his shoulder

again but couldn't face the sight of them all. Didn't know how he was going to walk out of Clarkson's office. This wasn't his fault, he knew that. But how many of them agreed with him these days?

62

17 December 2010

Adam had called everyone he knew. Whether they knew Louise or not didn't matter, he called them anyway. He'd knocked on doors and asked neighbours he'd never spoken to before. He'd been to the supermarket and walked up and down every aisle. He'd checked the library, the university, bookshops, the post office, the local shop. Anywhere that Louise went on a semi-regular basis, he tried. And then he called her phone again just in case she'd gone home.

His gut told him something was wrong but he didn't know what. Or why.

He walked into the police station and told the desk sergeant his problem. The man didn't seem particularly interested but he told Adam to take a seat and eventually a young, pretty officer came out and asked him to follow her.

Adam felt like an idiot, despite her kind smile, as she invited him to sit down. She introduced herself as PC Lawton and asked Adam to explain his problem. She reached into her pocket and retrieved a notebook.

Adam sighed as he finished telling Lawton what had happened. He knew as he'd driven over to the station that they wouldn't take him seriously, and despite Lawton trying to make the effort to look like she did, he could tell that she wasn't too concerned.

'So your girlfriend—' she started.

'Louise,' Adam said.

'Louise,' Lawton repeated. 'Louise's been missing since yesterday as far as you know?'

'That's it. I don't know. I was away for the night. I came back this morning and she was gone.'

'When was the last time you spoke?'

'Yesterday afternoon. And I know it's not long, but she just disappeared. The back door was left open, the door – the glass in the door's broken, her phone is still there, her purse is still there,' Adam said. 'Why would she leave of her own accord and not take them with her?'

Lawton gave him a tight smile. 'I don't know, Mr Quinn. You know your girlfriend better than I do. Is she forgetful? Impulsive? Does she have any medical problems?'

Adam rolled his eyes. 'No she's not impulsive or forgetful. If I thought she would do something like this I wouldn't be here. And she has no medical problems,' he added, wondering if he should've been checking the hospitals.

Lawton sighed. 'I'm sorry but I have to ask these questions.' She looked at the few notes she'd made. 'And you said you've tried friends and relatives,' she said.

'Yes, I've tried everyone. I've been everywhere she could've gone but she's not in any of those places.' He leaned forward again. 'Please. Something's happened to her. She wouldn't have just gone. The door was left open.'

'Were there any other signs of disturbance? Look like anything was taken?'

'No,' Adam said. 'Nothing like that.'

Lawton looked him over and he caught her glancing at his hands. 'Let me ask you, Mr Quinn, have you had any arguments with your girlfriend recently? Any fights? A dispute over where to spend Christmas Day, something like that?'

'No,' Adam said. 'We haven't argued. We're happy.'

Lawton looked Adam in the eye and Adam wondered if she could hear his thoughts. *Were* they happy? He thought they were, but Louise had been acting weird the last few days. Was that it? Was she unhappy with him? Was that what the address he'd found in her diary was about? She was planning to leave him?

No, he didn't believe it. If Louise wanted out of their relationship she wouldn't just go like that. She wouldn't leave everything behind.

'We're happy,' he said again.

Lawton sighed again. 'Your girlfriend's a grown-up, Mr Quinn. Unless she has some kind of mental health problem, there's nothing I can do for twenty-four hours.' She put her hand up as Adam started to argue. 'And I know you said you weren't there yesterday, but that doesn't mean Louise wasn't there.' She stood up. 'All I can suggest is that you go home and wait for her to come back. If she hasn't returned by tonight then give us a call and we'll see what we can do. We could always send someone to take prints from the door but if nothing was taken . . .'

Lawton opened the door and turned back when Adam didn't follow. Adam pulled out his wallet and found a picture of Louise. He dug in his pockets for a bit of paper but came up empty-handed and instead turned the photo over.

'Can I borrow your pen,' he said.

Adam wrote his name, phone number and address on the back of the photo and handed it to Lawton with the pen. 'Please,' he said. 'She wouldn't have just gone off of her own free will. I know she wouldn't.'

Lawton looked at the picture and nodded at Adam. 'I'll see what I can do,' she said and showed Adam out.

63

17 December 2010

Freeman pulled into the car park and turned off the engine. She looked at Gardner, who was staring ahead at the building like an arachnophobe about to be handed a box of tarantulas.

'You ready?' she asked and he nodded and climbed out of the car. 'We'll go straight to the cells. Mike Rogen is going to meet us there. You know him?' she asked.

'Nope,' he said and Freeman tried to think of something else to say to clear the air. She'd already assumed Gardner didn't know Rogen; he'd only been there six years. She'd been hoping it would put him at ease, knowing he wasn't about to face someone he knew, but she guessed he'd taken it as another probing question. That she'd been wanting to get Rogen to dish the dirt on him later.

'We shouldn't be here too long,' she said, trying to keep pace with him. 'We'll head to Alnwick as soon as possible. Try and catch up with Ben Swales.' Gardner just nodded and opened the door, letting her walk through first.

As they walked down towards the cells she heard a voice behind her call her name and she felt her stomach tighten. She turned around and saw McIlroy walking towards her. When he saw Gardner his face dropped.

'What the fuck is he doing here?' McIlroy said. Gardner

gave Freeman a look that told her he was about as happy as McIlroy. He probably thought she'd set it up. Set *him* up.

'DI Gardner is helping with the Emma Thorley investigation,' she said.

'DI?' McIlroy said. 'Who'd you screw over to get that?'

'Fuck you, Bob,' Gardner said with a weariness that made Freeman think he'd been asked it before.

'This is why you were asking about him?' McIlroy said to Freeman and she felt her face burn. 'I told you he was scum, told you what he did and you still bring him in here?'

'You didn't tell me anything,' she said, trying not to look at Gardner. 'But this is about an investigation which DI Gardner can help with. This has nothing to do with you.'

McIlroy turned to Gardner, getting up in his face. 'You seen Stu Wallace's kid recently?' Freeman saw Gardner's hands curl into fists.

'You seen your badge recently?' she said, and watched McIlroy's face turn red. 'Fuck off, McIlroy,' she said and moved between the two men. 'We've got work to do. Why don't you go and find a paper to read.'

McIlroy snorted and walked away. Gardner watched him go and then turned and walked in the opposite direction. Freeman caught up with him.

'I'm sorry about that,' she said.

'It's fine.'

'No, it's not. And I only asked about you because you'd worked on Emma's case and I needed to find you. I wasn't looking for—'

'It's fine,' he said again.

'I don't want you to think that I believe the bullshit that comes out of McIlroy's mouth. Whatever happened in the past, I don't care. I just—'

Gardner stopped, causing Freeman to almost walk into him. 'Leave it alone, Freeman,' he said and walked away, leaving her standing alone in the corridor.

64

9 December 1999

He couldn't take his eyes off her. He knew he shouldn't have come. For his sake as much as theirs. Of course he wasn't going to go marching into the chapel and make this harder for them than it already was. He had no intention of getting out of the car. But just seeing the look on her face as the car pulled up with the coffin was enough for his heart to break and for him to wish more than anything that none of this had ever happened.

She looked younger than twelve. She was short and skinny, had red hair like her mother. There was no trace of Stuart Wallace in the girl's appearance.

She clung to her mother's hand like her life depended on it. People came up to them, expressing sorrow, hugging and kissing, and still she didn't let go. She looked as though letting go of her mother would be the end of the world for her. Her mother was all she had left.

He watched as crowds gathered. Who knew Wallace had been that popular? Several representatives from the force had turned out. Of course Clarkson was there along with the rest of the team. Carol Smith clung to her husband and continually wiped her eyes. He wondered if she'd stopped crying at all since hearing the news. Gardner hadn't been into the office since the day the news broke. Clarkson had called and suggested taking some annual leave.

McIlroy stood against the wall of the chapel, chain-smoking until it was time to go inside. Gardner ducked down a little so McIlroy wouldn't see him. The last thing he needed – anyone needed – was him causing a scene. And Bob McIlroy wouldn't shy away from causing a scene, whether he was at his best mate's funeral or not.

And maybe he'd be right to this time. Gardner knew he shouldn't be here. Didn't really know why he was. But he knew he'd have to wait until everyone had filed into the chapel before he could drive away. If he did it now someone would notice.

It took a moment before he recognised her. She climbed out of a taxi dressed head to toe in black, including oversized sunglasses. Just as he was thinking what kind of drama queen wears sunglasses to a funeral in December, she took them off and he realised it was his wife. Or ex-wife, as she was now. She'd cut her hair short and coloured it. Anyone would think she was in disguise. Perhaps she was. He wondered how tasteful it was for her to be there with Wallace's wife and daughter and thought that it was good that the place was full of so many police officers as Annie approached Wallace's wife. He steeled himself for the slap. Instead the women embraced and Annie kissed Wallace's daughter on the cheek. No one seemed surprised. Maybe other people dealt with things more civilly.

Finally the coffin was taken from the hearse and the crowd started to gather to follow it inside. Part of him wanted to go and tell the family how sorry he was; to tell Annie. He wanted to touch her, wanted her to need him again. If only she would look up and see him there then maybe she'd come over, maybe they could talk. Instead she walked away, eyes on the coffin of the man she loved more than him.

Gardner slid the key into the ignition, ready to make his escape when all the mourners had gone in. But just before she went inside, Wallace's daughter turned and caught his eye. The expression on her face was as though she'd seen the devil, as though he had destroyed her world. And as she walked away to say goodbye to her father, he wondered how she knew.

65

17 December 2010

Gardner watched the drunken dealmaker, Stewart Thomas, as Freeman sat down in front of him. He seemed a little disappointed with her.

'What are you when you're at home?' Stewart asked her.

'I'm DS Freeman,' she said. 'I'm in charge of the Emma Thorley case.'

'What?' he said.

'I'm in charge,' Freeman said, slowly.

'Really?'

'That's right,' she said. 'Why, who were you expecting? Poirot?'

Stewart stared at her, oblivious, but Gardner was sure about one thing. The man in front of her was expecting a guy. He had the same look and hygiene as Neanderthal man, probably didn't even realise women were allowed to vote. He looked up at Gardner, who'd chosen to stand by the door. He was interested in hearing what Stewart had to say, but it was still Freeman's investigation so she would take the lead. Besides, he was still a bit pissed off. Not really with her. Well, maybe a little. But more at McIlroy. And at himself for agreeing to come.

'So,' Freeman started. 'You told my colleague that you knew something. About a body. Is that right?'

Stewart ignored Freeman and kept staring at Gardner. 'Who're you?' he asked. Gardner said nothing. He was trying to work out how old Stewart was. His manner made him seem young but he looked like he was heading towards fifty. Perhaps it was just the alcohol and whatever drugs it was that he'd been in possession of.

'This is DI Gardner,' Freeman told him. 'He's helping with the investigation.'

After a few seconds of staring, Stewart dropped his eyes and looked at the table. 'Yeah, I saw something,' he said.

'Where?' Freeman asked.

'Lime Court,' Stewart said and Gardner had a spark of recognition. If he remembered rightly, Lime Court and its surrounding area were a breeding ground for trouble. The force spent half their lives around there sorting out problems and looking for suspects.

'The flats on the estate?'

'Yeah.'

'Okay. And what did you see there?' Freeman asked. 'Tell me about that.'

'I saw something weird. And I reckon it was a body being brought out of the flat.'

Freeman sighed again and looked over her shoulder at Gardner. 'You're going to have to do better than that,' she said.

'What do you want to know?' he asked.

'Details. When was it? What did you see? Whose body was it? Who was carrying this body? Why didn't you call the police at the time?'

'I didn't know for sure,' he said. 'I never heard nothing about her so I thought maybe I was imagining it.'

'Go on.'

'It was ages ago. Like ten or eleven years, I think.'

Gardner yawned. He'd bet Freeman was rolling her eyes. Stewart had probably seen all of this on the news. 'I can't remember exactly when it was.'

How convenient.

'It must've been summer 'cause I was kicked out of the flat when our Kimberley went back to school and I had to move back in with my ex.'

Freeman sighed and made a gesture with her hand for Stewart to get to the point.

'It was late on and I was up watching telly and I heard this noise so I went and had a look. I saw someone carrying something; it looked heavy, they was struggling, but I couldn't really see what it was. The lights outside the flats never worked proper. It was ideal for muggers and that,' he said. 'But I saw someone carrying this thing and then they put it down and dragged it a bit. When they got down the end a light came on and I could see a bit more and I thought fuck me that's a dead body and then I started laughing. I remember that.'

'So you thought you saw someone carrying a dead body and that made you laugh?' Freeman said.

'No, it was just 'cause it was funny,' Stewart said and looked from Freeman to Gardner. 'You know, I thought it was a body but I thought, nah, you're being mental, man. It'd be mental if it actually *was* a body. So I just went back and watched the film I was watching. Never thought about it again. Thought maybe someone was nicking something or doing one in the night. Something like that.'

'And you didn't see who it was,' Freeman said.

'Nah, they had their face covered up and it was dark.' He shrugged.

'So what you're telling us is that you saw what *could've* been a body being moved out of a flat eleven years ago by an *unknown* person.'

'Yeah,' Stewart said.

'And how is that useful? How is that anything more than what we already know?'

Stewart frowned, considering the question, but Gardner thought actually, that *is* something more than we already knew. Kind of. If what Stewart saw *was* Emma Thorley's body being taken out of the flat, then they knew it was possible she was killed in there. Something they didn't know before. As far as he was aware they had no idea where she'd been killed.

'All right,' Freeman said and pushed her chair back. 'Thanks for your help.'

'What about me?' he asked. 'Can I go?'

Freeman shrugged. 'You'll have to take that up with Sergeant Rogen.'

'But what about our deal? I told you what I know.'

'You didn't tell us much, though,' she said. 'I don't think we can make a deal on the basis of what you gave us.' They both stood and looked down at Stewart. 'So unless you've got anything else . . .'

He looked down; his eyes darted about as if he was trying to stir up his brain into doing some thinking. 'Yeah, there's something else,' he said eventually.

'Go on then,' Freeman said.

'I saw this guy go in the flat earlier on.'

'This guy?' she asked, opening her bag, pulling out the photo of Lucas Yates. She slid it across to Stewart.

'Nah,' Stewart said. 'Not Luc—' He stopped and swallowed, probably not wanting to admit recognising a known dealer, despite the fact he'd been brought in for possession. 'It wasn't him,' he said and nodded towards the picture in Freeman's hand. 'It wasn't him.'

'Okay. So who was it?'

'I can't remember his name but I'd seen him about. Most

people on the estate knew him. He was always kicking about. He was from the drug place. Looked like a queer.' Freeman and Gardner looked at each other. 'I'd seen him earlier, the same day. Before I saw the body thing. Saw him at her flat.'

'Did he go in?' Freeman asked. 'This is important. Did he go into the flat or did he just knock at the door?'

Stewart shook his head. 'Nah, he definitely went in. Definitely. With some other lass. They was in there a while.'

'Who was with him? Who was the girl?' she asked, leaning on the table.

'Can't remember her name. One of the other slappers that knocked about with Lucas.'

'Her?' Freeman asked and passed him a photo of Jenny.

'Nah, not Jenny. It was *her* flat. Well, I say *her* flat but she was squatting. I was a proper tenant. Council put me there. Don't know how long she was there. A few months, probably. I saw her about sometimes. Asked her if she was interested in an exchange, you know,' he said and mimicked oral sex. 'For some smack.'

'Hang on,' Freeman said. '*Jenny Taylor* lived next door to you?'

'Yeah, that's what I'm saying. When I saw the body or whatever it was I thought, well, that was bound to happen sooner or later. Right annoying bint she was. But then I never heard nothing so I reckoned I was tripping.'

Freeman turned to Gardner, her face asking, *What the fuck?*

'Can I go now?' Stewart asked.

Freeman pointed to the picture of Jenny again. 'This is definitely the girl you lived next door to? You're sure?'

'Yeah,' Stewart said.

'And you're sure you saw Ben Swales at her flat?' She rummaged around and found the picture from Ben's driving licence. 'This guy?'

'Definitely. I remember thinking I better not answer the door. He might be trying to convert me.'

Gardner leaned over Freeman and found the photo of Emma Thorley. 'You recognise her?'

'Yeah, man. That's her. That's who went in the flat with the poofter.'

66

17 December 2010

Lucas slowed down to look at the street names. He had no idea where Ben's house was and had no intention of stopping to ask someone for directions. Last thing he needed was any witnesses.

After he'd been woken by Freeman, he realised he needed to get out of there as soon as possible. He couldn't believe he'd fallen asleep while Emma was getting away. But the bang on the head had obviously done some damage. His head was killing him. He'd started running towards the station as he had the previous night but stopped when he realised that Emma had probably had a head start. He needed wheels. And not only had he come across plenty of cars ripe for the picking, he'd managed to snag one that had plenty of space in the boot, an almost full tank of petrol, and was nice and non-descript. What else could a man ask for? There'd been no alarm, older than God's dog so it was easy to hot-wire, and despite the half a dozen people close by no one had seemed concerned about what he was doing. He was starting to like Middlesbrough.

He finally found the street he was after and parked down a side street before locating Ben's house. He knocked and waited. There was a car on the drive, someone had to be home. He wondered if she was there, with Ben, watching him from the window like the old days. Would either of them call the police? Unlikely. He knew what they'd done, they'd want to see the cops as much as he did.

Lucas was about to knock again, but thought better of it and headed round the back. None of the windows looked particularly secure but if he couldn't open them any other way, a brick would do.

He saw a figure moving in the darkness of the kitchen, near the back door. Lucas pushed against it as Ben lunged forward, realising too late the mistake he'd made leaving the door unlocked.

Ben tried to slam the door but Lucas was too quick, pushing it back and forcing his way in. He banged the door shut with one hand and shoved Ben against the wall with the other.

'Hello, Ben,' he said.

'What do you want?' Ben asked, not looking Lucas in the eye.

'No "hello"? No "how's it going"?' He slammed Ben into the wall again. 'Have it your way. Where is she?'

Ben was breathing quickly. 'Who?' he said and Lucas pulled him up straight, dragging him through to the living room. As he threw him to the floor, Lucas looked around, trying to work out if she'd been there.

'Who?' Lucas spat at him. 'Who do you fucking think?'

'I don't know what you're talking about.'

'Don't fucking lie to me.' Lucas loomed over Ben, his eyes never leaving him. 'Now, I've warned you once. Where is she?'

'I don't know,' Ben said. 'I swear.'

Ben flinched as Lucas raised his foot, letting it linger over Ben's body. 'Once more,' he said. 'Where is she?'

Ben closed his eyes. 'I don't know,' he repeated and Lucas brought his foot forward, kicking him in the ribs.

'I *will* find her again,' Lucas said. 'I've done pretty good so far. So you might as well just tell me.' He bent down and grabbed Ben's face, squeezing, making Ben look at him. 'You'll only make it worse for yourself.'

'I don't know where she is,' he said.

Lucas raised his foot again but this time used it to push Ben's head down, pressing against his neck. Ben gasped for air and tried to prise Lucas's foot away but the more he struggled the harder Lucas pressed. Eventually Lucas stepped back and Ben gasped for breath, grabbing at his throat. He curled up, protecting himself.

'So you don't know where she is,' Lucas asked. 'But you know what I'm talking about, don't you?'

Ben turned away from Lucas but he reached down and pulled him up straight. Lucas crouched in front of Ben and smiled.

'See, I was wondering how she'd done it, how someone like her had done something like that and then I realised. Of course, she had you,' Lucas said. 'But what I want to know is *why* you did it.' Ben said nothing. 'I know you didn't get laid,' he said, squeezing Ben's face again. 'Cause you're a poof, aren't you? A fucking bender.'

Ben's jaw clenched. 'I don't know what you're talking about,' he said and Lucas started laughing. He stood up and lit a cigarette.

'What? You're not a poof? Now I don't believe that,' he said and took a drag.

'Please,' Ben said. 'I don't know what you're talking about.'

Lucas jumped forward and bent over in front of Ben's face. He rammed the cigarette into Ben's cheek, causing him to scream.

'Stop telling lies,' Lucas said, 'and I'll stop hurting you.' He stepped back and picked up the cigarette butt. 'Now that was a waste,' he said and lit another. He sat in front of Ben, smoking, and then pulled out a piece of paper from his pocket and held it up in front of Ben.

'I found this in her house,' Lucas said, putting his cigarette out on the carpet. 'In her diary. Got me thinking maybe she was planning a trip.' Ben still said nothing. 'So either she's on her way, in which case I'll just hang around and wait until she gets here. Or else she's already been and you're lying to me.' He shuffled towards Ben and put his face in front of his. 'Either way, I think I'll stay for a while,' he said with a smile.

'She hasn't been here,' Ben said. 'I swear.'

Lucas nodded. 'All right. Then I'll wait.' He stood up, glanced around at all the guardian angel shit, and started to walk out of the room.

'Where're you going?' Ben asked him.

'None of your business,' Lucas said with a smile, walking into the kitchen. He was starving, wondered if Ben had anything worth eating. He was probably a vegetarian. He looked like one.

As he looked in the fridge, Lucas heard the door, the scrape of the wood across the floor as someone tried to pull it open. Was it someone coming back? It couldn't be Ben, he wouldn't be that stupid. Maybe it was her.

Lucas turned to check who was coming in and saw Ben disappearing out onto the driveway.

Emma stood across the street, watching the house, thinking it was stupid coming here. But where else was she going to go? She wondered if Ben would even want to see her. And who could blame him if he didn't? After the things she'd made him do. She wouldn't want to see her either.

She watched the house and wondered if Ben even lived there any more. It'd been such a long time since she'd seen him, since he'd given her a lifeline. Maybe she *should* just keep away from him. But she had nowhere else to go.

She stood staring at the house, wondering if she should just leave. Just start again like she had before.

And then she saw him.

The door opened and Ben came out. She almost smiled. Almost felt as if things would be okay. He always knew what to do.

But something was wrong. Ben ran down the driveway, slipping on the icy ground. She started walking towards him, almost called out. And then she saw what he was running from.

Lucas Yates.

67

17 December 2010

Freeman followed Gardner out of the room and closed the door on Stewart's voice, demanding a cup of tea if they weren't letting him out any time soon.

'So,' she said.

'You believe him?' Gardner asked.

'About what?'

'Any of it.'

'Well, I can't see why he'd lie about living next door to Jenny. If he was trying to make a deal, surely making something up about Emma would be the way to go.'

'All right, so he's telling the truth about Jenny living there. What about the rest?'

Freeman shrugged. 'If he's right and Emma and Ben went in there for whatever reason . . . Then what? Things get out of hand and Emma ends up dead? Ben panics and buries the body?'

'Might explain why he denied knowing Emma,' Gardner said. 'And you said it was no secret that Jenny hated Emma.'

'Yeah, but enough to kill her?'

'What about Ben? You think he could've killed Emma?'

Freeman glanced at him before walking away. 'I don't know. Maybe. But I wouldn't be willing to base a case on what Stewart Thomas says.'

'Who would?' Gardner said, looking back through the window at Stewart. 'You think it's worth checking the flat?'

Freeman shook her head. 'Knocked down a few years back.' She sighed. 'He knew Lucas Yates, though,' she said. 'It's possible he still has a part in this. Maybe Stewart knows Lucas's reputation and doesn't want to be the one to grass him to the police. Maybe he's lying about Ben.'

'Maybe,' Gardner said and checked his phone. One new message from Lawton, probably reminding him not to be late to the party. He slid the phone back into his pocket.

'It just doesn't feel right. Why would Emma go to Jenny's flat in the first place? And if Ben was there, why would he just stand by idly while Jenny killed the girl he'd been helping?' Freeman shifted her weight onto the other foot. 'You think we could go upstairs and talk about this?'

'I'd rather not,' he said.

Freeman sighed and leaned into the wall. 'It just doesn't make sense.'

'Is it possible Ben went to the flat to try and find Jenny if he was worried about her? You said she'd been going to the clinic for a while. Maybe Emma tagged along if he was also matey with her. And that's when Stewart saw them?'

'But Stewart said they were there for a while, that they went in.'

'He could be mistaken. And even if they *did* go in it doesn't mean anyone was murdered. Doesn't mean he was carrying a body out later. I think maybe we need to speak to Ben again.'

'Great. But first, I need to pee,' Freeman said and headed back the way they'd come, leaving Gardner alone in the corridor. Despite there being no one else around he felt like he was being watched, conspicuous. He checked his phone again and listened to Lawton's message.

'Sir, it's Lawton. Can you call me back as soon as you're free? It's about that address on Ayresome Street you stopped at the other day. Thanks.'

Gardner hung up. He started to call her back when Freeman returned.

'Ready?' she asked.

'Hang on,' Gardner said. 'Lawton just called. Something about Jenny's house.'

Freeman was about to speak, but he cut her off as Lawton answered. 'Lawton, it's me. What's going on?'

'I'm not sure, sir,' she said.

'Are you at the house?'

'No. Someone came in not long ago saying his girlfriend was missing. His name's Adam Quinn. He'd been away overnight so wasn't sure how long she's been gone but he said all her things were still there and the back door was left open, a window smashed. I didn't think much of it but he left a photo of her, wrote his name and number on the back. Plus his address. I recognised it.'

'This guy's Jenny Taylor's boyfriend?' Gardner asked and Freeman's ears pricked up.

'He said she was called Louise Taylor,' Lawton said. 'I just thought I should let you know.'

'Hang on a minute,' he told her and held the phone to his chest.

'What's going on?' Freeman asked.

'Someone reported his girlfriend missing from Jenny's address. Said her name was Louise Taylor.'

Freeman's brain whirred. 'Jenny's middle name is Louise,' she said. 'So it is her.'

Gardner got back on the phone. 'Lawton, can you send a copy of the photo to my phone?' Lawton said she'd get on it and he hung up.

'At least we know she was there,' Freeman said. 'Shame she's not any more.'

'Fuck,' Gardner said. 'I knew I shouldn't have left a note.'

His phone buzzed as Lawton's message came through. And Gardner's face dropped.

'Is it her?' Freeman asked and turned the phone in his hand to see. 'Shit,' she said and looked at Gardner. 'That's not Jenny. That's Emma Thorley.'

Freeman wondered if she looked as gormless as Gardner did at that moment. She stared at the photo again.

Emma Thorley was alive. Alive and apparently living as Jenny Taylor. Or Louise Taylor, to be precise.

'Emma's middle name was Louise, too,' Freeman said. 'I can't believe this. I just . . .' She turned and leaned her head against the cold wall. 'It's not her.'

'So it's Jenny?'

'Has to be,' Freeman said. 'Why else would Emma be using her ID?'

Gardner blew out his cheeks and shook his head. 'So now what? Are you looking at Emma as a suspect?'

'For what? Murder?' Freeman shook her head. 'It doesn't seem likely, but then . . . She's using her identity. She had to know Jenny was dead. So maybe Stewart was right. She did go into that flat.'

'You think she did it alone?'

Freeman shook her head again. 'No, I can't see it. She was a kid. She must've had help.'

'Who? Lucas? Or Ben?'

'Not Lucas. There's no way. She didn't have anything to do with him. But Ben? He'd helped her before.'

'True,' Gardner said. 'But helping someone get off drugs is one thing. Helping them murder a teenage girl is something else.'

Freeman turned and kicked the wall. 'Fuck,' she said. She couldn't get her head around it. All this time thinking Emma was dead, looking at Lucas. And she'd never once considered that the body wasn't her.

She took out her phone, pausing before dialling, trying to work out how to ask the question. When Angie Taylor picked up she just asked straight out.

'Mrs Taylor, it's DS Freeman. Did Jenny ever break her arm?'

'Yes, why?' Angie said.

'Left or right?'

'Left. Why?'

Freeman closed her eyes and mouthed one word. Shit.

Gardner followed Freeman upstairs while she spoke to the pathologist, asking him to locate Jenny's medical records and look at Jenny's X-rays to compare it with the bones on his table. As she hung up she grabbed DC Lloyd and told him to give Gardner a lift back to Middlesbrough. If Gardner had a problem with that, he didn't show it. Although he was on the phone to Lawton again.

'Head over to Adam Quinn's now. I'm on my way back. Don't tell him anything yet, just show some interest in his girlfriend and the door. Keep him there until I arrive,' he said and hung up.

'This is DC Colin Lloyd,' Freeman said when Gardner joined them again. 'He'll take you.'

'Where're you going?' Gardner asked.

'Ben's. If he was in on it with Emma, maybe that's where she's going. And I'm going to find her.'

68

17 December 2010

Lucas threw the glass he'd been holding onto the floor and ran after Ben, catching him just as he made it to the street. He grabbed Ben's shirt, pulling him back. Ben struggled, trying to pull away, but Lucas got his hand around his neck and dragged him towards the house.

'What the fuck are you doing?' Lucas asked and threw Ben inside, slamming the door behind him. He pushed Ben towards the kitchen and knocked him to the floor. Ben tried to stand, scrabbling about on the floor.

'I'm sorry,' Ben muttered and tried to crawl out of the kitchen. Lucas walked up behind him and slammed his foot onto Ben's back, pushing him to the floor.

'You're going to be more sorry,' Lucas said and turned Ben over to face him. He could see the fear in Ben's eyes and felt a ripple of pleasure. This was just a warm-up but he'd enjoy it anyway.

Lucas yanked Ben up by the hair into a sitting position and then slammed his fist into his face. Ben put his arms up to block the blows but he still managed to get a few nice ones in. Not enough though. He pulled back and took a breath before dragging Ben towards the table. He looked around the kitchen and then remembered something he'd seen in the hallway. He went out and got the scarf that'd been draped over the banister.

Bending down, he pulled Ben's arms behind his back and tied his hands, looping the scarf around the table leg. Ben was muttering. Lucas didn't know if he was talking to him or not. He didn't care. He twisted the knot tight and then looked Ben in the eye.

'Ready?' he said and smashed his fist into Ben's face again and again. Blood covered Ben's face, from his mouth, his nose. Lucas stopped after a few blows and admired his work. He looked at his fist, also covered in blood. He sat back and tried to control his breathing. He watched as Ben's chest moved with shallow breaths. He was crying. Lucas laughed.

'Don't cry, we're not done yet. I'm saving the best bit for last, don't worry,' he said and stood up. He wiped his face, smearing blood across it.

There was a noise upstairs, a creak of a floorboard that made them both freeze. Lucas looked at Ben. 'Are you hiding something from me, Benji?' he said. 'Is Emma up there?'

Lucas walked out of the kitchen and could hear Ben writhing around behind him, trying to get up. 'Please, don't,' Ben called after him. He walked up the stairs, his heart racing.

This was it.

He stuck his head around the door and stopped. An elderly woman lay in the bed, talking to herself. When she noticed him standing there she turned further towards him.

'Ben? I need the toilet,' she said.

Lucas walked into the room and stood over the woman. She took a moment to focus on him and then looked confused.

'Where's Ben?' she asked, her voice wavering.

'He's not here,' Lucas said and searched among the boxes of tissues and pill bottles for a phone. 'Who are you, then?' he said.

'I'm his mother. Where is he?'

'He's gone out,' he said.

'He can't go out. I need the toilet,' the woman said. She reached out for Lucas. 'Can you take me?'

Lucas waved at the woman and walked out, closing the door on her cries. He was about to go back down to Ben when he stopped. The other doors were closed. He walked to the first and pushed it open. Looked like Ben's room. Empty. He went to the next and checked inside. A lot of medical supplies, what looked like nappies and stuff, but no one hiding in there. He stopped at the last door. Must be the bathroom. He reached for the handle and the door opened.

No one in there.

Lucas left the door open and headed back downstairs, ignoring the old woman's whingeing. He went back into the kitchen and found Ben where he'd left him, slumped over, tied to the table. When he stopped in front of him, Ben looked up.

'What did you do to her?' Ben asked.

Lucas thought about telling him he'd shoved a pillow into her face or stuffed a whole load of pills down her throat but thought it'd be better to let old Ben's imagination run wild. What you imagined was usually worse than reality. Usually.

The old woman wouldn't be any bother. She was hardly likely to get up and come after him with her walking stick. There was no phone up there so the police wouldn't be coming any time soon.

He walked to the drawers and rummaged about. He found what he wanted in the second one. With both hands full he walked back around and stood in front of Ben. 'Which one should we play with first?' he asked and held the knives out to Ben. Ben sobbed and struggled against his bindings. Lucas laughed again. 'This is going to be fun,' he said.

He listened to Ben's screams, savouring each one. 'This is what happens when you try to set me up,' he said and Ben writhed beneath him. 'You and that little cunt are gonna pay for what you did.'

Ben cried out again, no longer using words, just noise. Lucas grinned at him and then put his hand over Ben's mouth. He could hear a noise, a wailing. He turned to the door and saw blue lights flashing outside.

Lucas got to his feet, knife still in hand. He ran to the back door, threw it open and made a run for it. Through the back garden, over the fence. He kept on running.

69

17 December 2010

Adam sat in the living room, watching the clock, wondering how much longer he had to wait until the police showed some interest. No, he didn't know exactly how long Louise had been gone, but that didn't mean anything. She could've been gone *more* than twenty-four hours for all he knew. For all the police knew. And there was the broken window. The copper had seemed interested when he mentioned that, but when he said nothing was gone, that there was no sign that a burglary had taken place, her interest had quickly waned. He should've lied.

He was staring at his phone, willing it to ring. So she didn't have her mobile, she could use a public phone. But would she know his number without her phone? Hell, he didn't know his own number. He didn't know her number. He didn't know any numbers any more. He used to write them in his diary but gave that up ages ago.

The diary.

Adam raced up the stairs and went into the bedroom. Louise's diary was next to the bed like always. He picked it up and flicked through, shaking it to see if anything came out.

Nothing.

There'd been an address in Alnwick. She was clearly trying to hide it from him, but why? Was that something to do with this? Was that where she'd gone? Who did she know that lived in Alnwick? She'd never mentioned it before. But if she was hiding something, she wouldn't have. Was there someone else? Was she cheating on him?

He put the diary down, refusing to think that way, and went back down to the living room and over to the window, pulling the curtain back. Where was she?

He dropped the curtain and went out into the kitchen. The windowpane in the back door was covered in the bubble-wrap he'd put up hastily before going out looking for her. Now he wondered if it was a mistake, if he'd messed up evidence. Not that the police gave a shit.

He opened the door and looked out into the yard, hoping there was something he'd missed earlier. Something he could take to the police and say, 'Look, someone took her.' Sure, he knew that a grown woman missing for a few hours wasn't going to set off a major investigation, but they could've shown some interest. The officer was nice enough but he bet she'd forgotten all about Louise by now.

He stood in the doorway and watched his breath steam out into the air. He didn't believe in God but he couldn't keep count of the number of times he'd caught himself thinking Please God, let her come through that door. He didn't care that he'd look foolish having to tell the police that she was back. He didn't care that she'd been selfish enough to just disappear like that. All he cared about was her coming back to where she belonged.

He thought he was imagining it at first. But on the second knock he realised that it was actually his door. He raced into the hallway, praying it'd be Louise on the other side, locked out.

He opened the door and found PC Lawton standing there. His heart sank. 'What's happened?'

'Mr Quinn,' Lawton said. 'Can I come in?'

Adam felt like the blood had stopped running through his veins. 'Yes,' he replied, his hand shaking, waving for her to enter. He led her into the living room and stood still, waiting for whatever it was she had to say.

'Have you heard from Louise yet?' Lawton asked, looking around the room as if she expected to find her there.

'No,' Adam said. 'I thought . . . You haven't found her?'

'No,' Lawton told him. 'Sorry, I should've explained. I think I was a little dismissive when you came to the station. We're a bit short of staff at the moment. But—'

'You think something's happened to her?'

'No,' Lawton said, head shaking like a bobblehead. 'I have no idea. That's why I'd like you to take me through it again.'

Adam slumped onto the chair. Why were they suddenly interested now? Something had to have happened.

'Mr Quinn?' Lawton said, notebook in hand.

Adam closed his eyes. 'Okay,' he said. As he started telling her his story again, he noticed Lawton glancing at the clock.

70

17 December 2010

Freeman was on her way to Ben's, still reeling, when Ray called her. She saw his name come up on her phone and she panicked. She needed to tell him it wasn't Emma's body, that Emma was alive and well and living as someone else. Or at least she was a few hours ago. But it wasn't something she wanted to do over the phone. And right now she needed to get to Ben's. She declined the call and felt the guilt welling up. He had a right to know, but not like this; she needed to tell him face to face. Plus she didn't want to get his hopes up. Lucas Yates was out there looking for Emma too. This wasn't necessarily going to have a happy ending.

She'd asked Gardner to organise getting prints from the house in Middlesbrough. She didn't even know whose house to call it – Emma's, Jenny's or Louise's. She wondered if Lucas Yates had been there. If he'd done something to Emma. Lawton had mentioned a broken door.

But how did he even know? She couldn't get her head around it all. She'd been sure Lucas was her guy and she was doing everything possible to prove it. It made sense after everything that'd happened between Lucas and Emma, everything he'd done to her. But now she knew it wasn't Emma who was dead.

Gardner had suggested that maybe Emma and Ben were

more likely candidates to have killed Jenny. Emma taking on her ID proved that she at least knew the other girl was dead. But if Lucas didn't kill Jenny, why had he been sniffing around? Why was he desperate to find Ben?

Her gut told her Lucas was still the most likely person to be the killer. Maybe Ben and Emma found out about it and Lucas was trying to find them to keep them quiet.

She tried to focus. Her head was all over the place. She'd have to inform Ray Thorley eventually that Emma wasn't dead. She didn't know what she would tell him about the rest of it – it would break his heart all over again.

Was it possible Emma would go there? And would Ray call Freeman if she did? Was that what he was just doing a moment ago? Calling to say Emma had turned up on his doorstep, alive and well? She checked the time. No. If Emma was in trouble the last place she'd go was home. She'd go to the person she'd gone to before.

She needed to get to Ben's.

71

17 December 2010

Gardner got out of the car outside Adam Quinn's house, DC Lloyd in tow, wondering what he was going to say to the man. Wondering what Adam would say to him. He knocked on the door and a slim man in his thirties opened the door. Lawton stood behind him, a concerned look on her face. Gardner felt bad about making Lawton babysit for him, but he'd needed Adam Quinn to stay put.

'Adam, this is DI Gardner,' Lawton said and Adam glanced back at her, questioning.

Gardner extended his hand and Adam shook it. Gardner nodded at Lloyd. 'This is DC Lloyd.' Adam glanced at the other detective before stepping back to allow them in.

'What's going on?' he said and closed the door.

Gardner noticed the movement in the kitchen, a SOCO he vaguely recognised taking prints. He glanced at Adam before looking towards the living room. 'Should we go through?' he asked.

Adam walked past Gardner, leading the way, but stopped in the doorway. 'Please. If something's happened—' He stopped and let out a slow breath. 'If you've found something, found Louise . . .' He looked from Lawton to Gardner, his eyes pleading.

Gardner realised what Adam thought he was there for and

felt a stab of guilt. He guided Adam into the room and they all sat down. 'Tell me what you told PC Lawton.'

Adam sighed and rubbed a hand through his hair, no doubt sick of saying the same thing. 'I came home and Louise was gone. The back door was broken; all her stuff is still here. Her phone, her handbag, money, everything. I spoke to her yesterday afternoon. She was fine.' He looked at Gardner. 'It's like she was here one minute and then she was just gone.'

Gardner frowned. 'Did she give any indication that she was unhappy, that she might want to leave?'

'No,' Adam said. 'She was fine. I've said all this. When we talked on the phone she was joking around, there was nothing wrong.' Adam looked at his feet.

'But?' Gardner said and Adam looked up at him and shook his head. 'Mr Quinn, if you don't tell me everything then I can't help you.'

Adam's jaw clenched and he looked over at the Christmas tree. 'She was a bit upset the other day. She wouldn't tell me what'd happened.' He turned back to Gardner. 'But then she was fine again.'

Gardner waited. He knew he should just tell Adam the truth but first he wanted to know what Adam Quinn knew about his girlfriend.

'I know it sounds stupid that I reported her missing after a few hours and that it seems like she might've run off, but I know she wouldn't do that. And even if she would, why would she leave her stuff behind? And the back door? What about that?'

'Maybe she wanted you to think that something had happened to her. Maybe she didn't want it to look like she just left,' Gardner said.

'Why? What reason would anyone have to do that?'

'You'd be surprised,' Gardner said.

Adam glanced at Lawton, who just looked down at her feet. 'Louise wouldn't do that.'

'Tell me about her,' Gardner said. 'Where did you meet, how long have you been together?'

Adam looked at the ceiling. 'We've been together four, four and a half years.' Gardner raised an eyebrow but said nothing. He was surprised anyone could keep up a lie that long. 'We met in Sheffield. I was teaching at the uni and she came to some of my lectures. I later found out she wasn't actually enrolled. She couldn't afford the fees so she just sneaked in to lectures, hoping no one would notice.'

'But you did,' Gardner said.

'Eventually,' Adam said. 'She was always very quiet. Never asked anything, never answered a question. One day I stopped her after a class and asked if she was all right. She looked like a rabbit caught in the headlights. I asked her name and then later I looked her up and found out she wasn't a student there. She didn't come back after that. But a month or so later I saw her in the university library and went to talk to her.' He shrugged. 'That's how we met.'

Gardner nodded. 'So what brought you up here?'

'A job,' Adam said. 'I was only part-time in Sheffield but I was offered a full-time position at Teesside so we moved.'

'And Louise didn't mind? How long had you been together then?'

'About eighteen months, slightly longer,' he said. 'But no, she didn't mind.' He paused.

'Adam?'

'She was reluctant to begin with.'

'About moving?'

'About everything,' Adam said. He looked away from Gardner again. 'She was shy. She was nervous about moving in together, she thought we were rushing things, but it made sense. She doesn't always make that much money.' He shook his head and frowned. 'I'm sorry, I'm rambling.'

Gardner shook his head. 'No, go on.'

'When I got the job here she was fine with moving. She didn't seem attached to Sheffield. But I suggested buying a house and she was less enthusiastic. I think she just fears being tied down,' he said and then looked at Gardner as if he'd just admitted something he shouldn't have. 'I mean, she wanted it but because she doesn't have a lot of money she felt like she'd be in debt to me. She didn't want that.'

'Okay,' Gardner said. 'What about her family? She ever mention them? Could she have gone to stay with a relative?'

Adam shook his head. 'No. She doesn't have any family. Her mum died when she was quite young, her dad a few years later. She doesn't talk about them much.'

Gardner sighed. He couldn't put it off any longer. Adam Quinn was clearly in the dark about his girlfriend's real life. He sat forward in his chair and waited for Adam to look at him.

'Mr Quinn, there's something I need to tell you about your girlfriend.' He noticed Adam stiffen. Gardner picked up the photograph that Adam had given to Lawton at the station. 'This is her, right?' he said, pointing at her on the picture.

'Yes,' Adam said. 'That's Louise.'

Gardner pulled another picture out, the much older photo sent from Blyth. He handed it to Adam, who frowned.

'What's this?' he asked.

'That's a picture of her when she was fifteen. Her father reported her missing and this was the photo he gave us.'

Adam swallowed and shuffled in his seat. 'So you're saying she's gone missing before?' His eyes went back to the photo. 'That doesn't mean she ran away now.'

'No, not necessarily. But that picture,' Gardner said,

nodding to the photo in Adam's hand, 'is of a girl called Emma Thorley.' Adam looked up. 'As is this one,' Gardner held up Adam's photo. 'Mr Quinn, your girlfriend isn't who she says she is.'

72

17 December 2010

Adam sat there, staring. *Your girlfriend isn't who she says she is.* Your girlfriend is not Louise Taylor. She's Emma Thorley.

His mind was racing. How could this be? Gardner kept on talking but he wasn't listening. His voice was just a noise in the background. Adam kept thinking it was a mistake. He knew her. He knew Louise. How could she be someone else?

And yet . . .

He thought about the news stories he'd heard the last few days. That was why the name Emma Thorley was familiar. Gardner reminded him that the police had originally thought the dead girl in Blyth was Emma Thorley. But it turned out it was likely to be Jenny Taylor. Jenny Taylor, his girlfriend. Her first name was Jenny but she said no one ever called her that. She said she'd always gone by Louise.

Except she hadn't.

Adam squeezed his eyes shut. Trying to process it, trying to make sense of it.

He guessed he knew why she was upset the last couple of days. But why would she lie about her name? Why would she become someone else?

'Adam?' Gardner said and brought him out of his thoughts.

Adam looked at the detective, unsure if he'd asked him a question or not. He wondered if Gardner was suddenly showing interest because he thought Louise was a criminal rather than a missing person. He was holding some pictures in his hand.

'Do you recognise either of these men?' Gardner asked, showing him two photographs. Adam took them and looked, wondering who they were.

'The one on the right is Lucas Yates. Does the name mean anything to you?' Gardner asked.

Adam frowned. 'No. Who is he?'

'He's Emma's ex-boyfriend,' Gardner said and Adam's head shot up. 'You're sure she never mentioned his name?'

'No,' Adam said. 'Never.'

'And Emma never had any visitors, men you didn't know?' Gardner continued.

'No,' Adam said. 'For God's sake. You think she was still seeing this guy?'

'No, I think it's unlikely. Let me ask you about this man,' he went on, pointing at the other picture. 'You recognise him?'

Adam glanced at this one, a photocopy from a driving licence. This guy was older. He didn't imagine he was also an ex of Emma's. He shook his head. 'No, I don't know him,' he said. 'Who is he?'

'His name's Ben Swales,' Gardner said. 'He worked at a drug rehab clinic in Blyth. He worked with Emma.'

Drug clinic? He looked at Gardner. 'When you say he worked with her . . .'

'Emma had a drug problem when she was a teenager. She attended the clinic that Ben worked at,' Gardner said.

Adam let the words sink in. They couldn't be talking about the same woman. The Louise he knew wasn't this girl. But that was it. She wasn't this girl at all. He could feel Louise slipping further and further away from him. The woman he loved was an illusion. We all have pasts, we all have secrets, but this? She was a drug addict, a runaway, a liar.

A killer?

No, that wasn't her. He knew it. She wasn't the person they said she was. They didn't know her.

'Did Emma ever go away by herself? Maybe not to stay, but trips for work or something?' Gardner asked. 'Did she ever go to Alnwick, for instance?'

'Alnwick?' Adam's head was spinning. He tried to make sense of the question, of everything they were throwing at him. 'No. No she's never been there.'

'You sure?' Gardner asked. 'She could've gone without telling you.'

'Then I wouldn't know, would I?' Adam shouted and stood up. 'Excuse me,' he said and hurried out of the room.

He'd been standing in the kitchen for a couple of minutes, head against the fridge door, when Gardner came in.

'You all right?' Gardner asked him.

'Fine,' Adam said without looking up. He wished they'd leave. They weren't helping. They weren't finding Louise. Or Emma, rather. They weren't bringing her back to him. They were just filling his head with crap. Saying things that weren't true. So she'd made some mistakes. Who hadn't? But he knew she wasn't a killer. You couldn't live with someone for four years and not know something like that.

'Why do you think she did it?' Adam asked. 'Took this girl's name?'

Gardner glanced back at Lawton before saying, 'I don't know.'

'The news said her ID was on the body,' Adam said, recalling the report he'd read. Gardner nodded. 'You think she put it there? Louise?'

Gardner shrugged again. 'I don't know. It's possible.'

'You think she killed her?' Adam asked.

Gardner blew out a breath. 'I couldn't say. Look, she

obviously had something to do with it being there or else she wouldn't be using Jenny Taylor's identity. What that something is, I can't say. Only Emma can. And she's gone.'

Adam flinched at her name. She wasn't Emma. She wasn't even Jenny. She was Louise. She would always be Louise to him. And he knew that Louise wouldn't have hurt anyone.

'Look, I'm not saying Emma killed anyone,' Gardner said. 'But she ran away for a reason. And whatever the reason she took this other girl's identity, now it's come back to bite her and she's had to run again.'

Adam shook his head. 'But what if she didn't run? What if someone took her? What if whoever killed that girl came after her? That could've been who broke in.'

Gardner sighed again. 'Maybe. But I think Emma had plenty of reasons to run on her own.'

73

17 December 2010

Lucas sat in the pub watching some idiot lose all his money in the fruit machine. He could wait for the muppet to leave and then get up and empty the machine into his own pocket, easy. But he wasn't in the mood. The buzz he'd felt with Ben had been immense. He hadn't felt that way for a long time. But it soon faded away when he realised he was no closer to getting what he really wanted.

He wondered who'd called the cops – whether Emma had shown up and seen him there or if it was some nosy neighbour. Either way, he'd scarpered. Didn't need the police on to him now. He didn't know what to do. If Emma was yet to show up, the best place to be would be Ben's house. But it was likely the cops would still be there, sniffing around. If Emma had been the one to call them, though, maybe she'd be at the hospital with Ben. He couldn't go onto the ward, Ben would kick up a stink for sure. Maybe he should wait elsewhere, see if she showed.

He drained the pint of Coke he'd been nursing for the last hour and ignored the fools on the fruit machine.

He pulled up the hood on the coat he'd nicked from the stool beside him. It looked a lot warmer than his jacket. He fished around in the pockets, hoping for a wallet or something. But all he found was a used bus ticket and an empty cigarette packet. He threw them both in the bin and walked across the road towards the hospital.

He was going to find her if it was the last thing he did. The bitch had fucked him over one too many times. She'd dared to leave him. Killed his baby. And now she'd tried to frame him for murder. He wasn't going to stop until she'd paid for what she'd done.

74

17 December 2010

Freeman found Ben's street and slowed down as she saw the police car in front of the house. She pulled over and jumped out. The house across the street from Ben's had turned on their Christmas lights and the whole street had an eerie glow.

'What's going on?' Freeman said, approaching a frozen-looking uniform. She flashed her ID and he looked her up and down as if he didn't quite believe her. Cheeky bastard. 'Who's in charge?' she asked and he nodded to a man in a crappy suit coming out of Ben's house. Freeman walked over and showed him her ID too.

'DC French,' he said and stuck out his hand. Freeman shook it and then asked what was happening.

'Got a call about an assault taking place. Arrived to find the guy on the kitchen floor. Pretty fucked up.'

'Ben Swales?'

French nodded. 'I think so. You know him?' It was Freeman's turn to nod. 'He wasn't really up to saying much. No sign of the assailant.'

'Who called it in?'

French shrugged. 'No idea. Anonymous call made from a phone box.' Someone behind them shouted to him. 'Excuse me,' he said to Freeman.

A middle-aged woman came out from next door, an

oversized sweater wrapped around her. 'You lot caught some-one yet?'

Freeman stepped closer to the woman and held out her hand. 'I'm DS Freeman; did you see what happened?'

The woman looked at her hand but didn't make a move to shake it. 'Maggie Paulson,' she said. 'Terrible thing. I just saw them take him out on the stretcher. Looked awful. His mother too,' she said, shaking her head.

'Shit,' muttered Freeman. So much for Williams doing her a favour.

'Probably one of those smackheads he worked with. I don't know why he bothers with them,' Maggie said.

'You saw who did it?' Freeman asked, but Maggie shook her head. Didn't matter, she knew who it was. 'But you saw them take Ben and his mother to hospital? Do you know which one?'

'Infirmary, it'd be,' Maggie said.

'Thank you.' Freeman turned to go back to her car before stopping. 'Wait,' she said as Maggie was just about to close the door. 'When you saw them take Ben away, was there anyone else here? Did anyone go with him? A woman?'

Maggie shook her head. 'No.'

Before Freeman walked back to the car, she gave DC French Lucas's name and bet him twenty quid he'd find his prints in Ben's house. French looked at her like she was mental but she knew if Lucas was still hanging around, he'd be arrested fairly soon. In the meantime she was going to speak to Ben and find out what was going on.

75

17 December 2010

Gardner excused himself as his phone rang. 'What's going on? Have you spoken to Ben?' he asked as he answered Freeman.

'Nope,' she said. 'Ben's in hospital. I'm just heading over there now.'

'What happened?' Gardner asked.

'I don't have the proof yet, but I'd say Lucas Yates happened. No sign of Emma so far. How's it going down there?'

'Well, I've just broken the news to Adam Quinn that his girlfriend's been lying to him for four years.'

'He had no idea who she really was?'

'Not a clue,' Gardner said. 'We're running prints on the broken window here. You think that was Yates' handiwork too?'

'Probably. Looks like he's on a roll.'

Gardner glanced through the gap in the door at Adam sitting there with Lawton and Lloyd. No one was saying anything any more. At least not anything important. Adam was in shock. Lloyd was talking about the weather.

'Listen,' he said. 'I think I've got everything I'm going to get from Adam for now. I could head back up there. That seems to be where all the action is.'

'Sure,' Freeman replied. 'Meet me at the hospital. Alnwick Infirmary.'

'I'll be as quick as I can.' He hung up, opened the door and the three of them looked up at him expectantly.

'Lloyd? Lawton? Can I have a word?'

They followed him into the hallway. 'Lloyd, can you take me back to the station? I'm going to head up to Alnwick and meet Freeman.'

'I could take you up there,' Lloyd said.

'No, no, then you'd have to bring me back later. Just drop me at the station and I'll get my car. Lawton,' he said. 'Can you stay here with Adam? I think it's unlikely but just in case Emma turns up I'd like someone to be here.'

Lawton nodded. 'Sure,' she said.

They went back into the living room and Gardner almost ran into Adam, who'd been standing by the door, listening.

'You know where she is?' Adam asked.

'No,' Gardner told him. 'But we *will* find her. I promise. PC Lawton's going to wait with you. I'll let you know as soon as we hear anything.' He nodded to Lloyd and they went to the door.

'You think she's in Alnwick?' Adam said. 'Why?'

Gardner just looked at Adam. If he really had no idea about Emma then he'd have no idea why she'd be up there.

'We'll be in touch,' he said and closed the door.

76

17 December 2010

Freeman's head lolled against the back of the cracked plastic chair. She'd arrived at the hospital full of hell, ready to get the truth from Ben Swales by any means necessary. Instead she'd been told he had just gone into surgery. Apparently Lucas had really gone to town on him.

She'd called Williams and asked in a not-too-charming manner why the hell no one had been watching Ben's house. Resources, she'd been told. It always came down to bloody resources. She'd spoken to French again but they still hadn't run the prints. She could've saved them time if they'd just accepted it was Yates but things didn't work like that. There'd be no conviction without some proper evidence.

So now she was waiting for Gardner, and for Ben. She'd drunk two cups of vile canteen coffee and wished she hadn't. She'd dialled her GP twice and then hung up. She'd called Williams back and apologised and asked if she could put an APB out on Emma as well as Lucas. Just in case.

She'd almost fallen asleep when Gardner's call woke her up.

'Where are you?' he said.

'Waiting outside theatre. Where are you?'

'Reception.'

'I'll come down,' she said and dragged herself to her feet.

Gardner was on the phone again when she found him.

'How long ago?' he asked and then sighed. 'All right, let me know if he comes back.'

'Now what?' Freeman asked.

'Adam's disappeared. Lawton went to the bathroom, came back and he was gone.'

'Where?'

Gardner shrugged. 'She said he'd been on his laptop but she's checked it and he wiped his browsing history. She's tried calling him but he's not picking up. Left about half an hour ago.'

'Maybe he needed some space,' Freeman said.

'Maybe. Anyway, what's happening here? Have you seen Ben?'

'No. They'd just taken him into surgery when I got here.'

'Surgery?' Gardner said.

'Yeah. So let's hope Lucas doesn't run into Emma before we do.'

77

17 December 2010

Adam felt a little sorry for PC Lawton. She'd been kind to him and now she'd probably get into trouble. But he couldn't just sit there, waiting.

Before leaving, he'd Googled street names in Alnwick. He remembered the address began with M and the number, but that was it. Fortunately there were only a few streets beginning with M in Alnwick. It didn't take long. He just had to wait for Lawton to leave him alone for a minute.

After what felt like hours of driving around, he finally found it. He parked the car and started walking towards the house, but stopped. What if she was here? What would he say to her? *'I know you're not who you say you are'? 'I know the police think you killed someone'?*

Maybe DI Gardner was right. He should've stayed at home and waited for her to come back.

He walked up the drive to the door and knocked. When there was no reply after a few moments he tried again. He walked up to the window and tried to look in but between the net curtains and lack of light, he couldn't see anything. There was a car on the drive.

He stepped back to see if there was any movement upstairs. Nothing. And then he noticed someone watching him from the house next door. He was about to go and knock on her door when he saw someone heading his way.

Lucas couldn't feel his feet. He needed to move. He'd been hanging around the hospital for hours and still she hadn't come. He pushed his sleeve up with stiff hands and checked the time. He was starving as well as freezing. There was probably a cafe of some kind but the idea of hospital food made his stomach turn. He remembered the stuff they'd served up to his nan when she was in. You couldn't identify it by sight or taste. It probably wasn't food at all. But more than a desire not to eat that crap he thought maybe he should check the house again. Maybe the police would've gone by now.

He pulled the collar up on his coat and walked out of the hospital grounds. He'd check the house, find somewhere to eat, and then come back. What else was he going to do? He had to find her. He'd been so close, he couldn't give up now.

He turned the corner into Ben's street and thought about what he'd do when he found her.

As he approached the house he stopped. There was someone there. Just not who he was expecting.

Adam saw the man walking quickly with his head down, battling against the cold wind. But there was something about him. Adam stopped and stared. The man looked up, caught his eye. Adam suddenly realised who he was. Gardner had showed him his photograph. This guy knew Louise. Her ex-boyfriend, he'd said. Lucas something.

'Hey,' Adam shouted and the man looked both ways before turning to run, back the way he'd come, back towards the town centre. 'Hey,' Adam shouted again and ran across the road, almost slipping on the icy surface.

A woman with a pushchair watched them run past, Adam

barely missing her as he passed her. But he couldn't stop, couldn't slow down. He'd just found the man who'd taken Louise.

He struggled to find his phone in his pocket as he ran. He felt his feet go from under him and put his hands out to break his fall, his phone skittering across the pavement. He cursed as the pain shot through him, up his arms to his shoulders. A couple of people stopped and looked and a man came over, bending to pick him up.

'Are you all right, son?' he asked. Adam nodded, picked up his phone and started to walk away, too breathless to thank him. He saw Lucas further down the street, getting away from him. He started to run again but he felt a stitch in his side, slowing him down. He was running towards the town centre, towards the crowds.

Adam tried to ignore the pain and picked up his pace. He couldn't lose him. This was the only way he was going to find her. The only way he'd find out what was going on.

He kept his eyes on Lucas as he darted in and out of groups of people. He had no idea what he'd do if he caught him. Sit on him until the police came? Twist his arm until he told him where she was? He knew he couldn't beat it out of him. He'd never even been in a fight. Not a proper one anyway. A scuffle at school that was stopped before it ever started, that was it.

He kept running. His chest was burning. He tried dialling Gardner as he ran, getting it wrong twice before he finally managed it. He could barely hear anything. The phone just kept ringing. Why wasn't he picking up? He had to be somewhere in Alnwick, somewhere close by.

He looked ahead and realised Lucas had turned a corner. He sped up, ignoring his heart, which was almost bursting out of his chest. He couldn't lose him. He turned the corner and scanned the street. There were too many people, he couldn't take them all in.

He was gone.

Adam bent over, trying to catch his breath. The wind was stinging his eyes and his legs felt like jelly. He couldn't run any more. Gardner's voicemail kicked in.

'DI Gardner, it's Adam Quinn. I'm in Alnwick and I just ran into that guy. Lucas whateverhisnameis. He's here.' He walked to the side of the street and leaned against a wall. Shoppers passed by and some looked at him, but most ignored him, too busy navigating the streets and trying to work their way through the rest of the crowd. He kept walking and found a quiet spot. There were no shops, just the backs of buildings and piles of rubbish waiting for collection.

'I'm somewhere in the town centre now. I lost him but—' His phone was knocked out of his hand. He started to turn and felt an arm around his neck, someone grabbing him from behind.

78

17 December 2010

Emma sat huddled over the Formica table in the hospital cafe, her hands cradling a cup of coffee. She was freezing. As she'd run from Ben's it had started to sleet and she was soaked again. She'd now spent the last of her money on coffee and she didn't know what to do. She had no money, no ideas. Nowhere to go. She felt like she had all those years ago when she'd left for the last time. When she'd left her dad for the last time.

Her chest felt tight at the thought of him. She'd seen his name in the paper when they thought it was her who'd been buried in the woods. What must he be going through? What had she put him through all these years? She'd never wanted to leave. After the abortion she'd come back thinking everything would be okay. That she'd go back to school and at least try to make up for lost time. That she'd rebuild her relationship with her dad, make up for everything she'd done. Things didn't quite work out. But how could she ever have been so selfish? He'd lost his wife and then she'd abandoned him too. She didn't deserve the kind of love he'd shown her. The kind of love Adam had shown her. She was worthless.

She wondered if Lucas would find her here, if he'd stick around, waiting for her to show her face. And what about Adam? She should call him, let him know she was all right. But how could she possibly explain it? How would she even

288

start? She didn't want her life with Adam to be over. Didn't want to have to run again, become someone else. She'd been happy. Or at least as happy as she could ever be. She didn't want things to change. But it was too late for that. Things *had* changed. Her secret was out.

Maybe she should've stuck around at Ben's after she'd called the police. Instead she'd run, as far from Lucas as she could get. She should go to the police now. But not to save herself from Lucas. She deserved to be punished for what she'd done. To her dad, to Adam, to that girl and her family. To Ben. She'd got him into it. Got him involved with her fucked-up life. If he'd never met her he wouldn't be in hospital now. Wouldn't have spent the last eleven years of his life living in fear. Living with the image of that girl's dead body in his mind.

She needed to hand herself in. Tell them what she'd done. But she couldn't involve Ben. Couldn't let her mistakes ruin the rest of his life. She'd go and find him and tell him what she was going to do. Explain to him it was better that way. She didn't want him to contradict her story when they came looking for him. And they would. She would tell them it was her. All of it. It was her idea. Her plan. Her alone who buried Jenny Taylor in the woods.

79

17 December 2010

Adam felt the wind go out of him as Lucas slammed him against the wall. He bent over, the pain coursing through his body. He could see the feet of passers-by, people hurrying through the street at the end of the alley. He wanted to call out but he doubted anyone would hear him or do anything, even if he could find his voice.

He saw Lucas's fist before it cracked into his cheek. His brain was telling him to do something but his body was slow to respond. The blow knocked him to the ground and he lay there looking up at the grey sky and tops of buildings until Lucas moved into his view and looked down at him. He could see spit at the side of Lucas's mouth and for a second all he could think was *I hope it doesn't drip down on me.*

'Where is she?'

For a second he thought he'd managed to speak but then he realised it was Lucas who had asked the question.

'Where is she?' he asked again and bent down to pull Adam up.

'I don't know,' Adam said.

Lucas grabbed Adam's face and squeezed. 'Don't fucking lie to me,' he said. 'You don't want to know what I did to the last person that lied to me.'

Adam managed to push himself up and pulled away from Lucas's grip. 'What did you do to her?'

'I haven't touched her. Yet,' Lucas said and grabbed Adam's coat, forcing him against the wall again. 'Did she tell you what she did?' His face was inches from Adam's. 'She tell you that she was a junkie? A fucking slag? A killer?'

Adam pushed forward, trying to get Lucas off him. 'Bullshit,' he said, though he knew part of what Lucas was saying was true.

'Yeah, she was a proper little slut.'

Adam clenched his fists. He could hear heavy breathing but he wasn't sure if it was his or Lucas's.

'She was a good fuck, though. I don't blame you for wanting that back,' he grinned and Adam took a swing at him.

Lucas stumbled back and laughed. 'You'll have to do better than that, mate.' Then he launched at Adam, hitting him in the gut, knocking him to the floor. 'You're as fucking stupid as he was,' he said and slammed his fist into Adam's face.

Adam could taste blood in his mouth and spat it out, wanting to get rid of the coppery tang, but Lucas just hit him again and again. He tried to put his hands up, to defend himself, but Lucas had his knee on one of Adam's arms and held the other down with his fingers digging into the skin. He could hear Lucas panting hard and fast and when he sat back a little to catch his breath, Adam brought his knee up, watching Lucas's face pale. He pushed him off and scrambled to his knees but Lucas was already up and his foot swung at Adam, catching him under the chin.

Adam fell forward; he didn't need to spit the blood out any more, it just poured. He gagged on it and recoiled as Lucas booted him again in the ribs.

Somewhere behind him he heard a noise, a woman's voice, footsteps pounding on the pavement. His head was spinning.

He closed his eyes and when he finally opened them there were two women in expensive-looking scarves standing over him, one scrambling around in her bag, the other just staring. They didn't look the type to run towards brawling men.

Pain shot through his head as he turned to look for Lucas, but he wasn't there any more and Adam realised it was him he'd heard running away, not the women running towards him.

'I'll call the police, love,' one of the women said. 'God, where's my phone?'

Adam rolled onto his back and reached out for his phone, finding it on the ground beside him. He found Gardner's number. 'It's okay,' he said, his voice thick with pain. 'I can do it myself.'

As he turned and spat out more blood, his phone started to ring.

80

17 December 2010

Gardner followed Freeman into the canteen where she promised him some mediocre coffee. She looked knackered but he didn't tell her that. She'd looked pretty pissed off when the doctor had told her Ben would be in surgery for at least a couple more hours. He didn't fancy winding her up any more.

'So what now?' he asked instead as she passed him a plastic cup of brown swill.

'I guess we wait,' she said, dropping into the nearest chair. 'Williams reckons everyone's got their eyes peeled for Lucas and Emma. So until one of them shows up, or Ben's up for a bit of storytelling . . .' She pressed her face into her hands and groaned.

'We'll get there,' Gardner said.

'Will we?' She looked up at him. 'This is a complete mess.'

Gardner wanted to offer some wise words but he was at a loss. He had less idea than she did what was going on. It seemed clear to him that Emma had at least been involved in Jenny's death, even if she hadn't killed her herself. Which left Ben and Lucas.

Lucas was the most obvious candidate, but not with Emma. So if Ben and Emma had done it, why did Lucas Yates care so much? Gardner doubted he was avenging Jenny's death.

Freeman's phone rang and she looked at it before excusing

herself. Gardner checked his own and noticed he had a voice-mail, probably received while he'd been upstairs in the land of no signal. He dialled his voicemail and was listening to his message when Freeman came back.

'That was Tom, the pathologist,' she said, oblivious to the fact that he was on the phone too. 'He got hold of the X-ray and it's looking good. Or bad. Depending on which way you look at it. Looks like a match for Jenny Taylor.'

'Shit,' he said.

'Well at least we know now.'

'No,' Gardner said. 'That was Adam Quinn. He's in Alnwick. And he also found Lucas Yates.'

'What? What happened?'

'I don't know. He got disconnected,' he said as he rang Quinn back. 'But I wouldn't be surprised if he was on his way here too.'

81

17 December 2010

Lucas pushed his way through the pub, past the Christmas shoppers and work parties. His hand was throbbing as much as the bass coming through the speakers. He found the toilets and shut himself into a cubicle to inspect the damage. There was blood all over his hand, though most of it wasn't his, a fact that did little to make him feel better.

He'd lost her. He knew that now. She'd got away from him again, could be anywhere, and now the fucking boyfriend was looking for her, as well as the cops. He'd considered letting the little prick go so he could follow him but the idiot seemed to have about as much idea where she was as he did.

He slammed his fist into the cubicle door; the pain shot up his arm but he didn't care. He was still pounding the door when he heard a couple of guys come in, shouting and laughing. If they noticed him smacking the door they didn't care. He leaned back against the door, listening to them taking a piss and then leaving without washing their hands.

Lucas opened the cubicle door and went to the sink. He washed the blood off his knuckles and stared at himself in the mirror. For a second he thought he could see the blood pumping through his veins, pressing against his skin, making it bulge. He blinked as the sound resonated in his head.

He wasn't giving in. She wouldn't beat him again. He smashed his fist into the mirror, causing it to crack; the pain radiated through his hand and this time the blood was his own. He looked at the river of red that started to pool in the dirty white sink. He wasn't giving in.

He'd been starting to think he was wrong, that Emma hadn't come to Alnwick at all, hadn't come to find Ben. But after he'd seen the boyfriend he was certain. Why else would he be here?

He turned and walked out of the toilets and back through the busy pub, knocking into people too drunk to make an issue out of it. As he got to the door he saw a couple of coppers standing there, trying to calm down a pair of slappers having a catfight. Lucas stopped, tried to find another way out. As he turned back to make sure they hadn't spotted him, one of the slappers launched herself at the other. As she stumbled backwards, causing a domino effect, Lucas dodged her and tried to sneak past.

'You all right, mate?'

Lucas kept his head down, tried to pretend he hadn't heard him, but the copper was as wide as he was tall and blocked the exit.

'I'm all right,' Lucas said and tried to get around him, but he wasn't having any of it. Behind them the other copper had hold of both girls, trying to keep them apart. Lucas saw another police car pull up outside. He had to leave. Now.

'You'll need stitches in that,' the copper said, nodding at Lucas's hand. He looked past Lucas for a moment as his colleague helped one of the girls towards the door. Her face was covered in blood, looked like her nose was broken. 'Looks like we're going to A&E,' the copper said. 'You might as well join the party.'

Lucas's stomach clenched. Why the fuck wouldn't he leave it? When did the police get so helpful?

'We've got another one,' the copper said to his mate as he led the girl outside to their car. 'Come on,' he said to Lucas. Lucas watched as the other coppers walked around the pub, asking people for ID.

'All right, mate – thanks,' Lucas said and followed him out. If the stupid bastard wanted to give him a lift back to the hospital, who was he to argue?

82

17 December 2010

Gardner called Adam Quinn back, his foot tapping as the phone rang a few times. He was about to hang up when Adam answered. 'Adam? It's Detective Gardner. You all right?'

'Yeah,' Adam said and made a noise as if he was spitting. 'I'm in Alnwick.'

'Yeah, I got your message. What the hell happened? I told you to stay at home.'

'I couldn't just sit there. I needed to do something, so I decided to come to Alnwick and look for her myself. I saw an address in her diary the other day. When you mentioned Alnwick I figured it was as good a place as any to look.'

'And you didn't think to mention it to me?' Gardner heard more spitting and held the phone away from his ear. Adam clearly wasn't going to answer the question so he moved on. 'What happened with Yates? Where is he?'

'I don't know,' Adam said. 'I saw him in the street and chased him. We had an altercation and he ran off.'

'An altercation? Are you hurt?' Gardner asked and Freeman stared at him, questioning.

'I'm all right,' he said but Gardner doubted it, realising what the spitting sound was. 'He asked me where Louise was. She's not with him. Where are you?'

'At the hospital. The guy whose address that was – Ben,

the drug counsellor I told you about – he's in surgery. Lucas Yates got to him too. Do you need to go to the hospital? How bad is it?'

'I'm fine,' Adam said.

'Where are you?'

'Somewhere in the town centre. I've kind of lost track of where I left my car.'

Gardner rubbed his eyes. 'All right, hang on and we'll come and get you, take you back to your car. Where exactly are you?'

Adam paused before answering. 'I don't know. Hang on, there's a pub down here.'

'All right,' Gardner said when Adam told him the name. 'Stay there, we'll come and get you.'

'Okay.'

'Do *not* go back to Ben's house alone. I doubt Yates will go back but don't take the risk. We'll be as quick as we can.' He hung up and looked at Freeman, who was watching him like a dog watches a biscuit.

'So,' she said. 'Is he okay?'

'He said he was.'

'And what about Lucas?'

'In the wind. Again.'

'Shit,' Freeman said. 'So what happened?'

Gardner shook his head. 'Adam decided to come and play detective. Ran into Lucas Yates and had an altercation. I'm guessing Lucas won. But Adam managed to find out one thing.'

'Which is?'

'Lucas doesn't have Emma. He has no idea where she is.'

83

17 December 2010

Lucas gave a fake name to the A&E receptionist and waved his friendly copper goodbye. Obviously he was heading back to the mean streets of Alnwick. It was Christmas – made everyone go mad. He looked around the waiting room, at the old people slumped over with their mouths open, already halfway to death; at the drunks puking all over themselves at five in the afternoon. The receptionist didn't even bat an eyelid. Lucas wondered if he should enquire about his mate Ben. She'd probably be able to tell him where he was, how he was doing. But he didn't want to draw attention to himself so he just sat there and waited for his turn.

When the young doctor was finished with him, Lucas went outside and lit a cigarette underneath the 'No Smoking' sign. Leaning against the cold, stone wall, he was trying to work out his next move when something caught his eye.

Getting out of a car a hundred yards away was DS Freeman. Lucas flicked the cigarette butt and moved behind the wall. What was she doing here? Had she heard about Ben or had someone recognised him inside?

He watched as the other copper got out of the car, followed by Emma's boyfriend. Lucas ducked down as they started walking towards the entrance. He went back into A&E and stood behind a vending machine, watching as the three of them stopped outside. Freeman said something to the boyfriend and then they all walked on. When he was sure they'd left, Lucas went back outside. There were a couple of other ways into the building, fortunately. As he cast his eyes towards another entrance, making sure it was safe, he felt like his heart had been attached to one of those electric shock machines you see on telly. His mouth went dry, he couldn't move.

Emma.

She had her head down and her arms wrapped around herself. She looked like she'd been crying. He wanted to run over and grab her by the hair and smack her in the face but he couldn't. Not yet. Not here.

He watched as she disappeared from view, back towards the main road. Lucas followed her. His heart was racing. He could see his breath in front of his face as he walked behind her. She didn't turn around once, didn't seem aware she was being followed.

He kept his distance until she almost got to the end of the path and back onto the main road. Almost. She turned and looked up at the hospital, fear in her eyes. Maybe poor Ben was dead.

And then her gaze dropped, she saw him and he knew she had suddenly been reminded of what fear actually was. For a few seconds she was too stunned to move.

'We meet again,' Lucas said.

He gripped Emma's arm and pulled her down the street, searching for another car. They'd passed maybe two people near the hospital but no one had noticed anything; they were too busy staring at the ground, trying to keep their faces out of the wind as much as possible. She'd tried to call out to them but he just wrapped his arm around her neck, like they were two young lovers, and put his hand over her mouth. She still struggled against him, her elbow dug into his ribs, but he kept hold of her and no one said a thing, no one even blinked.

He stopped at the side of the road as a car approached. He hadn't noticed until now that she was crying. As the car moved towards them Emma pulled free of him and stepped out. The driver honked and swerved slightly but Lucas grabbed hold of her and pulled her back. The driver threw his arms up and mouthed something through the window before speeding off.

Lucas had hold of both her arms, hugging her close like he'd just saved her life. He could feel her trying to pull away but he held tight, his face close to hers.

'That was stupid,' he whispered. 'Try anything else and I'll not only kill you but I'll come back for your boyfriend. Did I mention we met earlier?' Emma whimpered and he pushed her across the road where someone had left a car running as they made a delivery. He wished he hadn't dumped the car from Middlesbrough but it was bound to be hot by now.

As they got up close and he opened the car door, Emma pushed away from him and screamed. Across the street a couple of women turned around. For a moment one looked like she was going to come over but instead she just raised her hand to her mouth.

Lucas tried to subdue Emma but she struggled against him, pulling away. As she made it around the back of the car he put his leg out, tripping her. With one hand he opened the boot, the other grabbing the back of Emma's jumper. The car's owner dropped his parcel and ran towards them.

He saw the women across the road pull out phones. He thought about going over, smashing them up. No time. He needed to go. Now.

He threw Emma into the boot and slammed it closed before jumping in the front seat. The driver grabbed Lucas, trying to pull him out. Lucas punched him in the face and kicked him away from the car. He looked up to see the two women pointing out the car to a man built like a brick shithouse, just as he got the driver's side door shut.

As the man crossed the road, Lucas slammed his foot on the accelerator. He saw the man reach out for the car but it was too late. Lucas turned a corner and felt the butterflies in his gut once more. It had been close. He'd nearly blown it again. He let out a laugh. It all added to the excitement.

84

17 December 2010

The receptionist almost rolled her eyes as Freeman approached the desk again, this time with *another* person in tow.

'Any news?' Freeman asked and the receptionist sighed.

'He's just come out of theatre. But he'll be out of it for a while, so . . .' She shrugged at Freeman as if to say 'piss off and stop asking me questions'.

'Thanks,' Freeman said and started to walk away.

'He's a popular guy,' the receptionist said behind her.

Freeman turned. 'What's that?'

'Someone else has been in asking about him.'

'Who?' Freeman snapped. 'A man?'

'No, a woman. Youngish lass.'

Freeman looked at Gardner and Adam. She was about to show the receptionist the photo of Emma but Adam beat her to it, whipping his phone out. 'Was it her?'

The receptionist looked from Adam to Freeman, baffled. 'Yes, her. Why?'

'How long ago was she here?' Freeman asked and the receptionist shrugged.

'Not long,' she said. 'Twenty minutes, maybe.'

Freeman told the security guy to go back half an hour, starting with the cameras near the exits. At least this guy – Wayne, she thought he'd said – was helpful, even if he was a little too keen. The other one had seemed more interested in finishing his curry.

She tried to zone Wayne out as he explained the intricacies of the hospital security CCTV system and instead focused on the activity on screen. Dozens of people came in and out but no Emma so far. The fast motion on screen was making her eyes lose focus and there was a sudden rush of activity she couldn't make out.

'Stop it there,' she said. 'Go back and play in normal time.'

Wayne ran the tape back and pressed play. 'So who are we looking for?' he asked and Freeman had to suppress the urge to say, '*We're* not looking for anyone.'

'Young woman, about five-two, five-three, brown hair,' she said. Her eyes skimmed the throng of people but she didn't see her. Would Emma think about the security cameras? Would she think to hide amongst groups of people?

She tried to focus on another section of the screen but still there was nothing that stood out. The group dispersed and the corridor was suddenly empty save a doctor talking on a phone, pacing up and down.

'Should I speed up again?' Wayne asked and she nodded. As the people moved about at Benny Hill speed her eyes darted after them. 'Stop,' she said and put her hand over Wayne's. 'Go back.' On screen a woman came into shot, head down and walking quickly. 'Pause it.' He squinted at the fuzzy image. 'That could be her,' she said. 'Press play again.' Wayne started the tape and they watched the woman walk around the corner out of view.

'Where's the next camera?' Freeman asked and Wayne twiddled with buttons and mumbled to himself about the time code.

'Okay, I picked her up again here,' Wayne said, pointing at

a figure on the screen. 'Here she is on the main corridor, heading towards the exit.'

Freeman leaned forward. The image was still grainy but as she got closer to the camera it became clear they were looking at Emma Thorley.

'We lose her here when she walks behind the pillars but there's a camera outside if you bear with me . . .' Wayne played around with the controls, letting the corridor tape run.

'Wait,' Freeman said and leaned forward, pointing at the screen as it changed to the exterior. 'There.' She saw a man walk towards Emma.

'Shit.'

85

17 December 2010

Lucas listened to the noises Emma made from the boot. She was doing his head in. He wondered if anyone else could hear her. He'd been driving around trying to find somewhere to go for what seemed like forever. He wanted to do it right. Wanted to show her that she couldn't get away with fucking with him. But there were people everywhere and he didn't have a clue where the fuck he was. He was going to run out of petrol shortly and unless the police were complete idiots they were going to catch up with him soon. He wondered how he'd got clear of the city after those busybody bitches had interfered.

He passed by streams of traffic, thankfully no cop cars, until he got to the smaller roads and the number of cars dwindled. He was running on fumes now. He could stop here. There was no one around. They hadn't passed another car for ten minutes. He slowed down and pulled in to the side of the road. They'd been passing woods for a long time. Maybe he'd found the perfect place.

Emma wanted to play dead? Playtime was over. He was going to give her precisely what she wanted and then he'd disappear. Be free from it all. And no one – especially Emma Thorley, Detective Freeman, or any of the other stupid bitches that thought they could get to him – would ever fuck with him again.

He was going to put her in the ground – just like she'd done to Jenny.

Freeman ran out of the security office, back into the corridor, and bumped into Gardner, who hung up the phone as she appeared.

'Lucas was here. He's found her,' she said.

'I know.' Gardner held up his phone as they headed towards the exit. 'Local police got a report forty minutes ago about a possible abduction not far from the hospital grounds. Two women saw a couple fighting. The man dragged the woman to a car, kicking and screaming, threw her in the boot and drove away.'

'Description?'

'Matches Lucas and Emma,' Gardner said, dodging an old lady who was trying to find something in her handbag.

'They get a licence plate?'

'Yep. Assaulted the driver before he went. The car was spotted heading north on the B1340 about fifteen minutes ago.'

'I guess that's where we're going, then,' Freeman said, as they ran out into the cold.

'Have you found her?'

Freeman and Gardner stopped short and turned around to see Adam staring at them.

'I told you to wait upstairs,' said Gardner, walking towards the car.

'We're going to look for her now,' Freeman told Adam and opened her car door.

'Where is she?' Adam looked scared.

'We'll let you know as soon as we get any information,' Gardner said and climbed in the passenger seat. 'Go back upstairs. Wait for us here.'

Freeman pulled away, seeing Adam standing there in the car park, watching them disappear.

86

17 December 2010

Adam walked onto the ward and looked down at Ben Swales. He'd lied to the nurse, said he was his brother.

He saw Ben's eyelids flutter. Slowly, Adam walked towards his bed and took a seat beside him. Compared to Ben, it looked like he'd got off lightly in his altercation with Lucas Yates. It was almost a relief until he thought of her out there . . . somewhere . . . with him. What would he do to her?

Ben coughed and Adam turned to see if there was a nurse about. He looked back at Ben. 'Do you want me to get someone? Do you need anything?'

Ben shook his head. 'Who are you?' he asked.

'Adam,' he replied. 'I'm Louise— I'm Emma's boyfriend.'

'Emma?' Ben said and looked past Adam. 'Is she here?'

'No,' Adam told him. 'But she's been here.' He looked out of the window. He didn't know who this guy was, how he was involved. What he *did* know was that this man knew Louise, Emma, whatever her name was, better than he did. He knew about her past, her family, her secrets. He'd been the one person she trusted with her life. What did that leave him with?

'Where's she gone?' Ben asked.

'He took her. They're looking for the car.'

Ben struggled to sit up. 'Lucas found her?'

Adam gave a slight nod. 'I heard them talking. Someone

309

spotted the car; they've gone after them. Detective Freeman. And Gardner.'

Ben looked like he wanted to get out of bed. 'He'll kill her,' he said, closing his eyes. 'He's going to kill her.'

Adam couldn't fight it any more. The tears came and he was gasping for breath. He felt useless. He'd failed her. He should've done something. Should've stopped Yates when he had the chance. Should've known something was wrong with her from the start. But he'd done nothing. He was helpless. No wonder she couldn't trust him, couldn't tell him the truth.

'She didn't do anything wrong,' Ben said.

Adam just stared, his face red hot with tears. He shook his head. 'She lied to me. All this time she pretended to be something she's not. They think she killed that girl.'

Ben's eyes filled up. 'She's a good person,' he said. 'If she lied to you, it was to protect you from the truth. Everything she did was to get away from him. Lucas. They have to stop him.'

Adam felt a stab in his heart. *She* was protecting *him*. It should've been the other way round. He looked out of the window to the car park, which was thick with sleet. Adam pushed back the chair and thanked Ben before running out of the ward and down the stairs. Maybe it wasn't too late. Maybe he could do something after all.

87

17 December 2010

Lucas dragged Emma through the woods, spade in the other hand. The car he'd stolen had been full of gardening shit. If Ben had been there he might've said it was his guardian angel looking out for him.

The branches scratched at his face and kept catching in Emma's hair. He'd gagged her with a rag and some twine from the car but he could still hear her muffled cries. In the distance ahead he could see lights, though he was sure the road was behind him. He turned slightly, moving away from the lights. He'd got this far, he didn't need someone seeing him and calling the cops now.

Emma tried to dig her heels in, slowing them down. The ground beneath them was slippery, the muddy sleet spattering his jeans. It was starting to snow again but he didn't care any more about the cold. After he'd finished with her he wouldn't care about anything. He'd disappear and start again somewhere new.

They came to a clearing. It wasn't a big space, maybe eight by ten feet, but it was big enough for what he wanted and still had the cover of trees. He doubted anyone would be out walking in this weather. Not unless *they* were burying bodies too.

Lucas let go of Emma, throwing her to the ground. She

landed face down, putting her hands in front of her to break her fall and then scrambled to her feet, trying to run away.

'I don't think so,' he said and grabbed hold of her. He held her tight against his body but she struggled and tried to elbow him in the guts. He pulled the twine from his pocket and pushed her down, straddling her. She tried to claw at him. He brought his fist down on her jaw and she stopped. He turned her over, pulling her arms behind her back and tied them up. She flailed about in the mud, writhing on her stomach, and he took a second to laugh at her before moving down to her feet and binding her ankles. When he was done he flipped her over and straddled her again. He couldn't tell if she was crying or if it was the rain streaking her face but he could see the fear in her eyes and it was all he wanted. He pressed himself into her and leaned forward, his mouth next to her ear.

'The last thing you're ever going to see is the soil I throw down on your face,' he said and she started to squirm against him. He laughed and got off her, pulling her up to a seated position, leaning her against a tree. He took one last look around. He could no longer see any lights. They were alone. Completely. He started digging. Under the slush at the top the ground was hard. Each time he struck it reverberated up his arm. But with each strike he felt more and more excitement. He kept his gaze on her, enjoying the terror in her eyes. He'd get the grave dug; that was the important thing, to get that done. And then maybe, just maybe, there'd be time left for some fun.

88

17 December 2010

Gardner looked at the map in his hand as Freeman swerved around another corner. She had that look you get when things snowball, when suddenly things start to happen. He knew the look well; he'd seen it hundreds of times. He was probably wearing it himself.

'So far they've been picked up on the cameras three times. First heading north. Then west. And then going north again on the B6346. That was almost half an hour ago. There're units heading that way but so far, nothing,' Freeman said.

'B6346,' Gardner said and spread his map out. 'Plenty of woods around.' He stopped as Freeman's phone rang.

'The car's been spotted,' she said, after speaking to someone at the other end. 'Officer approached the vehicle but it was empty.'

'How far?'

'About ten minutes.'

'All right,' Gardner said, 'let's go.' Freeman did a U-turn and Gardner hung on for dear life.

Adam checked the road signs, trying to make out where he was. He'd heard Gardner say the car was spotted on the B1340. But that was a while ago. They could be anywhere now. But surely someone would've seen them? Someone would notice her struggling? He tried not to picture what Lucas might be doing to her.

There'd been a part of him that felt relief when he'd discovered what was going on. When he knew that she hadn't left him by choice, that she hadn't wanted to disappear with Lucas. The relief was huge. But maybe he'd have preferred it if she had gone with Lucas voluntarily. At least then she might not be in danger. She might not be dead.

Adam felt sick at the thought. Images of her dying alone and thinking he'd done nothing to help her rushed through his head. He needed to find her. He pulled over and grabbed his phone to call Gardner. As he answered, Adam could hear traffic rushing in the background.

'What's going on? Have you found her?' Adam asked.

'Not yet, but the car we believe they were in was spotted outside some woods not long ago. We're heading that way now. Stay put with Ben and I'll call you as soon as possible.'

Adam listened as Freeman spoke in the background, asking for back-up at Shipley Woods. He hung up and looked down at the map, trying to make out his location.

He tried not to think about how much time she'd been in there with Lucas, how much time she'd been suffering, alone. At least they were on their way. They were going to find her. *He* was going to find her. He just hoped he'd get there in time.

89

17 December 2010

Lucas wiped the sweat from his face with cold hands. He'd dug maybe a foot. If that. Who'd have thought digging a grave would be so fucking hard. He stepped back and wondered if he should just leave her there. The police would be onto him by now. It was unlikely she'd be left to rot as long as Jenny anyway.

He turned to Emma and watched as she tried to tear the twine off her wrists and ankles, tried to pull them apart. He wiped his face again. It was pitch black now; he could barely see past the tree she was sitting against. His arms were aching and he'd pulled a muscle in his back. This wasn't how he'd imagined it would go down.

As he threw the spade onto the ground he thought about everything she had done to him. How she'd rejected him. How she'd murdered his baby. How she'd gone running to that prick Ben for help. How they'd set him up.

He looked over at Emma, still struggling, still crying under her gag. She thought she was better than him but she wasn't. She was as guilty as he was. Worse, even. She'd picked at that girl's bones like carrion.

Lucas stood over her, looking down. Emma stopped moving. He crouched down in front of her. He wanted to pull the gag from her mouth but he was afraid she'd scream, afraid someone would hear and come running. But he needed answers.

'Did you think you'd get away with it, Em?' he said. 'Did you really think I wouldn't work it out? Wouldn't find you?'

Emma whimpered and he pulled the gag away.

'You always thought you were better than me. Better than everyone. But you're just as bad. A liar, a killer.'

'I didn't kill her,' she said, her voice shaking.

Lucas punched her in the stomach. She cried out and keeled over and Lucas grabbed her by the throat. 'Don't you fucking lie to me.' Spit came out as he screamed in her face. He let go of her and sat back, wiping his mouth. 'And then you have the fucking gall to set me up.' He pulled her upright again.

'How did you know what'd happened with us? Why her?' he asked, and she just looked at him like she didn't know what he was talking about. 'I know you set me up. You put your ID on her body. You wanted them to think I'd killed you. Didn't you?'

'I just wanted to get away,' Emma said.

'But how did you know about me and her? How did you know to do it to her?'

'I don't know what you're talking about. I swear,' Emma said through her sobs. 'We found her. Ben was trying to help her. We went looking for her and we found her in the flat.'

'So you and the bent lad helped her by killing her? Finishing her off? Finishing what I started?'

'No. It wasn't like that. We found her like that. She was already dead.' Emma looked confused before the realisation hit her. 'It was you. You killed her. You killed Jenny.'

Lucas sat back, his hands on his head. After all this time, he was starting to understand. He looked at Emma, squinting to see her face in the gloom. And it was a picture. They both knew. After all this time they were finally on the same page. Lucas started to laugh.

90

8 July 1999

Emma jumped up from the bench as Ben came out of the clinic. She'd rather have spent the day in there instead of loitering outside, but Ben couldn't watch her 24/7 and after she'd sat in the waiting room for a couple of hours, Ben's colleagues started getting uppity. So much for helping those in need.

After walking around for hours the night before, she'd finally gone to Ben's and told him about Lucas. She knew she couldn't go home. Not after Lucas had threatened her dad, too. She couldn't bear knowing she would be responsible for her dad getting hurt. Ben had tried to get her to go to the police but it was pointless. They never did anything. A slap on the wrists and he was free to do whatever he wanted. If that man hadn't come out of the bookies when he did, Lucas would've done something there and then. She'd seen him angry before; that was pretty much all he ever was these days. But it had been different the other day. She'd seen something new in his eyes and she was sure that he wouldn't stop coming after her. She wasn't sure Ben would be able to protect her from Lucas if he found her, but at least she wouldn't be alone.

Ben nodded at her and glanced over his shoulder as his boss locked up the clinic. Emma walked across to him. His boss was trying to pretend she wasn't watching them but was failing miserably. Emma turned her back to the other woman. 'Can we go now?'

'See you tomorrow, Ben,' his boss said as she passed them.

'Bye, Jessie,' Ben replied and waited until she was out of earshot. 'There's something I need to do first. Maybe you should go home.'

'No,' Emma told him. 'I can't.'

Ben looked away from her and she wondered if she should just leave him alone. He'd already done so much for her. Lucas had hurt Ben once, she couldn't bear for it to happen again. But she was scared. She didn't know how she'd cope by herself. And how could she be sure Lucas wouldn't find her eventually?

'I need to go and find someone,' Ben said. 'A girl who's been coming here. I'm worried about her.'

'I'll come with you.'

Ben sighed. He looked like he didn't have the energy to argue. Or maybe he knew he wouldn't win. Emma felt strange being the one in control.

'I don't even know where she is,' he admitted. 'Someone mentioned seeing her over at Lime Court. You don't know her, do you? Jenny Taylor?'

Emma stuck close to Ben as he asked around. She'd recognised a few faces. Lucas's customers. She wished she hadn't come. Someone might see her, tell him she was there. No one was talking to Ben anyway. It was a waste of time. And she really didn't want to see Jenny.

'Up there?' Ben said, distracting Emma from her thoughts. She watched as a young kid walked away, stuffing a tenner into his pocket. 'Come on,' Ben said and she followed him up the concrete steps, wishing she had somewhere else to go.

Ben knocked on the door and it creaked open. Emma felt a fly buzz past her face and caught a whiff of something foul. Worse than the rest of the estate. She saw someone watching from the flat next door.

'Wait here,' Ben said and stepped into the flat. Emma ignored him and followed him inside. The smell was stronger. They both covered their faces and edged further in.

'Jenny?' Ben said, though not quite loud enough for anyone to hear. Emma felt her stomach churn. It wasn't just the smell. It was more than that. A feeling.

She followed Ben through the flat to a half-open door at the back. She could hear buzzing. More than just one trapped fly.

She heard the noise from Ben before she saw her. He turned, gagging, and Emma saw her too. Her blonde hair spread across the pillow like Sleeping Beauty. Only Jenny wasn't sleeping. Her face was caved in. Flies were making themselves at home on her corpse. Ben brushed past her as he ran out. She could hear the sound of him retching.

She couldn't move. She was mesmerised by her. By the mess of her body and the brilliant shine of her hair where the sliver of sunlight between the curtains hit it. The girl who had been so big, so angry. All she could think was, That's what I'd look like if I were dead.

She felt Ben come up behind her. He pulled gently at her elbow. 'We need to call the police,' he said.

Emma didn't move. She felt like she was seeing her future.

'Emma?'

'That could be me,' she said. 'That's what Lucas will do to me.'

Ben stepped in front of her, blocking her view of Jenny. 'We need to go,' he said. 'You shouldn't have to see this.'

'That could be me,' she said again and stepped around him, looking at what was left of the girl.

'No,' Ben said. 'It won't be. We'll call the police. We'll tell them about Lucas. I won't let it happen to you.'

'No, you don't understand,' she said, finally looking at Ben. 'That could be me.'

91

17 December 2010

Lucas moved closer to Emma and put a hand on her cheek, unable to stop the grin spreading across his face. 'The best thing you ever did for me, Em. You got rid of the body, the evidence. Any trace that I was ever there. If you'd left well alone I probably would've been banged up for it. But instead,' he said with a smile, 'here we are. Think about that before you die.'

'You killed her,' she said again and looked past him at the grave he'd started to dig. Her elbow cracked into his face before he had time to react. He fell backwards and she kicked out at him, pushing him further away.

Lucas struggled to stand up straight, watching as she kicked out again, the twine starting to fray. He lunged at her and her foot caught him in the jaw. 'Fucking bitch,' he said and grabbed her legs. She reared her head back at him, catching him on his temple, knocking him off her. Pulling her feet apart, she ripped the twine and scrambled to her feet.

Lucas grabbed for her, catching her ankle, pulling her back to the ground. She kicked out again but he got his footing and slammed into her back. She started to scream and he pushed her face into the mud. 'Shut up,' he said. He rolled her to the side and they both slipped into the ditch. He pushed her down and then reached up for the shovel, raising it above his head.

She cowered beneath him and he climbed out of the ditch. It wasn't deep enough but it'd do. He brought the shovel down and felt the vibration up his arm as the metal made contact with her skull.

She was still.

Lucas stood over her, his breathing out of control. He thought he could hear a noise coming from somewhere behind him. How far was he from the road?

He turned back to the grave and started shovelling the soil back in, watching her slowly disappear.

92

8 July 1999

Emma sat on the bus, trying to hold back the tears. With one hand she held onto the bag with everything she owned in it – Jenny's dole book, Ben's savings, and an address in Alnwick where his mother lived. The other hand clutched at her neck where her mother's necklace should've been. Ben had put her bus pass in Jenny's pocket but he said it wasn't enough. He'd asked for the necklace. She didn't want to but she was giving up everything else. Giving up being Emma Thorley. She had to do it. The only way she would escape Lucas, the only way she'd live, was by pretending to be dead.

She'd convinced Ben it could work. There'd be no DNA to ID her as she didn't have any real family. Not that that made it any less painful. She knew it would destroy her dad. She kept telling herself that it was for the best. That one day she'd find a way of telling him she was okay. But what if that day never came?

And what about Ben? She'd left him to sort things out again. Only this time he wasn't passing on messages. He was going to break the law. He was going to bury Jenny.

Emma realised she was crying when the old lady in the seat next to her held out a tissue.

What had she done?

She got up and moved to the front of the coach, stopping beside the driver. 'I need to get off.'

'No unscheduled stops,' he said without looking at her.

'It's an emergency,' she said. 'Please.'

'Next stop is Sheffield. You need to sit down.'

Emma made her way back to her seat. She'd get off in Sheffield and come back. She needed to stop Ben. Needed to stop him from ruining his life.

She leaned against the cold window and thought about her dad. Ben had asked her over and over if she could do it. If she could walk away from her life. She'd felt so sure. But now?

She looked at her watch. It was late. She wondered where Ben was. If he'd gone back to the flat yet. If he'd started. She sobbed as she thought of him burying Jenny. How could she have agreed to let him do it alone?

Ben had promised he'd sort things out, but what if someone found the body too soon and worked out it wasn't her? Still, she'd be long gone by then. Maybe Lucas would've given up.

And what was so good about being Emma Thorley anyway? She might not have her own life, but she'd be free.

93

17 December 2010

Gardner looked across at Freeman as they drove. Local police had been helpful, and it was one of their officers that'd spotted the car, but as they approached the woods he saw they hardly had the cavalry to help with the search. He saw one parked police car at the side of the road, and an officer standing beside it looking like he was freezing. Freeman pulled in and Gardner jumped out.

'What's the situation?' he asked the officer.

'I've checked the car, no one inside, no sign of any damage but then the light's not great.' Gardner nodded and Freeman caught up with him.

'Can you wait by the car?' Gardner asked the officer, and he nodded as if he was always in charge of waiting by cars.

'How far away is back-up?' Freeman asked, looking at her watch. 'We need to get in there.'

Gardner sighed. He looked up and down the road for any sign of a car. Nothing. He turned to the officer again. 'We're waiting on some support. When they show up, tell them we've gone in looking for her. Tell them to secure a perimeter first and then anyone else should come in and start looking too. All right?'

Gardner started walking towards the car that Lucas had dumped. He ducked down and looked inside, shining his torch around the interior. He turned and looked at the fence surrounding the woods. 'Shall we?'

Gardner climbed over first and put out a hand for Freeman, which she ignored and jumped down behind him. They both had their flashlights on but still couldn't make out much beyond a few feet in front of them. The trees were closely planted, and though the branches were bare they hung low, dipping down under the weight of recent snow.

Behind him Freeman cursed as another branch hit her in the face. He only had to deal with them hitting him in the chest. That was something. He could feel his feet sinking into the sleet-soaked earth and every time he stood on a rock or bit of rubbish he'd drop his light to the ground, wondering if he'd found Emma.

'There's a light over there,' Freeman said and pointed to the left.

'It's probably from a car.' He turned to look back at the road. He couldn't see any sign of it now, even though they'd only been walking a couple of minutes. He wondered where the back-up was. They were going to need more than two pairs of eyes. They needed another team to start at the other side at the very least. He'd chosen to start here because of where the car had been dumped but that didn't necessarily mean anything. She might not even be here. He tried to push the thought out of his mind.

'Did you hear that?' Freeman said and stopped walking. She shone her light to the right, moving it back and forth. 'I thought I heard something.'

Gardner looked over to where her torchlight shone. 'I think you've been watching too many horror films,' he said. Then he heard a rustle. 'Okay, I heard it that time.' His heart beat fast.

Freeman started walking towards the sound. Gardner followed.

There was nothing there but ahead they could see a clearing. Freeman turned back to him.

'I see it,' he said and they started running towards it. Freeman slowed at the edge of the clearing; her light showed a mound of earth. 'Shit,' she said and shone her torch on a piece of twine discarded on top of the soil.

Gardner spun around, checking for any movement, any sound, while Freeman knelt down.

'Gardner?' she said, her voice low. He turned back and saw it. The arm sticking out from beneath the soil.

He dug away the mud and turned Emma over and Freeman checked for signs of life. 'Very faint,' she said.

Gardner pulled his phone out and called for an ambulance. 'We need to get her out of here,' he said and bent down to pick Emma up. 'I think he's still here. She can't have been under there long.'

'Get her out, I'll check for Lucas,' she said.

'I'll go,' Gardner said, but Freeman shook her head.

'No. You need to get her out. I can't carry her.'

Gardner glanced down at Freeman's stomach. Couldn't help it.

'I'll be fine,' she said. 'Go.'

Gardner picked Emma up and started to make his way out of the woods, hoping he could find his way. He looked back over his shoulder as Freeman edged her way through, flashlight in hand. That was the only weapon she had. He hoped she wouldn't need it.

94

9 July 1999

He'd been thinking about it for days. The morning after had been a blur. The power of vodka. But bit by bit things were coming back and he couldn't stop thinking about it. About her. What he'd done to her.

He remembered seeing her in the pub. He'd just seen Emma. Finally caught up with the little bitch, told her he knew what she'd done. But Mikey had got in the way and she'd run off, leaving him with his anger and nowhere to direct it. And then he saw Jenny in the pub. She was already fucked up. Obviously her trips to see Ben hadn't helped. She was all over him the minute she saw him. He didn't want to know.

He sat there in the pub among all the scumbags who paid his wages and let it stew. He could barely hear the pounding music, the inane chatter, the clatter of the fruit machines. All he could hear was the blood pumping through his veins, his pulse thumping.

He got up to leave. She started to follow. He knew she was there but he let the door slam into her face. She didn't care. Kept coming. Knew he could give her what she wanted.

'Fuck off, Jenny,' he said and lit another fag.

'Where you going?' she asked, catching up to him. She took the fag from his hand without asking. Took a drag. Gave it back.

'Fuck off,' Lucas said.

'I'll give you a blow job,' she said, skipping in front of him. His hand curled into a fist. She thought she was sexy but she wasn't. Wearing a dress a hooker wouldn't be seen dead in, topped off with a filthy tracksuit top. She was a skank. She'd had her roots done. He wondered how she'd paid for it. How many blokes she'd had to shag for that?

'Piss off,' he said and turned back the other way. He should go to Emma's. Show her he meant what he said. Show her she wasn't going to get away with it.

Jenny came up behind him, slid her hand round onto his chest. 'Come on, Lucas,' she said. 'You know you want it.'

Lucas grabbed her wrist and swung her in front of him. He could see fear in her eyes that quickly dissipated. She started laughing and pulled him towards the estate.

'Come on,' she said again.

Lucas stood still and she bounced back as if she were attached by elastic. He stared at her. He'd done her before. Used her while Emma was gone.

They were standing below the flats where her filthy squat was. He stared at her fake hair, her desperate smile, and something made him want her.

He pushed her inside and she stumbled against the wall, giggling. He grabbed her wrists and forced her onto the bed.

'Emma,' he whispered.

'Whatever,' Jenny said and let him hold her down.

And then it went black. A blank until he was running down the piss-stained concrete stairs from the flat. He pulled a tab out of the pack and dug around his pocket for the lighter. He came up empty-handed. Fuck. He must've left it in the flat. He wasn't going back for it.

He made his way through the estate, ignoring the shouts from all the fuckwits wanting something from him. He knew it wouldn't make any difference. They'd always be back. There was no such thing as customer service in this business. Besides, most of them would be too pissed to remember in a few hours.

The offy on the corner was still open. He went inside for a lighter, wondering if he had enough cash on him for a bottle of something.

He slid the lighter onto the counter and pointed at the bottles of booze lined up across the back shelf. 'One of them,' he said, pointing vaguely in the direction of the vodka. He didn't much care what it was. He just needed something to forget about things. Forget what had happened.

He didn't drink much these days. But seeing Emma like that had pushed something inside him. If it hadn't been for her he wouldn't have got so angry. Wouldn't be drinking half a litre of cheap vodka in the street like the fucking homeless.

Lucas unscrewed the lid and tossed it over a fence. He doubted he'd save any for later. He kicked a black bag across the street, the contents scattering. Bits of old kebab and dirty nappies.

He hated this place. He needed to get out. Needed to leave. The place was a shithole. Nothing to do. He had to move on, forget about Emma. Get out before the cops came looking for him. And they would, sooner or later.

Now, three days later, there was still a sickness in his stomach and it wasn't the vodka. Curiosity got the better of him.

He looked around the estate, but it was deserted. Too early for the scumbags to be up and about. He'd wondered if anyone would've noticed yet. If the place would be crawling with coppers. But there wasn't a soul about.

He climbed the stairs, dodging the shit, presumably dog's, possibly not, and went to the door. It was unlocked. He pushed it open with his elbow, though it was probably too late for that. He knew he shouldn't have come here. He should've gone, left town.

But he had to see for himself. Had to see what he'd done.

He walked inside. There was a smell but he couldn't tell if it was anything different to the usual stench of the place. He ignored the living room, the kitchen, the filthy bathroom. He paused outside the bedroom. He could taste bile in the back of his throat.

What if he was right?

He pushed the door open, expecting her to be there, waiting for him; expecting to see her half-naked, decaying body on the bed.

But there was nothing.

No dead girl.

Lucas let out a breath. He'd been wrong. He hadn't killed her.

There was no dead girl.

95

17 December 2010

Lucas kept moving. The lights had freaked him out. It had to be the cops; no one else would be walking about in the dark. But if the cops were there, then how was he going to get back to the car? He could walk away, head in another direction, but he had no fucking idea where he was and he'd probably freeze to death before he found civilisation.

He heard movement; like someone running. They were going to find her. They were going to find her and get her out and she wouldn't be dead. He should've just finished her off, smashed her fucking head in. He slashed at some branches with the shovel.

All this time and he thought he'd been wrong about Jenny. Thought she was fine, that his imagination had got the better of him. That maybe he'd just wished he'd done it. But he was wrong. He *had* killed her. He'd known it was her as soon as DS Freeman showed him the picture of the trackie top. He remembered his fists pounding at her face, the blood spattering onto the grubby nylon. But how she'd ended up out in the woods? That was something he hadn't been able to get his head around. Not for a while. And then it'd clicked. Emma's things were on the body. They didn't get there by mistake. She was setting him up. And for a while there he thought she'd really grown a pair. That she'd finished what he'd started. But instead she just cleaned up his mess. Maybe Ben really was right about guardian angels.

He could hear voices somewhere behind him, snapping him back to reality. He needed to get out. He started moving faster. He thought he could see a light ahead but he'd lost his sense of direction. He had no idea if he was heading back to the road. He could be walking straight into a trap.

Lucas pushed aside the foliage and after a few more minutes found himself looking at the road he'd stopped on. He could see flashing lights. He crouched down and crab-walked to the fence, trying to see how many of them were out there. To the left he could see his car parked at the side of the road, maybe a hundred yards away. There was one cop car to the right, another just behind it, much closer to him than his own car. He'd never get to it.

His fist curled around the handle of the shovel. He couldn't see anyone else around. Maybe they were all in the woods. He looked behind him. He couldn't see any lights coming towards him. It was now or never.

He edged along the line of the fence, keeping his eye on the officer standing by the road. When he was directly behind him, he stood. A twig cracked beneath his foot and the officer turned.

'Hey,' he said and came towards Lucas. Lucas's arm shot out, the shovel cracked the officer's head and he staggered back. Lucas jumped over the fence and stood over the cop. He raised the shovel again and brought it down; the sound seemed to echo along the empty road. The cop fell back, blood pooled around his head. Lucas stood over him for a second, watching the cop's eyes flicker. Then he turned and ran for the car.

As he approached it he heard movement coming from the woods. He turned and saw someone climbing the fence, a woman. For a second he thought it was her, back from the dead, and he tripped. He picked himself up and ran for the car. He could hear the woman shouting.

Fucking Freeman.

He could see headlights reflecting on his car, another vehicle coming towards them. Another cop car? He climbed in and saw Freeman coming at him in the mirror. Lucas tried to start his car but the car behind didn't stop. Instead it sped up and Lucas felt the blow as it careened into his rear bumper, forcing him forward. His head cracked the windscreen and he was spinning.

He could see a familiar face in the other car – Emma's boyfriend. He could see Freeman coming towards him. He could see blue lights flashing. And then as he span one last time he saw Emma being carried out of the woods and he knew it was over.

She'd got away from him again.

96

17 December 2010

Gardner wasn't sure who to visit first. Adam was being treated for whiplash. He hadn't needed to speed up to hit Lucas's car, just nudging him would've given Freeman enough time to get to him but Gardner suspected he hadn't been thinking about helping Freeman anyway. The doctor had also patched up Adam's other cuts and bruises and had said nothing when he'd explained they were from an earlier incident.

Emma was being treated for concussion, and several cuts and bruises of varying severity. Fortunately the blow to the head hadn't appeared to do any lasting damage. He wasn't sure the same could be said about the experience as a whole.

Ben was still on the ward and Freeman had been to inform him that they'd found Emma and she was okay. She'd agreed to wait to take his statement. The doctor had offered to clean up the scratches on Freeman's face from the low-hanging branches in the wood, but she'd refused.

Lucas was in A&E but unfortunately he'd live. He hadn't said anything so far but then the doctors had given him some strong painkillers. He doubted any confession given by Lucas under the influence of the drugs would be admissible.

The officer who'd been clobbered by Lucas was also being treated, but according to his wife was going to be okay and seemed pleased to finally have a real story to tell.

Only Gardner hadn't been seen by a doctor and though his back was killing him from carrying Emma through the woods, he wasn't going to mention it lest anyone thought he was feeling sorry for himself.

He watched Freeman walk up the corridor towards him. She looked exhausted and as soon as she reached him she slumped into one of the chairs he was pacing in front of.

'They're keeping Adam in,' she said. 'He doesn't have anywhere to go and his car's knackered so they're giving him the B&B treatment.'

'What about Emma?' Gardner asked.

Freeman shook her head. 'The doctor's still in there. I haven't spoken to her yet.'

'Lucas is doped up. No chance of getting him to talk tonight.'

'What're you going to do?' Freeman asked.

'Wait here, I guess,' Gardner said and sat down in the chair beside her. 'Has Adam seen Emma yet?'

'I think they let him in briefly to convince him she's okay. But they haven't had the big reunion yet.' She paused. 'You think they'll stick together after what's happened?'

Gardner shrugged. 'He came after her, didn't he?'

Freeman closed her eyes.

'How about you? Are you all right?' he asked.

She opened one eye. 'I'm fine. Although I am pregnant. So . . .' Gardner nodded but kept his mouth shut. 'But you already knew that,' she said.

'I took a wild guess after your vomiting interlude.' He paused, knowing it was both irrelevant and none of his business. 'You think you should get checked over?'

'No point,' she said, staring straight ahead.

They sat in silence for a while and Gardner thought she'd dropped off, but as a porter wheeled a bed past them she stirred.

'What did McIlroy tell you about me?' he asked eventually.

'Not much,' Freeman said. He could tell she was lying. 'Whatever happened, happened. McIlroy reckons you're an arsehole but that's like the pot calling the kettle an arsehole. Plus McIlroy's the dumb-arse who let Lucas get hold of his badge, so he's hardly worth listening to about anything.' Freeman finally looked Gardner in the eye. 'Anyway, you seem all right to me.'

Gardner smiled. They sat in silence again. Part of him wanted her to press him. Part of him needed to let it out. Maybe she'd understand. Maybe she'd pardon him.

She didn't speak.

Gardner let out a breath and started telling her his story, staring straight ahead. For something that'd cast a shadow over the last eleven years of his life, it was a pretty quick story to tell.

'I guess some people thought Wallace deserved to be sent down for what he did. A few didn't. But even those who thought I was right to shop him, I think they questioned my motives. Would I have done it if it had been someone else?'

'And would you?' Freeman asked, speaking for the first time.

Gardner shook his head and turned around to face her. 'I don't know. That's the million dollar question,' he said. 'I've seen other people, other coppers, doing stuff they shouldn't – we all have – and I turned a blind eye. But that was petty stuff. And maybe that makes me a hypocrite.' He shook his head again. 'I never wanted anyone to get hurt, not like that.'

'But that wasn't your fault. He made his own bed. He didn't have to kick the shit out of that kid. He didn't have to top himself. He made his own decisions. You shouldn't feel sorry for him.'

'I don't,' Gardner said. 'I don't even feel sorry for myself. Well, not really. I didn't care about leaving Blyth.'

'Who would?' Freeman said.

'It meant I didn't have to see Annie any more; I didn't have to see the arseholes like McIlroy. I got to start again. But it was *her* that I felt sorry for. Wallace had a daughter, Heather. She was twelve years old when he killed himself. And she's the only reason I wish I could change what happened. As much as I believe I did the right thing when I told the truth about Wallace, if I could change it now, I would. Just so that kid could have her dad back.'

'You think she blames you?' Freeman asked.

'Probably.'

'You should go and see her.'

'No.' Gardner shook his head. 'I've thought about it, but I doubt it'd do either of us any good.'

'You never know,' she said as his phone started ringing.

'Excuse me. Gardner,' he answered.

He listened to Harrington ramble on for almost a minute before hanging up. He could hear his colleagues shouting and laughing in the background at Lawton's party. The party he should've been at. 'Shit,' he said and sat back down.

'Problem?' Freeman asked.

'It's nothing,' he said. 'There was just somewhere I was meant to be tonight.'

Freeman raised an eyebrow. 'Somewhere with young PC Lawton, I presume. Are you and her—'

'No,' Gardner said before she went any further. 'It's her birthday. The whole team was going out. I said I'd be there.'

'Well that's you in bother, then,' Freeman said. 'I think she likes you. She got all mother-bear protective when I was loitering by your desk.'

Gardner squirmed in his seat and wished he hadn't mentioned anything. Fortunately Freeman dropped it and stood up, stretching.

'Well, I think I might see if Emma's ready to talk. Coming?'
Gardner nodded.

'Oh, and about Blyth,' she said. 'You shouldn't let it get
to you so much. It was a mistake. It's in the past. Everyone
has skeletons.'

97

18 December 2010

Gardner and Freeman sat opposite Lucas and waited for him to start talking. They'd heard Emma's story, now they wanted his. Most of his injuries were superficial. He had quite the nasty bruise across his forehead where he'd hit the windscreen, but all it had done was make him less attractive to the ladies. Freeman didn't think it was possible to do any more damage to his brain than he already had. And despite the broken arm and dislocated shoulder, the hospital had released him into their custody. The nursing staff were probably as sick of him as the detectives were. They'd been there for an hour already and he'd said nothing useful. He hadn't denied any of the charges. Attempted murder, kidnapping, assault, theft. Anything that'd happened in the last couple of days he just shrugged at. They had enough evidence to convict him on each one of those charges, something he knew as well as they did. So maybe it didn't matter what he said about Jenny Taylor. They had enough to put him away for a very long time.

But *she* wanted to know and she knew Gardner did too. It was her case and she wanted to close it, wanted to solve it, to find out what had really happened to Jenny Taylor. They had part of the story from Ben and Emma, although their versions differed slightly. Emma claimed it had all been her idea but Ben was saying it was his and that Emma was long gone on a bus by the time he moved the body. Freeman knew they were just trying to protect each other; she would keep working on them. But they still didn't have all the pieces. Emma claimed Lucas had confessed to killing Jenny while they were in the woods, but he wasn't saying anything now.

'So why did you kill her, Lucas?' Freeman asked again and Lucas just stared at her. 'We know it was you. Emma told us what you said. I just want to know why.'

Freeman watched as Lucas dug his fingernails into his skin. She wondered why he was so bothered about being caught out on Jenny's murder when he knew he was going down for the rest.

'I didn't kill her,' Lucas said. 'Show me some proof I killed her. They were trying to set me up. They put her ID on Jenny's body. They buried her. Looks to me like *they* killed her.'

'Post-mortem indicated that whoever killed Jenny was left-handed. You're left-handed, aren't you, Lucas?'

Lucas shrugged. 'So are a lot of people.'

'Also, the results came back on Jenny's tracksuit top. There were traces of semen on it. Your semen.'

Lucas's eyes narrowed. Trying to work out if she was bluffing. 'So what?' he said. 'We fucked. Doesn't mean I killed her.'

Freeman stared at him until he looked away. She knew he was lying but he was also right. Nothing she had proved absolutely that he'd killed Jenny. She stood up to leave. They were getting nowhere. He wasn't going to tell them anything.

'Tell Emma she lost,' he said as they went to walk out.

'No, I don't think she did,' Freeman said, leaning over him. Getting in his face. 'Emma's fine. You're in here. You lost, Lucas.'

98

19 December 2010

Adam followed Emma's instructions and drove through the estate. She'd been relatively quiet the whole way but her chatter had declined even further the closer they got to Blyth. After they'd visited Ben in hospital to say goodbye and promised to keep in touch with him, she'd asked if he'd take her home. At first he thought she meant to Middlesbrough, back to the house they shared. But she meant to Blyth, to see her dad. Detective Freeman had assured her that he'd want to see her, but Emma was scared he'd be angry with her. She'd abandoned him eleven years ago, why should he just open his arms to her now? But she knew it was something she had to do, another step in becoming Emma Thorley again.

Emma. He was going to have to get used to calling her that. Every time he opened his mouth 'Louise' came out and he had to correct himself. He wondered how long it'd take to get used to it. Whether she'd even stick around long enough for it to happen.

'Here,' she said and pointed at a house with an overgrown garden. Adam stopped the car outside and they sat watching the house in silence. Adam looked at Emma and he felt as scared as she looked. What was going to happen when she went into that house? Emma was afraid of how her dad would react but *he* was afraid of what would happen afterwards.

They hadn't talked about it yet. Once she became Emma again, then what? Did she still want to be with him? Would she want to come back here to be with her dad? She'd already called it home.

He knew she was scared about what might happen to her and Ben. She'd been crying as she left Ben at the hospital. Apparently he'd been telling the truth when he said it was just him who'd buried Jenny. He'd put Emma on a bus and gone back to the house alone. Adam had to admit he'd felt relieved when he'd heard that. It was enough dealing with her being someone else. He didn't think he could cope with the thought of her digging graves too. Ben had told the police Emma hadn't been involved and no matter how much she argued, Ben was determined to take the blame. He wanted Emma to move on. To finally find the happiness she'd been looking for. Whereas he seemed to be needing the punishment, to finally be at peace with what he'd done. Though he felt sorry for Ben, Adam hoped that Emma would accept his plan. He couldn't stand the thought of losing her again.

Whether she was Louise or Emma, it didn't matter to him. He loved her. He put his hand on hers and she turned to him. 'I just want you to know that whatever happens, I'm going to be there for you,' he said and Emma frowned. 'I don't want to lose you and I don't care what happened in the past. I love you. I don't want this to be over.'

Emma smiled at him. 'Neither do I,' she said and leaned over to kiss him. 'I thought you'd want out.'

'Never,' he said.

'But all the lies I told you. I got you hurt,' she said, brushing her fingers across his face.

'I don't care,' he said. 'I want to be with you, whoever you are.'

She smiled again and looked back at the house. 'Will you come in with me?' she asked and he nodded.

They knocked on the door and Emma squeezed his hand as they waited. The door opened and her dad stood there and looked at Adam first before shifting his eyes to Emma. She smiled at him. 'Hello, Dad,' she said and he grinned at her, throwing his arms around her.

'Come in, come in,' he said and let them past. 'I was just about to have some tea. You should've used your key, pet.' He closed the door. 'So this must be your new fella, then,' he said and reached for Adam's hand. 'I hope you're taking care of my girl.'

'I'm trying,' Adam told him, and her dad threw his arms around Emma again.

'I've missed you, Em.'

Emma hung on to her dad and Adam smiled at her. 'I'll get the tea,' said Ray and shuffled into the kitchen. Adam took her hand. A tear rolled down Emma's face as her dad talked to her about the weather.

She was going to be okay. Some things are meant to be forgiven.

99

23 December 2010

Gardner parked the car and sat watching the station. He'd only been there a week before but it felt like the past was staring down at him. He didn't know why he'd come back again. He'd been thinking about what Freeman had said and managed to convince himself that she was right. But now he was having second thoughts. Maybe third thoughts. He should've stayed at home.

Gardner watched people come in and out of the station, none of whom he recognised. He wondered how many people he knew were still in there, how many he would have to face when he walked in. Of course McIlroy was still there, though God only knew how. He hadn't been any good at his job back then, and he seriously doubted the tubby bastard had got any better over the years.

He watched the clock on the dashboard change from 10:28 to 10:29. He promised himself he'd go in when it got to thirty. Or he could just turn around and go home. He could go back and face the music with Lawton instead. He'd apologised profusely for not getting to her party and she'd said it was fine but it clearly wasn't. She obviously thought he'd had no intention of going and maybe she was right. She'd thawed somewhat when he gave her the gift he'd bought – he'd finally settled on a scarf. But he still wasn't totally forgiven. She still hadn't made him any coffee.

He checked the clock again: 10:30. 'All right,' he muttered to himself and got out of the car, walking slowly to the old brick building.

It still had the same musty smell and peeling paint, and the faces had the same look of resignation even though they were different people. He walked towards the offices he used to sit in, that once upon a time he had a laugh in and had mates in. The walk was easy, as if he were just going in for a normal day of work. Someone held the door open for him, maybe mistaking him for someone else, someone who was meant to be there.

He stopped in the doorway and looked across the room but no one looked up. Phones rang at both ends of the office, people swung on chairs while they were on hold; the sound of fingers on keyboards was different, hardly anyone typed with one finger any more. He looked across to his old desk. Some bald guy he'd never seen before was sitting there, scribbling something down, his face creased with concentration.

'Hi.'

Gardner turned around and saw Freeman standing there with a pile of folders under her arm and a cup of coffee in her hand.

'Hi,' Gardner said.

Freeman beckoned him to follow her and walked to her desk. She pulled up another chair from the desk behind her. 'What can I do for you?' she asked.

Gardner took another look around the office before sitting. There was no one he knew and he felt a little relieved. Facing your demons is easier when they're not around.

'I thought about what you said. About going to see Heather Wallace. I was wondering if you'd come with me.' Freeman looked surprised. 'You think I should go alone?' he said.

'Probably. But I'll meet you for a drink afterwards. You can tell me how it went.'

Gardner agreed to call her and walked back out into the corridor. Coming towards him was Adrian Hingham, who'd still been a green PC when Gardner knew him but was now wearing a flashy suit. He remembered Hingham working with Wallace on a number of occasions and felt his fists ball up as he approached.

'Michael Gardner,' Hingham said and extended his hand. 'I heard you'd been hanging around the place. How you doing?'

Gardner shook his hand and tried not to look as surprised as he felt. 'I'm good. How are you? Clearly making too much money,' he said, nodding at the suit.

'Yeah, I've made it all the way up to the dizzy heights of DC. The suit was a gift from the missus. She thinks my taste in clothes is appalling,' he said with a grin. 'Anyway, I'd better run. But it was good to see you.'

Hingham trotted off down the corridor while Gardner thought maybe he'd killed another demon. Maybe seeing Heather Wallace wouldn't be so bad. Or maybe he was pushing his luck.

He got in his car and drove towards the big house Heather had lived in with her mother. Heather would be what, twenty-three, twenty-four now? She probably didn't live there any more. Maybe her mother didn't even live there any more. He pulled up across the street and looked at the house. There was a car on the drive so *someone* was there. He sat watching for a while and then made a deal with himself. He'd go and knock and if she was there, he'd talk to her. If she wasn't, he'd drive home and forget about it. Let sleeping dogs lie. He crossed the road and knocked on the door.

A tall, skinny woman with red hair opened the door and

Gardner wanted to turn and run. He knew it was her; she didn't look any different except for being taller and happier than the last time he'd seen her.

'Yes?' Heather said and smiled at him. For a moment he contemplated asking if she was happy with her electricity supplier or if she wanted to let God into her life.

'Heather Wallace?' he asked and she nodded, the smile fading slightly. 'I'm Michael Gardner,' he said. 'I'm a police officer, I—'

'I know who you are,' she cut him off. The smile had gone completely and her arms were folded across her chest.

'Right,' he said. 'I was just . . . I've been working on a case with the local police and I wanted to come and . . .' What? What did he want? She just stared at him, waiting for his point. 'I just wanted to see that you were all right and to tell you I was sorry about your dad. I never got to tell you at the time but I *am* sorry about what happened.' He waited for her to speak but she didn't, she just stood staring at him and he couldn't stop talking and suddenly he knew how it felt to be one of his suspects. 'I never wanted that to happen and if I could change it I would. I really would. I just wanted you to know that—'

'What do you want me to say?' Heather snapped. 'That I forgive you?'

'No. I just—'

'Because I don't,' she said and slammed the door. Gardner stood there on the doorstep and felt like he'd been punched in the gut. His hands were shaking. 'I'm sorry,' he said. As he turned to walk away he tripped on a waving snowman ornament, knocking it onto its side. It wished him a merry Christmas.

As he climbed into the car he could hear a ringing in his

ears. He shouldn't have come. For her sake as much as his own. He shouldn't have come. Some things just aren't meant to be forgiven.

100

23 December 2010

Gardner spotted her sitting in the corner, looking out of place amongst the Christmas revellers. She nodded in his direction and he noticed she'd already got the drinks in.

'Got you a Coke,' she said as he walked over.

'I could do with something stronger,' he said and sat down, throwing his coat on the seat beside him.

'Well, unless you're going to spend the night with me, you've still got to drive home.' Gardner raised an eyebrow and Freeman shrugged and pushed the pint glass towards him. He raised it in a half-hearted toast. 'So?' she asked. 'How did it go?'

'About as well as could be expected,' he said. 'I shouldn't have gone. Especially now. Christmas.'

'So there was no goodwill towards men? It was worth a try.'

'Was it? I feel worse than I did before. It's the last time I take advice from you.'

Freeman tried to smile over her glass of Coke. 'Well, I'm the last person to be handing out advice.' She looked away, towards a group of men and women shrieking and giggling by the bar, probably on a work Christmas party.

'Shit, I'm sorry,' he said. 'I shouldn't have come up here moaning about my own crap.'

Freeman shook her head. 'It's fine. It's done now.'

'I'm sorry.'

'I'm not,' she said and started tearing up a beer mat.

'Did the father go with you?'

Freeman laughed. 'The father,' she said. 'Fat lot of good he'd be.' She threw the bits of cardboard across the table. 'Anyway, I didn't tell him.'

'He's out of the picture?'

'He is now. We broke up before I found out.'

'Oh.'

'Oh, what? Don't look at me like that.'

'Like what?'

'With that judgey face. Brian was a dick. He cheated on me.'

'But still,' Gardner said, then regretted getting into the conversation as Freeman sat up straight like she was ready to fight.

'You think I was wrong. That I should've told him. That I'm a total bitch for not letting him have any input.'

'Woah. How did we get to that?' Gardner held up his hands. 'Let's just drop it. I don't think anything. It's none of my business.'

'You're right. It's not.'

They sat in silence for a while and Gardner finished his drink. He wondered whether he should just go. His people skills had done him proud once more. He tapped the edge of the table and tried to judge whether it was safe to speak.

'I'd already made up my mind and anything Brian said wasn't going to change that. So what would have been the point?'

Gardner got the feeling she wasn't arguing any more. From the time he'd spent with Freeman he gathered she wasn't some shrinking violet. Didn't need anyone to back her up, to validate her. But whatever front she was putting on now, clearly the decision hadn't been easy. He knew that. He'd been there. Last year of university with the first girl he'd been in love with. Holly Hughes. She'd told him ten minutes before a lecture before bursting into tears and running off. He'd sat there listening to some drivel about Shakespeare and wondered what the hell he was going to do, whether his life was over. And more to the point, how the hell he was going to tell his mum that he'd knocked up some girl she'd never even met. By the end of the lecture he'd decided that it was going to be fine. Good, even. He didn't have a clue what else he was going to do with his life after uni, so why not be a dad? Unfortunately, Holly had other plans. She *did* know what she was going to do with her life after uni, and it didn't involve kids. She made all the arrangements herself. All he had to do was borrow a mate's car to drive her to the hospital and that was it. She'd made her decision.

She kept asking him afterwards if he was angry with her. He wasn't. Not really. It was the right decision. Just not his decision. She broke up with him three months later. But Freeman probably didn't want to hear all this.

'You're right,' he said and stood up. He dug in his pocket for some change. 'Another drink?'

He came back with two more Cokes and his spilt across the table as he put it down.

'I saw Ray Thorley yesterday,' Freeman said. 'Emma's been staying there. He's a new man. It's nice.'

'That's good. What about Adam? Has he stuck around?'

Freeman nodded as she slurped the full glass. 'Him and Emma are staying for Christmas. She's also changed her story.'

'Really?'

'Yep. All lines up with Ben's. She was on a bus out of town before the body was moved.'

'But she was still involved. Still took on Jenny's identity,' Gardner said.

'Yeah, she's not quite out of the woods yet. So to speak.'

'What about Ben Swales?'

Freeman shrugged. 'He's out of hospital. But he's still waiting for all this to end. I think part of him wants to go to prison. He thinks he should be punished. I still can't believe he smashed Jenny's teeth in. Didn't think he had that in him.'

'So you think it's really true? That he planted the ID and buried the body, but didn't kill her?'

'You *don't* believe him?' she asked.

Gardner blew out his cheeks. 'Sounds far too convenient. Finding a dead girl just when you need one.'

'I guess if you work with heroin addicts you're bound to come across one eventually,' Freeman said. 'Especially if they know Lucas Yates.'

'What's happening with Yates?' Gardner asked. 'He's still not talking?'

'Nope. But I know it was him, I can feel it. But,' she shrugged, 'we don't have enough. There's Emma's testimony about what he told her in the woods but she's hardly a reliable witness. There's the semen, but that means squat.' She sighed. 'I just wish I knew what'd happened. It's pissing me off.'

Gardner's phone beeped and he checked his message. An email from the dating site. Some woman from Guisborough had been in touch. Did he fancy meeting for a drink sometime? Gardner smiled.

'What's up?' Freeman asked.

'Nothing,' he said and slid the phone back in his pocket.

They sat back in silence and listened as 'Fairytale of New York' came on the jukebox. In the corner the office workers started singing along and Freeman and Gardner finished their drinks.

EPILOGUE

6 July 1999

She lay back on the sunken mattress, her fingers touching her neck where his hands had been. As he'd slammed into her, with his hand around her neck, she thought he would kill her. She didn't need this. It wasn't just sex. It was anger. It was hate.

Bitch. Slut. Junkie. Whore.

Emma.

Between the vitriol he called her Emma. For a moment it verged on tenderness until his fury took over again and the name took on the same spiteful tone as the other names he'd called her.

And then it was over. He pulled out of her, pulling the sheet across his legs, leaving her naked body exposed. He lit a cigarette and tossed the lighter between them. She waited a moment before she spoke – allowing him to calm down, allowing time for the nicotine to kick in.

It hurt when she swallowed. He was a fucking animal. But she knew that already. She wasn't expecting anything else. She'd given up on anything else a long time ago. Her life now was pain followed by pleasure. A lot of one, a little of the other. But what pleasure.

He closed his eyes and she figured it was enough time.

'Have you got any, then?' she said, her voice catching in her throat. She pulled her tracksuit top out from under him and put it back on.

He opened his eyes as if he'd forgotten she was there. He stared at her for a second before sitting up, reaching for his jacket and pulling out the small packet. Her heart started to race. She reached out but he pulled back, out of her grasp.

'Give it to me,' she said, her voice stronger.

His hand stung her cheek and she knew she'd been too forceful.

'Don't,' he said, his fingers wrapped around her face. He threw the packet at her and climbed off the bed. He pulled on his jeans, muttering to himself. 'Stupid fucking cunts. I've had it with the lot of you.'

'Aw, poor Lucas. Did your little girlfriend dump you?' She giggled and sat up, opening the tiny plastic bag.

'Shut up,' he said and turned to leave.

'Poor Lucas,' she said again, in a singsong voice. 'Doesn't she love you any more?'

He was back on her in a flash. Her head snapped back against the mattress as he held her down.

'Don't you fucking dare,' he whispered.

His hands were hot against her neck. She could see herself reflected in his eyes. She wanted to beg him to stop but no words came out. She saw spots flit across her vision. His body was heavy on hers; she could see the veins in his neck bulge. She tried to push him away, kicked at him. She caught him in the balls and he fell away from her. She started to run, tripped over her shoes thrown carelessly on the floor.

She screamed as he grabbed hold of her, throwing her back on the bed. 'Fucking bitch.' He slammed his fist into her face, spitting out 'Emma' as he pounded. She tried to call out, tried to make it stop but he just kept going until she couldn't see, until her face was hot with blood and tears.

Her eyelids fluttered and suddenly there was nothing. She felt the world darken and his hands fell away. She could feel him, feel his fingerprints on her, feel the life draining from her body, feel death coming over her.

She wished for the first time in so long for her parents. She wondered if they'd ever know or care.

She heard the front door slam.

She was alone.

And as she finally found her voice for the very last time, all she could say was, 'My name's not Emma.'

ACKNOWLEDGMENTS

Thanks to everyone who helped make this book happen. I'm sure I'll forget someone for which I apologise, but special thanks to:

Mam, Dad, Donna and Christine.

To my unofficial distributors Jonathan (Yorkshire and Bulgaria regions) and Maria (North East and Australia regions).

To Diane (best boss ever), Andrea and Barbara for lending their names to characters – and just for the record, the real Andrea Round is nothing like her namesake and does *not* like to be called Anders.

To everyone at James Cook Hospital who's supported me and always asks how the next book is coming along – you know who you are.

To New Writing North and Moth Publishing for continued support.

To all the crime writing friends I've made over the last year – you're all marvellous.

To all at Mulholland/Hodder for believing in my work and making it happen, especially my editor Ruth Tross, who I knew I'd get along with after she confessed her love for *Buffy the Vampire Slayer*.

To my agent, Stan, for general awesomeness and all the cider he kindly provided me with. I'm sure it helped the book in many ways.

To Cotton, who will be in one of the books one of these days.

And lastly, to Stephen, for everything you are and everything you do – thank you so much. xx

You've turned the last page.

But it doesn't have to end there . . .

If you're looking for more first-class, action-packed, nail-biting suspense, join us at **Facebook.com/ MulhollandUncovered** for news, competitions, and behind-the-scenes access to Mulholland Books.

For regular updates about our books and authors as well as what's going on in the world of crime and thrillers, follow us on **Twitter@MulhollandUK**.

There are many more twists to come.

MULHOLLAND:
You never know what's coming around the curve.

HODDER

www.mulhollandbooks.co.uk